THE OC

ALSO BY D.P. LYLE

The Jake Longly Series
Deep Six
A-List
Sunshine State
Rigged

The Cain/Harper Series
Skin in the Game
Prior Bad Acts

The Dub Walker Series
Stress Fracture
Hot Lights, Cold Steel
Run to Ground

The Samantha Cody Series
Original Sin
Devil's Playground
Double Blind

The Royal Pains Media Tie-In Series
Royal Pains: First, Do No Harm
Royal Pains: Sick Rich

Nonfiction
Murder and Mayhem
Forensics For Dummies
Forensics and Fiction
Howdunit: Forensics; A Guide For Writers
More Forensics and Fiction
ABA Fundamentals: Forensic Science

Anthologies
Thrillers: 100 Must-Reads (contributor); *Jules Verne, Mysterious Island Thriller 3: Love Is Murder* (contributor); *Even Steven; For the Sake of the Game* (contributor); *Bottom Line*

THE OC

A JAKE LONGLY THRILLER

D. P. LYLE

OCEANVIEW PUBLISHING
SARASOTA, FLORIDA

ISBN 978-1-60809-460-8

Published in the United States of America by Oceanview Publishing

Sarasota, Florida

www.oceanviewpub.com

10 9 8 7 6 5 4 3 2 1

PRINTED IN THE UNITED STATES OF AMERICA

THE OC

ACKNOWLEDGMENTS

To my wonderful agent, Kimberley Cameron of Kimberley Cameron & Associates, for her guidance, advice, dedication, and friendship. KC, you're the best.

To Bob and Pat Gussin and the great folks at Oceanview. Thanks for your hard work and creativity in making this book the best it can be.

To my always first reader and editor, Nancy Whitley.

To Nan for everything.

CHAPTER 1

"She likes you."

"Everybody likes me."

"Yeah, but she likes you in that I-want-to-sit-on-your-lap way."

"So do you."

"Hmmm. Sounds like a plan."

"These seats aren't that big."

Okay, a little perspective here. I'm Jake Longly, ex-pro baseball player, restaurant/bar owner, and lover of women. Well, the one sitting next to me anyway. That would be Nicole Jamison. Funny, smart, and insanely beautiful. Sometimes annoying. Actually, she excels at that.

We were seated in first class, Row 5, Seats A and B, on an American Airlines flight into Orange County, California's John Wayne Airport. The OC, baby.

We had started out early this morning in Gulf Shores, Alabama, where my restaurant, Captain Rocky's, sits on the sand, and where we both live. This trip was in part a vacation from—I'm not sure from what. I work very little. My manager, Carla Martinez, runs the joint so I have essentially zero to do. Except hang out with Nicole and Pancake. Nicole is my girlfriend, or whatever. We haven't yet decided what we are. Let's say, she likes me. See? I told you, everybody likes me. Tommy "Pancake" Jeffers is my best friend. All the way back to when we terrorized the neighborhood as kids. He likes hanging out at Captain Rocky's, too. Mainly because the food and drink are free. My God, that boy can eat. Gnaws on my profits. If there are any. I'm never very sure since Carla rarely tells me. I don't worry too much about it since the place is always packed. Also, I share the profits with her, so I figured that if we were bleeding out, she'd let me know.

Nicole, besides being smart and hot, and at times snarky, also writes screenplays. That's the other reason for our trip to the left coast. Her new film was teed up to begin shooting in three weeks. Her other two screenplays had been minimalist productions, indies that made it to a couple of small film festivals. This one was on an entirely different level. It would be shepherded by her uncle Charles Balfour, the A-list producer and CEO of Regency Global Productions, RGP for short. He's the driving force behind the multibillion-dollar *Space Quest* series. Yeah, billion with a B.

Me and Uncle Charles go way back. I've never actually met him but I've spent many a night in the home he owns near Gulf Shores. That's where Nicole lives. Or hangs out anyway.

Nicole also lives in The OC, in a Newport Beach condo, but she's rarely there. For the past year or so, that's how long we've been together, she's mostly stayed in Uncle Charles' mega-mansion very near my Gulf Shores home.

"These seats aren't that small," Nicole said.

"There's no leg room."

"That's because you have long legs."

"You don't?"

She laughed. "If memory serves, you do pretty well in tight spaces."

I looked at her "I'll let that one slide by."

The flight attendant returned, smiling, saying, "Can I get you anything?" Her gaze locked on me for a beat too long. Her name tag said she was Maryanne.

"I think we're good." I smiled back.

She moved on down the row.

Nicole elbowed my ribs. "See? What'd I tell you?"

"Maybe she's using me to get to you?"

"Could be. Maybe I should be glad you have the aisle seat," Nicole said.

"Pancake's better at running interference. He's built for it."

"In this situation, I think you'll do fine."

Through the opening that led into the galley, I saw flight attendant Maryanne lift the microphone from its wall perch. She looked at me and smiled. Her announcement informed us that we would be landing in thirty minutes so any last-minute trips to the restroom might be a good idea.

"I think she wants you to join the mile-high club," Nicole said.

"She's doing her job."

"The aforementioned restroom is right behind her. Looked like an invitation to me."

"Might disturb the pilots," I said. "Besides, speaking of tight spaces. Not much room to maneuver."

"Bigger than the front seat of my car."

Nicole drives a Mercedes SL convertible. More than once, or twice, or thrice—I love that word—we've watched a sunset from the front passenger seat, her settled on my lap.

"We could try the one in back," she said. "See if it'll work."

"And get cuffed by those TSA folks when we step off the plane."

"You're no fun."

"Wait until we get to your place."

"Your girlfriend's headed this way." She nodded toward the galley area. "I think she wants your phone number."

I looked up as Maryanne approached, a scrap of paper and a pen in her hand.

"I hate to bother you," she said. "But could I get your autograph for my son. He's a big baseball fan."

I guess she didn't want my number.

This happened from time to time. Less so with each year that flowed by since my days in the Bigs. Still felt good though. I mean being an old, washed-up athlete is better than being a *forgotten*, old, washed-up one.

"How old is he?" I asked.

"Eight. Going on thirty." She gave a headshake. "He's much more mature than his father." She laughed. "He can be such a goof."

"It's a guy thing," Nicole said. "They only mature until about age fourteen. That's their ceiling."

I would have defended my manhood but I was outnumbered, surrounded, and couldn't think of a clever comeback. Which was likely their point.

"Don't I know it." Maryanne extended the paper toward me.

"What's your son's name?" I asked.

"Scott. We call him Scotty."

"What position does he play?"

"He pitches and plays shortstop." She beamed. "He's really very good."

I started to sign the paper but then said. "I have something he'll like more." I foot-tugged my carry-on from beneath the seat and lifted it into my lap. I unzipped it and rummaged inside until I found what I was looking for. A baseball.

I always traveled with several baseballs. Rarely to sign one for a fan but mostly to throw at bad guys. Like Victor Borkov's crew. Baseballs are great weapons. But I didn't tell Maryanne any of that. Instead, I said, "I always carry a couple of these for just such occasions."

"You don't have to do that," she said.

"My pleasure." I signed the ball to Scotty and handed it to her.

"He'll be thrilled." She gave me another smile and a quick nod. "Thank you so much."

"I think you just made her day," Nicole said as Maryanne walked away.

"Scotty's, too, I hope."

"Definitely." She hooked her arm in mine. "You deserve a reward."

"Like what?"

"The usual."

Me likey the usual.

CHAPTER 2

THE USUAL TURNED out to be unusually wonderful. The unusually part wasn't exactly true. Anytime I crawled in the shower with Nicole it was memorable.

After we landed at John Wayne, said goodbye to Maryanne, and grabbed our luggage and our rental, we drove the few miles to Nicole's condo. We had opted for a Range Rover, figuring with all the driving around we would be doing, LA, Malibu, and wherever else we might have to go, the extra room would come in handy. We didn't bother to unpack, but rather dumped our suitcases on the living room floor, shed our clothes, and climbed in the shower. The fun started there and ended on her bed.

Now, we lay on the sheets, the covers having been kicked to the floor, Nicole resting in the crook of my arm.

"That was fun," she said.

"It was. Not sure what revved your engine but I like it."

"Flying always cranks up my rpms."

"Everything seems to redline your rpms."

She tilted her head upward. "You complaining?"

"Not even remotely."

"What time is it?"

I scooped up my iPhone from the bedside table and punched it to life. "Almost four."

"We better unpack and get ready."

"I'm ready."

I was. She reached down and squeezed me. "Put it away, cowboy." She laughed. "Until later."

"What about now?"

She rolled out of bed in all her magnificent nakedness. "We're meeting Megan at five thirty. I need to call Mom and Dad, and Uncle Charles, and let them know we made it."

I swung around to sit on the edge of the bed. "You're no fun."

"That's not what you said a little while ago."

"That was then. This is now."

"Quit pouting and get ready to go."

I wasn't pouting. Not much. "Okay, okay. I need to take another shower."

"Or I can simply throw cold water on you."

"A hot shower sounds better."

"Make it quick, I'm right behind you."

I stood. "Or, you can join me."

"No. That thing might get in the way."

"What thing?"

"Get in the shower, Jake."

I did, then dressed, and walked out on the deck while Nicole made her calls. Her condo, top floor, the third, in a fairly large cluster, hung along a narrow boardwalk and looked down on a line of Newport Harbor boat slips. The late-day sun glinted the water and cast long mast shadows over its surface. Down a few slips, a couple seemed to be prepping their sailboat for a sunset cruise. Popular around here. The guy lifted a blue cooler over the gunwale and settled it on the stern seat. That reminded me, I was hungry. Made me wonder what the boaters had on the menu. Sandwiches and beer would be fine with me, but I suspected Nicole would have wanted lobster, some sort of cheese I couldn't pronounce—Frenchy and nasty-tasting—and Champagne.

Toss in some avocado and quinoa and it would be like so California. Not that Nicole was all that high-maintenance, actually far from it, but out on the ocean in a cool-looking sailboat, she'd likely want to climb up the cuisine food chain.

Well before five, Nicole was all spiffed up and ready to go. Didn't take long because she didn't need much spiffing.

Took all of three minutes to walk to The Cannery, a Newport Beach institution. It was an old fish canning facility built a century ago that nearly fifty years ago evolved into a popular restaurant/bar. Even had its own boat slips so folks could sail or motor up and have lunch, dinner, drinks, whatever.

The hostess led us to a waterside table on the covered deck that looked down on the water. We ordered drinks, and since it was a half hour before Megan was due, Nicole added a dose of extra-crispy French fries.

"How is everyone?" I asked.

"I talked with Mom. She's so excited about the movie."

"As she should be. It'll be great."

"You're saying that to tamp down my anxiety about it."

"No. It's true. It's a great story."

It was. Based on a real Hollywood murder case. An unsolved one. Of course, Nicole's screenplay only loosely followed the real events. Poetic license at its best. She had transformed the complex and confusing case into a first-rate script. Lots of quirky characters and a thrill-ride plot.

Our drinks and the fries appeared. Our waitress, an attractive young lady named Willa, asked if we wanted to order any food.

"We're meeting someone," Nicole said. "We'll wait for them."

Willa nodded and disappeared toward the bar area.

"It'll be good to see them again," I said.

"Mom can't wait." Nicole smiled. "She has a crush on you."

"As I have on her."

That was true. Connie was basically Nicole in twenty years. Trim, fit, blond, and funny. Nicole had a good template to age into. Made me say a silent prayer that I wouldn't grow into Ray. Not likely. I was taller and leaner and took more after my mom. Sometimes the inheritance roulette wheel spun in the right direction. Not that Ray wasn't a good-looking guy, and smart, and oh so tough, but Mom had a sense of humor and calmness that seemed to have filtered down to me. Which rankled Ray on a daily basis. He, of course, loved my mom and losing her hammered him hard. Me too. But he had always hoped I'd get the sense of urgency and focus that defined his life. That ship sailed long ago.

"Uncle Charles is hosting a party at his place on Saturday. Mom and Dad will be there."

"Good."

"So will Kirk Ford."

Kirk Ford. The star of Uncle Charles' mega-hit *Space Quest* series. A couple of billion dollars worldwide, so far, and still counting. Uncle Charles had not only played the domestic and foreign market game to the hilt; he held the episodes closely and milked each through rereleases as long a possible. Then on to cable and the various streaming services and he needed 18-wheelers to roll in the money. Not literally, of course, but I liked that image.

All systems hummed, the franchise growing like kudzu, and then it jumped the rails. Kirk's involvement in the whole Kristi Guidry murder case down in New Orleans nearly did the franchise in. His reputation, and the reputation of Uncle Charles' Regency Global Productions, took a hit. Big-time. Now, Uncle Charles was gradually pasting it all back together and was planning the next installment for next year. As a way to reintroduce Kirk to the world and test the water temperature, Uncle Charles slotted him to star in *Murderwood*, Nicole's movie.

"Well, he is the star," I said. "How's he doing?"

"According to Uncle Charles, well. Seems to have put it all behind him and is eager to get back to work. Hopefully, the public is ready for his return."

"They will be. He's a certified superstar."

"I guess we'll see."

"It's been a rough road for him, I'm sure."

"Oh yeah. But Kirk's resilient."

"And pretty."

Nicole laughed. "He is that." She munched on a fry. "So we're off to Malibu."

"Can't wait to see Uncle Charles' place there. Bet it's nice."

"You have no idea. Makes the house I stay in look like a beach shack."

The beach shack in question was Uncle Charles' mansion in Gulf Shores. In The Point, the high-dollar, beachfront enclave where Tammy, my ex, also lived. Despite that, the neighborhood was envied by all who didn't, or couldn't, afford to live there. Uncle Charles' home was one of the biggest and classiest in the area. Massive, modern yet warm and cozy, with a large deck that hung over the beach, and best of all, a large hot tub, where Nicole and I had passed some quality time.

"That's hard to imagine," I said.

"Here comes Megan." Nicole waved

CHAPTER 3

"SORRY I'M LATE," Megan said as she walked up.

Megan Weatherly. I had last seen her six months earlier when Nicole and I were in The OC for a few days. Back when Nicole's movie project was in the early development stages. We came out to "take a few meetings." See? I know Hollywood-speak. Megan, as pretty as ever, was nearly as tall as Nicole's five-ten and had flowing mahogany hair, bright green eyes, and a perfect smile. She wore her "on-screen" clothes—ivory blouse, navy blue slacks, and a matching sports coat. Still had the Channel 16 button on the lapel.

Nicole and I stood, we exchanged hugs, sat again.

"You're not late," I said.

She glanced at her watch, shrugged. "Guess not. Sure feels that way."

"One of those days?" Nicole asked.

"Yeah. The show had a brief technical issue. One of the cameras went out right in the middle of my report." She laughed. "Scared the hell out of me. It sputtered and fumed and smoked. Good thing we have backups."

"Knowing you, you soldiered on without difficulty," Nicole said.

"Did my best. Then we had a brief editorial meeting. That's why I didn't have time to change."

"You look very professional," I said.

"Yeah well, I'd rather look more casual." She scanned the room. "Right now I need a drink."

I saw Willa, our waitress, taking an order at a nearby table. I gave her a quick wave when she glanced my way.

Megan snatched a French fry. "I'm starving."

"Have all you want," Nicole said. "Jake hasn't been much help. I don't think he likes them."

"I do," I said. "I was afraid to eat too many. You do have sharp instruments at hand."

Megan smiled in my direction. "Glad to see you haven't lost your smart-ass sense of humor."

"It's ingrained," Nicole said. "But he's pretty so it's okay."

Good lord.

Willa appeared. "Can I get you something?" she asked Megan.

Megan nodded toward Nicole's glass of wine. "I'll have whatever she's having."

"Anything else?"

"I'll have a another," I said, indicating my glass of Makers Mark.

"Cool. I'll get those right up and bring some menus."

"Grab an extra one," Megan said. "Someone's joining us."

"Will do." And Willa was gone.

"I hope you don't mind," Megan said. "I asked my new intern to join us. You'll like her."

"Intern?" I asked.

"Yeah. It's a new program at the station. The owners want to establish a training program for future broadcasters." She raised a shoulder. "Somehow I got nabbed as the guinea pig."

"Because you're good," Nicole said. "And experienced. I'm sure she'll learn a lot from you."

Willa rolled by, ferrying a platter piled with fried calamari to another table. "I'll be right back with your drinks," she said as she passed our table.

"Apparently, it's part of my promotion," Megan said.

"That's right," Nicole said. "I'm sorry I didn't mention it but congratulations."

"A good promotion?" I asked.

"Very. They made me Editorial VP and Co-Director of programming."

"So cool," Nicole said.

"What's her story?" I asked. "Your new girl Friday?"

"Her name's Abby. Abby Watson. She graduated from Oregon with a degree in journalism. Then she worked at a couple of small-market stations. Mostly behind the scenes. Now she wants to move around and face the camera. So, she applied for the internship and management hired her."

Our drinks appeared. Willa placed four menus on the table. "Anything while you wait for your other guest?"

"The calamari looked good," I said.

"Oh my. It's to die for."

"Sound good?" I asked Nicole and Megan.

"Absolutely," Nicole said.

"On it." Willa sped off again.

"Anyway," Megan continued. "She's a very attractive young lady. She seems smart like she really has it together. I think she'll do well in front of the camera. Seems to have some moxie and isn't afraid of the lights."

"Sort of like you," Nicole said.

"And here you are moving the other way," Megan said to Nicole. "From facing the camera to being behind it."

"I'm just the writer."

Megan glanced toward me. "Listen to her. She's *just the writer*. Only the most important part."

"It's a very good script," I said. "It'll be a great movie."

"Jake's trying to flatter me. Earning points for later."

Megan flipped her hair back over her shoulder. "Like he needs them."

"You know me too well," Nicole said.

I knew that was true. Nicole had often referred to Megan as the sister she never had. When Nicole lived here in Newport Beach—of course, technically she still did even if she now spent virtually all her time in Gulf Shores squatting in Uncle Charles' house—she and Megan had grown tight. Hanging out at the beach, cruising bars, and mostly offering each other shoulders to lean on when need be. They still talked on the phone almost weekly and occasionally helped each other with crises. It crossed my mind that Nicole never had crises. She seemed to go with the flow. But Megan had had a few bumps along the way. I remembered one night, what, maybe a year ago, when Nicole had to talk Megan off the ceiling after a tough breakup with a guy Nicole described as a "douche." I had laid in bed next to her while Nicole offered a degree of comfort and rationality to Megan's world. Seemed to work. By the time Nicole hung up, they were both laughing.

"So tell me about the movie," Megan said. "What's going on?"

"We begin shooting in three weeks. Then we have a ten-week production schedule."

"You'll be here the entire time?"

"Probably not. Maybe for about half of that."

"Kirk Ford is going to star in it, right?" Megan asked.

"He is."

"Ballsy move. After all the trouble he had."

"Yeah," Nicole said. "But Uncle Charles needs to get him back on the screen and his face out in public again. He figured this would be a good project for him. An action thriller."

"You okay with that?"

"I am. Kirk's actually a good guy. He simply made a mistake." She nudged me. "The kind most guys make. Thinking with their dicks."

"I thought you liked that about me," I said.

"I do. But then none of your conquests ended up dead." She shrugged. "As far as I know."

"Conquests? That's me. The knight-errant, knocking down castle walls and bedding all the maidens."

Nicole shook her head. "Jake has a vivid imagination."

"I need to if I'm going to keep up with you."

The calamari appeared. Steaming, aromatic, and delicious.

"This will be Kirk's first movie then?" Megan asked. "Since the New Orleans fiasco?"

Nicole nodded while wrestling a calamari tentacle into her mouth.

"Speaking of being a guinea pig," Megan continued.

Nicole swiped her lips with her napkin. "Sort of. But a win-win for sure. Kirk gets to have a PR trial run and I get to have a true mega-star in my movie. Not to mention it'll be done by Uncle Charles. With those two names attached, it has a good chance to be successful." She shrugged. "But if it flops, I couldn't be in better company for the flame-out."

"Never heard of a flop by Charles Balfour," Megan said.

"First time for everything."

"I doubt it." Megan's phone buzzed. She looked at the screen. "That's Abby. She's five minutes away."

CHAPTER 4

"THERE SHE IS," Megan said.

I followed her gaze. A broad smile led Abby Watson our way. An attractive young lady, with lively brown eyes, black hair cut short and feathered around the edges, and a compact, fit body. Maybe five-four and a buck-ten. She wore snug jeans and an untucked purple shirt. She lugged a large black purse over one shoulder.

"Sorry I'm late," she said. She settled in the chair between Megan and Nicole, across from me.

Megan made the introductions.

"Megan's told me all about you two," Abby said. "Good to finally put faces with the names."

"She speaks highly of you, too," Nicole said.

"She has to. Company policy."

Megan laughed. "That's actually true. You know, all that 'safe space' and 'micro aggression' crap."

"I mean really," Abby said. "If you can't piss someone off every now and then, what's the purpose of life?"

I liked her. She seemed energetic and witty. The glint in her eyes revealed a bit of irreverence. Add to that a healthy dose of cuteness and what wasn't to like?

"That's essentially Jake's motto," Nicole said.

"Me? What about you?"

"I'm all peaches and cream."

"I see. And me?"

"Rhubarb."

Abby giggled at that. "Just as advertised."

"Oh?" I said. "*Advertised?*"

"Yeah, Megan said you two were Tracy and Hepburn reborn."

"You are," Megan said. "All those word jousts you guys love."

No way I could deny that. We did like to jab each other. Well, Nicole did most of the jabbing. She said I was a target-rich subject, whatever that meant. I was afraid to ask.

But I did wonder if that was part of the Longly Investigations company manual. Was there one? Did Nicole have to read it to sort-of, kind-of work for Ray? I can see it now. Article two: hammer Jake at every opportunity.

Willa the waitress returned. She took Abby's order, the same as Nicole and Megan, and added another round for the rest of us.

"Before you go," Nicole said. "Can you take a group picture for us?"

"Sure."

Nicole passed Willa her iPhone. She and Megan scooted close to Abby while I moved around behind the trio, bracing my arms on the chair backs and leaning forward. Once arranged, Willa snapped a couple of shots and returned Nicole's phone.

"Thanks," Nicole said.

"No problem. I'll be right back with your drinks."

"Oh," Abby said. She twisted and rummaged inside her purse, which she had hung on the back of her chair. She lifted what was obviously a wrapped gift. Shiny white paper, red bow, and a matching red envelope taped to the front. "From Mr. Wonderful."

I saw script on the front of the card that read, "For Megan, My True Love."

"A new guy in your life?" Nicole asked.

"Not what it seems."

"He's her celebrity stalker," Abby said.

"No, he's not." Megan gave a headshake. "He's simply an admirer."

"A crazed admirer."

"Let's say devoted."

Concern creased Nicole's brow. "What's this about?"

"Just some guy," Megan said. "A fan of the show and apparently me. Sends notes from time to time. Flowers, candy." She lifted the box. "This feels like candy."

"Not to mention the emails and texts," Abby added. "You've had about a million texts just since I got here."

"How long have you been interning?" Nicole asked.

"What?" Abby glanced at Megan. "Three weeks?"

"About that."

"This guy?" I asked. "Who is he?"

"I don't know. He simply signs everything 'A Devoted Fan.'"

I nodded toward the gift. "Or 'My True Love,' it seems."

"Creepy," Nicole added.

"Exactly," Abby said. "But she refuses to take this seriously." She rolled her eyes. "I've told her over and over that this is how stalkers start. Some of them can escalate and become dangerous."

"Voice of experience?" Nicole asked.

Abby nodded. "An old boyfriend. I broke up with him because he was actually a dick disguised as a normal guy. He kept following me, texting me, putting all kinds of crap on Facebook. Sent me things like flowers and candy." She nodded toward Megan. "Like this dude is doing."

"Anything more threatening?" Nicole asked.

"Oh yeah. He'd show up at my home, my work, at school. He'd leave notes on my door, in my mailbox. He'd even send things to my mom telling her that he was her future son-in-law. Crap like that." She forked her fingers through her hair. "He flattened my tires once. At a mall of all places. He must've followed me there. He then offered me a ride. Like he was my savior or something. I said no way and called a friend."

"Did he ever try to harm you?" I asked.

"Not directly. I put a restraining order on him and he smashed the windshield of my car." She shrugged. "I could never prove that it was him but it had to be."

"What eventually happened?" Nicole asked.

"I finished school, moved away. Far away. I got a few more texts from him so I got a new phone and shut down that email account. Never heard anything again."

"This guy isn't that way," Megan said. "He's merely a fan."

"Didn't I say that's how they start?" Abby said.

"What does the card say?" I asked, indicating the box resting by Megan's left elbow.

She detached it, finger-nailed the flap, and slid the card out. White with a red rose on the front. She opened it and read:

The TV does you no justice. A camera cannot capture your true beauty. Only the eyes of the beholder can do that. I love you madly and always will. Your most loyal fan and lover.

Megan frowned. "Well that's different. First time he's used the word 'lover.'"

"See?" Abby said. "He's getting all weird."

"Have you met him?" I asked.

"No. Not that I know anyway."

"Well, he's seen you. In the flesh, so to speak."

"Sounds that way," Nicole added. "That could mean he's following you."

Megan reread the note. She sighed. "Okay, so he's quirky and infatuated. I still believe he's harmless."

"They seem that way at first," Abby said. "But then they grab on more firmly."

Megan raised an eyebrow. "A little dramatic."

Abby shook her head. "Not really. Look at the words he used." She took the card from Megan and examined it. "He says things like 'eyes of the beholder,' 'love you madly,' and calls himself your 'lover.' Seems a bit obsessive to me."

"I think you're overreading it," Megan said. "He's simply some infatuated dude."

"I'm afraid that I agree with Abby here," Nicole said. "I've had stalkers in the past. Back when I was still acting. The worst one started with notes and flowers, but before long he somehow found a way onto the studio lot where we were filming. With all the security around, that was no small task. He actually made it to the sound stage several times. He was repeatedly warned. The studio even got a trespass order that banned him from the property. Didn't work though. He returned a couple of more times and was ultimately arrested. That pissed him off so he became even more aggressive. He started showing up at my condo. This was when I lived in LA. Creating chaos. Even scratched some pretty awful words into my front door with a knife."

"I never knew that," Megan said.

"Not something I dwell on. Or care to think about. Ultimately, he broke in to my condo. Middle of the night. Fortunately, I had started keeping a short aluminum baseball bat by my bed and whacked him a couple of times." She smiled. "A couple of good shots if I say so myself. He took off but only got a few blocks before the police arrested him. Thank God he pled guilty and there was no trial. I didn't want to face him again. Not to mention all the paparazzi that would have turned it into a semi-circus." She shrugged. "Not that I was a big name. Not even close. But I was Charles Balfour's niece and that would have attracted the flies."

"What happened to him?" Abby asked.

"The judge sent him away for five years."

I knew the story. Nicole had talked about it, and a couple of other less scary stalkers, but hearing it again gave me chills. Always did. Raised my blood pressure and made me wish I had been there with a real baseball bat.

"That's why you should take this seriously," Abby said to Megan. "These guys always escalate." She nodded toward the note. "Like Mr. Wonderful here. He seems to have started climbing that ladder."

"You guys are overreacting," Megan said. "He's harmless. Not all fans become obsessed stalkers."

"That's true," Nicole said. "Jake's been stalking me for over a year now."

"Me?" I said. "If memory serves, you started it. Took advantage of my predicament."

"Oh, there's a story I'd like to hear," Abby said.

"Jake was doing surveillance," Nicole said.

"Surveillance?" Abby asked.

"My father's a P.I. He roped me into watching a house. Still not sure why I caved in and did it, but Ray can be persuasive."

"Jake in his infinite wisdom—" Nicole gave me a glance and a smile—"managed to park right in front of his ex's house, which was just a few doors away from the house he was watching. She saw him and beat his car to a pulp with a golf club. A cop showed up. The whole deal."

"Really?" Abby's eyes were wide.

"Really," I said. "That's when Nicole pounced. She saw me all helpless and vulnerable. Used her wiles to trap me in her home. I felt like Hansel without Gretel."

Nicole gave a headshake. "Jake has a vivid imagination. Also a vintage Mustang. Tammy, that's his ex, trashed a couple of windows and it was beginning to rain. I offered my garage as a safe haven."

"Among other things," I said.

"Just being a good Samaritan."

"You were a great Samaritan."

"That's how you guys met?" Abby asked.

"It is. Jake's been obsessed with me ever since." She laughed.

I started to protest but really couldn't since I was guilty as charged. But in my defense, look at her. Who wouldn't be obsessed with Nicole? Megan and Abby, too, for that matter. Which I guessed was the point of this entire conversation.

Also in my defense, I never sent Nicole flowers or candy or creepy notes. She wasn't a flower and candy girl anyway, preferring whiskey and ribs.

"So, you see," Nicole said, "you have to take these stalker types seriously. They're hard to shake."

"Like you've tried," I said.

"Look," Megan said. "This guy's harmless. It's simply a momentary infatuation. He'll soon move on, I'm sure. Besides, I need all the fans I can get."

"Have you had any others like this?" I asked.

"Sure. A dozen over the past couple of years. Most send a handful of emails and then go away. A couple kept it up for a few months but even they gave up." She shrugged. "I guess they realized I was a TV image and not their friend."

"But this guy looks at you as his lover," Abby said. "That's creepy and scary."

CHAPTER 5

THE NEXT MORNING, Nicole and I decided to take a walk along the Newport Beach bike path. It ran virtually the entire length of Balboa Peninsula, a spit of land that embraced Newport Harbor, as well as Lido Isle and Balboa Island, both packed with seven-figure, some eight-figure, homes, and protected the harbor from the Pacific's sometimes churning waves. The pathway, a thin ribbon of concrete, separated the broad sand beach and the multimillion-dollar houses that stood shoulder to shoulder like beachy row homes. A few million didn't buy you much land around here but enough zeroes could get you a great view.

Nicole wore black Lycra knee-length shorts that appeared to have been spray-painted on and a gray cropped tee shirt. A black baseball cap and gray New Balance jogging shoes completed her outfit.

Wow, just wow.

Me? Shorts and a tee shirt. Nothing special. No one was going to notice me anyway with Nicole alongside.

We headed over to the Newport Pier, only a five-minute walk from Nicole's condo, where we could jump on the bike path. But that wasn't our destination. Not yet. Nicole needed nourishment first. Even though we had had a rather substantial meal last night, I was hungry too.

Near the base of the pier and nestled among a few shops and other eateries was Charlie's Chili. Like The Cannery, a Newport Beach institution and famous for their massive and perfectly spicy Chili Cheese Omelet. Nicole's favorite restaurant and dish. Every time we came out to the left coast, a stop at Charlie's was mandatory.

We found a booth along the back wall. Our waitress poured coffee and took our orders.

"I think you like this place better than Captain Rocky's," I said.

"I do right now."

"You do?"

"We're here. That makes it number one."

"My feelings are hurt."

"No, they're not. I eat enough meals at Captain Rocky's to own stock."

"But like Pancake, you eat for free."

"Here too. You're buying."

"Why me? You're the big Hollywood mogul."

"Oh, I forgot. Okay, I'll buy. But you'll pay later."

"I'll pay later anyway."

"That's true."

Our omelets appeared, coffee cups refilled, and we dug in. I had to admit, it was outstanding. Nicole shoveled in a couple of bites then said, "Heaven. Pure heaven."

"Spicy."

"Wimp." She pointed her fork at me. "You should serve breakfast at Captain Rocky's."

"I do. We have breakfast burritos on the menu."

"Yeah but you don't open until eleven. Open at seven. Serve real breakfast."

"Carla would mutiny."

Carla Martinez, my manager, and the one who really kept the doors open and the books balanced. I was simply the "face man." If I told her we were opening four hours earlier, she'd shoot me. Literally.

"Probably true," Nicole said. "But if you did, you'd have to put this on the menu."

"You might get fat if you ate this everyday."

She smiled. "I'd find a way to work it off."

"Would that include me?"

"It would."

"Then I'd better eat up."

"You go, cowboy."

We each cleaned our plates, and then Nicole did indeed pay the bill. We walked outside.

"Okay, let's walk this off," Nicole said.

"When you said work it off earlier, I had something else in mind."

"I did too. But right now, I need to walk."

The typical morning marine layer blocked the sun and the light onshore breeze felt cool. That would soon change as the sun burned away the cloud layer and heated up the sand. We followed the bike path for the next half hour, down the peninsula past the Balboa Pier and way out to the peninsula's tip, to The Wedge. One of the many surfing cathedrals along the Southern California coastline. A place where the western swell shoved the water against the elbow created by the harbor's rock-pile breakwater barrier and the sandy beach. An arrangement that created churning waves and a beach break. Meaning the water slammed directly onto hard-packed sand. Dangerous, The Wedge had caused more spinal injuries than folks cared to talk about. Yet it still attracted body surfers and boogie boarders of all skill levels.

We stood on the beach and watched a group of teenage boys get thrashed by the waves. A couple of them smacked the sand fairly hard

but came up spitting and coughing and laughing. One, a skinny kid
with stringy blond hair and dark blue baggies, kissed the beach with a
firm whack—off the top of a wave and flat against the sand. He rolled
over and sat up, while his buddies whooped and hollered, one shout-
ing that it was an epic face-plant. It was. Fortunately, the kid shook
it off and dove back into the surf. Kids that age, especially boys, are
indestructible, or at least think they are. Growing up, Pancake and I
were exactly the same. The difference being that Pancake actually was
indestructible. I tried to picture him thumping the beach like that.
Wouldn't be pretty. Pancake one, beach zero.

Pancake and I didn't have big waves like those at The Wedge along
the Gulf Coast so we found other venues for our stunts. Like jumping
off the roof of the garage. Yeah, we actually did that. Thought it was
fun. Go figure. Or swinging on a rope lashed to a tree limb to propel
ourselves out over a shallow creek. The drop was a rush, the water
cool, the bottom hard and craggy. Seemed we did such crazy crap all
the time. Sort of explained many a southern boy's final words: "Here,
hold my beer and watch this."

We retreated to the bike path and turned toward home. Nicole
took my hand.

"What do you think about what Megan said last night?" she asked.

"That dude?"

"Yeah. Her stalker."

"That's a little harsh, don't you think?"

"No. I didn't feel comfortable with the note he included with the
candy. It sounded a little too desperate."

"Guys with crushes do and say all kinds of stupid stuff."

"You'd know."

I looked at her. "What does that mean?"

"It means you're a guy. You think with the wrong head way too
often."

"In our defense, we can't help it. It's biological. Besides, I thought you liked that about me."

"I do." She slapped my butt. "But your advances aren't exactly unwelcome."

"Maybe this guy's aren't either."

"Really? Don't you think Megan's uncomfortable with all this?"

"Is she? Nothing she said last night made me think she was upset or concerned in the least."

"Hmmm." Nicole seemed the think that over. Maybe mentally running through last night's conversation. "She's at least not taking him very seriously."

"My point. The truth is there is no way to know who or what this guy is. Or even form a coherent impression. We just heard about it, and only the highlights. She's been living with it for a few weeks."

"She's a pretty together woman. Not one to go all crazy about anything."

"So she might be right? This is a big nothing?"

"Maybe." She sighed. "I don't know why, but for some reason I have a bad feeling about it."

"Why?"

"Maybe it's the stalkers I've had. That could be coloring my reading of this."

"Still, you have good instincts."

She smiled. "Sometimes."

"Most times."

She kissed my cheek. "You're sweet."

"I am. I'll tell you what. Let's go see Megan today. Take a look at all the communications she's had from this guy."

"So, you're concerned, too?"

"Not really. Well, maybe a little. But if you're feeling things are wrong, it warrants looking into."

"Isn't that what P.I.s do?"

"I'm not a P.I.," I said.

"We'll see."

"Ray isn't anywhere around here. In fact, he's two thousand miles away."

"Yeah, but he's like Santa Claus. He's everywhere."

That I couldn't deny.

CHAPTER 6

THE WALK BACK up the bike path was pleasant. The morning marine layer began to break up and the sun made a sketchy appearance, its orb visibly pushing through the low clouds. Looked like it was going to be a great day.

Why wouldn't it be? Every day in The OC bordered on perfect. Well, except for June. The exception that made the rule. A month when the marine layer would hang around for days, relegating the sun to forgotten visitor status. Locals called it the June Gloom. Not sure why it happened, but it was a seasonal phenomenon. Fortunately, this wasn't June so another stellar day hung on the horizon. Besides, we had had an excellent breakfast, a pleasant walk, and when we got back to Nicole's place we would need a shower. Oh yeah.

"What are you smiling about?" Nicole asked as we strolled past the Balboa Pier and the Fun Zone, a collection of shops, restaurants, and even a small Ferris wheel. Also, the peninsula terminus of the ferry that slid back and forth to nearby—meaning a hundred or so yards—Balboa Island. The area was quiet this time of morning, just a few walkers out and about, but it would soon crank up and become chaotic.

"I was smiling?"

"You were."

"Just thinking about the shower when we get back."

She bumped a hip against mine. "Of course, you were." Another bump. "Me, too."

Yes, it was destined to be a perfect day.

Then it wasn't.

My cell buzzed. The screen read "Tammy." My ex. Tammy the Insane. Past history dictated that ignoring her was not an option. She would only call and call and call. A war of attrition that she always won. I mean, how many chimes and buzzes could you stand? Soon the anticipation of the next call became worse than the chirping itself. She once called every two minutes for well over a half an hour. As I said, Tammy the Insane.

Nicole and I veered off the bike path, away from the other walkers, and moved across the beach toward the water. Out of earshot. I punched the speaker button, but before I could say anything, Tammy jumped right into the issue of the day.

"Jake, where are you?"

"California."

"Oh. I forgot."

She knew Nicole and I were coming out for the shooting of Nicole's movie.

Tammy continued. "I need you here."

"Why?" As soon as it escaped my mouth, I regretted it. Never a good idea to encourage Tammy. Never ask a question, never offer advice, never seem interested, never, never, never. Yet, with a single word, I had opened the door. Stupid is as stupid does.

"I don't know what to do," Tammy said. "I want you to talk to Walter."

Walter Horton. Tammy's husband. A mega lawyer along the Gulf Coast. The one that took me for a bundle when he handled our divorce. Then married Tammy. In the end, not all that bad for me.

"Walter and I don't talk," I said.

"That's because Walter's busy. And smart. You're neither."

Gotta love her. She can insult you and ask for help and never take a breath between. "So, why would I talk to Walter now?"

"Because he needs you."

My brain screamed "Don't ask." But I had to admit the old cat curiosity thing reared its head. "Needs me for what?"

"He's talking crazy. About closing his practice and retiring."

"Okay."

"Don't you see? How will we live? If Walter quits, we'll be destitute."

Depends on your meaning of destitute. Walter probably had eight figures in the bank, a multimillion-dollar house on The Point, and likely a pile of accounts receivable that exceeded my net worth. Hard to muster much sympathy for the Horton clan.

"I think Walter will be fine," I said.

We reached the firmer sand near the waterline and turned up the beach, toward the Newport Pier.

"What about me?" Tammy said. "What will I do?"

"Maybe get a job."

That stopped her for a few seconds. Such brief moments of silence is all you could ask for in any conversation with Tammy. A fleeting hope, but then doesn't that always spring eternal? Or explodes in your face.

"Jake, be serious."

Hmm, I thought I had been. But then Tammy and work were like oil and water.

"All I'm asking is that you talk to him," she went on. "Tell him everyone has bad weeks."

I failed to see how I would have any insights into Walter's issues with his practice, his mood, or his life. But this is Tammy's world. Nothing ever really makes sense. Or to be charitable—rarely does. Her brain is like the cloud of electrons that whirl around an unstable plutonium nucleus. See, I did pay attention in school. The point is that somewhere in her head there's a lot of swirling and flashing and chaos, and every now and then a couple of those electrons collide, and an idea pops out. Not always one that makes sense though.

"What are you talking about?" I asked.

"Walter's had a couple of difficult cases. Pro bono so he did them for free. I keep telling him not to. That he doesn't owe anyone anything." That's the Tammy we know and love. Always so warm and fuzzy. "He spent a lot of time on them. Even lost one of them. He's depressed and thinks he's too old and should walk away."

"Maybe he should."

"Jake, whose side are you on?"

"I don't have a side."

"You never do."

"Okay, I'll bite. What could I possibly say to Walter that he'd listen to?"

"Tell him that bad times don't mean the end of anything. Tell him about the time you gave up four home runs in two innings."

Not my best night. Yankee Stadium. I hung a couple of curveballs and the Bronx Bombers made me pay. Three single homers and one two-runner. Before the second inning was over, I was in the showers.

Tammy reminded me of the night all too often. Her way of saying I wasn't as good as ESPN said I was.

"Walter doesn't want to talk to me about anything, much less his life choices," I said. I thought about adding that his decision to marry Tammy pretty much meant he made poor ones, but I held that in. Wasn't easy.

"But you have some insights that might help him. You know, about losing and all. Granted, yours were silly baseball games and his are more serious lawsuits, but still, he might like to hear how you handled it."

"You don't remember?" I asked. Dammit, Jake, just shut up.

"The brunette?"

"Redhead."

A moment of silence and then, "Oh yeah, the stripper."

"She wasn't a stripper. She danced on Broadway."

"In *A Chorus Line*. Isn't that about strippers?"

Does her brain ever work? "No. It's about chorus line dancers. They're serious professionals and work hard."

"Just one of your many dalliances."

"If memory serves, you were packing all my shit in boxes and changing the locks."

"So?"

"Sort of meant the marriage was over, don't you think?"

"Well yeah, but still."

"Look, Tammy. I could walk down memory lane all day but I don't see the point. Neither do I see the point in talking with Walter."

"So you aren't going to help him? Help me?"

"I will give you some advice. I think your major worry is that if Walter isn't working, he'll be home all day and you don't know how to handle that. So back to my original suggestion—get a job."

"It's not that easy. I've never really had a job. What on earth could I possibly do."

"Maybe a stripper?"

That did it. She railed and spewed for a good five minutes, closing with, "You're such an ass." She hung up.

"That was fun," Nicole said.

"I need a shower."

She grabbed my hand. "Poor baby, you sure do."

CHAPTER 7

CHANNEL 16, DEFINITELY a small market enterprise and touted as "OC's Most Reliable Local News Source," broadcasted to all of Orange County as well as much of Los Angles, San Bernardino, Riverside, and San Diego Counties. From what I read, the broadcast hours ran from 8:00 a.m. until midnight. Except for several daily news reports and some local interest stories, most programming appeared to be prerecorded and packaged. Things such as community service and educational spots, travel stories, and locally produced infomercials for everything from the SoCal AAA to a local hairstylist to how to make money in the always hot—their word—Orange County real estate market. They also aired classic movies, high school stage productions, and highlights from local high school sporting events. Some of Megan's reports were prerecorded but most were live during the Monday through Friday 4:00 p.m. to 6:00 p.m. time slots. Typically five to ten minutes long, her show broadcast times varied daily and moved around within that two-hour window.

The studio, located just over a block from the intersection of Newport Boulevard and 19th Street in Costa Mesa, hung on the end of an industrial strip center next door to a printing company. The sign that stretched over the entryway read: "Channel 16 Local News You Can Trust."

Inside, Nicole and I encountered a pleasant receptionist who sat at a small desk behind a counter. Her name tag read: "Phyllis P."

"Can I help you?" Phyllis P asked with a welcoming smile.

"We're looking for Megan Weatherly," Nicole said.

"You must be Nicole and Jake."

"We are."

"She said you were coming by." Her phone rang. She answered, saying, "Please hold for a sec." She pressed the phone against her chest and pointed toward the door along the far wall. "Through there. She's in the last room on the right."

"Thanks," I said.

Phyllis P returned to her call.

We found Megan in a rather large room that held four desks, one near each corner. Obviously, a multi-user office. She sat at one desk, a legal pad and pen in hand. To her left, Abby worked on a computer.

"There you guys are," Megan said. "Any trouble finding this place?"

"Not really," Nicole said.

"We're tucked back here off the beaten path."

"You know," Nicole said, "when we pulled up, I realized I'd never seen where you work."

"Here it is." She waved a hand. "My humble abode."

I looked at Abby, who had swung her chair around to face us. "How're you doing?"

"Megan's making me work too hard." She smiled. "Sort of a slave driver."

Megan matched her laugh. "You know? The youngsters? Got to stay on top of them."

"You're not that much older than me," Abby said. "Only a few years." She shrugged. "But in terms of experience in this business? Light-years."

Megan stood. "Let me show you around." She nodded toward the two unoccupied desks. "We have two rooms like this. We don't have the space or the funds for everyone to have a private office so we sort of dorm room it." She shrugged. "It can get chaotic at times, but for the most part it works."

We followed her back into the hallway. Another nearly identical four-desk office space was across the way. It sat empty. Back toward the entry were three recording studios. Two smaller ones to our right and a large one to our left. Only one of the smaller ones was in use, the other dark. A woman and a man sat in matching comfortable chairs, angled forty-five degrees from the camera and from each other. Behind them was an easel with a large sign that read "Regal Real Estate Partners."

"Pretty quiet right now," Megan said. "They're recording a fifteen-minute commercial spot."

"From what I saw," I said, "you do a lot of those."

Megan nodded. "Got to keep the lights, and the cameras, on. These commercial slots really keep our head above water."

"How else do you bring in revenue?" I asked.

"Some public funds from the PBS world. Donations, of course. We sell our logo hats and shirts and things like that. And we do several fundraisers every year."

"Things going okay? Financially wise?"

"So far so good. But it's a constant battle."

Megan moved to the smoked glass wall that peered into the larger studio. "This is our main studio. Where I do my reports. Where we do major recordings and all the live stuff."

"It looks well equipped," I said.

It did. Three cameras, several mic booms, and a main set that included a long desk with space for four or more people. For interviews, I assumed. The Channel 16 logo fronted the desk. A smaller set with two director's chairs and a backdrop, also with the station logo, sat near the far wall.

"We are blessed there," Megan said. "The owners didn't scrimp on electronics."

We returned to Megan's office.

"Anything new from that guy?" Nicole asked.

"A couple of emails this morning."

"Can we see everything you have so far?" I asked.

"Sure."

Megan settled in her chair and spun to face her computer. Nicole and I pulled up chairs, Abby rolled in behind us, looking over Nicole's shoulder.

"I can't imagine you'll see anything in these," Megan said.

"Probably not," I said. "But it doesn't hurt to look."

"Let's go through them chronologically," Nicole said.

"Okay." Megan tapped the keyboard and called up her email program.

"How many are we talking about?" I asked.

"A couple of dozen or so. Many more texts."

There were actually nineteen emails. Over the past three weeks. The first few were benign, saying things like he was a "big fan" and "love your style." The fifth one said that he would "love to meet you sometime." A couple of days later, an invitation to drinks and dinner. Megan had replied to each, being very formal and even standoffish but always considerate. Treating him like a fan and nothing more.

"Looks pretty harmless so far," I said.

"Let's see the rest," Nicole said.

Number sixteen suggested a change in tone and attitude. Just yesterday. It followed a couple of other invitations to hook up.

It read:

I'm truly injured by your refusal to see me. I'm confused and hurt because I know we could be friends. Maybe more. Who

knows? Romances have blossomed from less. What if we were
meant for each other and your stubbornness prevented either
of us from ever experiencing that? Makes me sad to even think
about. Please reconsider and join me for a nice, quiet, romantic
dinner. If we have sparks then fine and if not, at least we will
both know for sure.

"That's a little more desperate," Nicole said.

"Exactly what I told her," Abby added. "It reminds me of my stalker. All nice and kind but then more demanding." She shook her head. "Then it only got worse."

"You guys are overreacting," Megan said.

"I agree," I said. "Maybe he's a little desperate, but this suggests a degree of ineptness more than anything else."

"Says the voice of experience," Nicole said.

"You're saying I'm inept?"

"More so the opposite. You have a knack for engaging people. Apparently, this guy doesn't." She raised an eyebrow, and then said to Megan, "Jake has a way with women."

Megan laughed. "That's obvious."

"It's because he's so handsome," Abby said.

"Also pretty," Nicole added.

"Yeah," Abby said. "That, too."

The three of them shared a laugh.

"Are you finished picking on me?" I asked.

Nicole roughed my hair. "Poor baby. Always put upon."

"You'll pay for this later," I said.

"That's the plan."

Another round of laughter.

"Let's look at the two from today," I said.

The next one was somewhat apologetic for him being pushy. Even contrite, promising not to pressure her. But the final one, which had come in a half hour ago, was definitely more aggressive.

It read:

Please don't ignore me. Please meet me. Only then will you see that I'm a real and caring person who only wants what's best for you. For us. We could have a future together if you would only open the door and let me in. I'm trying so hard to not let your refusals spike my anger but it isn't easy. I don't want to feel that way about you. I want to love and cherish you. Please, I beg of you, don't push me away.

"Oh," Abby said. "I hadn't seen that one. That is major-league creepy."

Megan sighed. "Maybe not all the way to creepy."

"I take back what I said earlier," I said. "He's more than simply inept."

"Unstable is the word," Nicole said.

"Absolutely," Abby added. "This one has an entirely different tone than the earlier ones."

Megan sighed. "I hate this. I wish he'd simply go away."

"He won't," Abby said.

"What about texts?" I asked. "You said you've gotten those also."

"Yeah. Maybe forty or so."

"Let's see."

Megan opened her messaging app on her computer. "This is synced to my phone so all of them are here."

There were eight threads and a total of forty-seven messages. I immediately noticed that they came from several different phone numbers. Looked like a dozen from one, the next dozen or so from another, and so on. All from the 720 area code.

"The area codes are the Denver area," I said.

"I never noticed," Megan said.

"I played ball with a guy from Denver. That's how I know."

"You're becoming a real P.I.," Nicole said.

Was she poking fun at me? She smiled, proving she was.

Back to the business at hand, I scanned through the texts. Most were benign, simply letting her know he was thinking of her. Some said he had watched her show and that she was "wonderful," or "perky," or "oh so beautiful." A few invited her to meet him at some bar or restaurant. These were mostly last-minute contacts, him telling her he was out somewhere and thinking of her and thought he'd see if she was free. She never was. All of Megan's replies, to her credit, were polite and noncommittal. As with the emails, his tone underwent a change over the past forty-eight hours. Abby's use of the term desperate seemed appropriate.

"You have no idea who this is?" I asked.

"None." She shrugged. "All I know is what you've seen right here."

"Has he called?" Nicole asked.

Megan shook her head. "No. Other than these there were only the brief notes that accompanied the presents he's sent."

"Do you have those?" I asked.

"I tossed them. The only one I have is from last night. The one you saw."

I struggled with what to say. Should I assure her that this was simply a devoted fan with suspect social skills? Or that he might be some deranged stalker who should be taken seriously? I mean, most, nearly all, of his communications had been friendly and nonthreatening. Only a few had crossed that line. Maybe those were when he was having a bad day. A little cranky and frustrated with Megan stiff-arming him. But did any of this make him truly dangerous? Truth was, I was on the fence. Apparently, Nicole wasn't.

"I think we should try to track this guy down," Nicole said.

"How?" Megan asked.

"Open up one of the emails," I said.

She did. I now saw that he had a Gmail account and his user name was "DevotedFan998877."

"Now click there and scroll down to 'show original,'" I said.

She did. A page appeared with all sorts of letters and numbers and computer gibberish.

"What's this?" Megan asked.

"It's how he can be tracked, I think," I said. "This should show his IP address and maybe who he is."

"Looks like a mad scientist's notepad to me," Abby said.

I laughed. "It does and truthfully it makes little sense to me." Then to Megan, I said, "Can you forward me all of those? Both emails and texts?"

"Why?" Megan asked.

"So we can begin tracking down his email and phone services. Maybe find him."

"You know how to do that?" Abby asked.

"No. That's above my pay grade."

"And mental capacity," Nicole said.

"You're funny. You really are."

"Okay, you two," Megan said. "But all that begs the question, how are you going to find this dude?"

"I got a guy."

"Who?"

"Pancake." Nicole and I said it in unison.

"Ah, the mysterious Pancake," Megan said.

"Who's Pancake?" Abby asked.

I did my best to describe him for her. Size, weight, red hair, need for constant food. Also, that he was a P.I. who worked for my father. In the end, my description seemed anemic. Pancake isn't easily reduced to words.

"He's an investigator?" Abby asked.

"Very skilled with computers, too."

"So, he'll know what all this means?"

"Probably. If not, he knows people who do."

Abby laid a hand on Megan's shoulder. "Now we're getting somewhere."

"I bet it'll be some fourteen-year-old video gamer," Megan said.

That for sure would be the best-case scenario, but I had a feeling that wasn't the case. I was beginning to catch Nicole's creep bug and beginning to feel that Megan's secret admirer wasn't just some infatuated fool. Not sure why, but that was the sensation that crept up my back.

CHAPTER 8

"THIS IS CURIOUS," Pancake said.

"This case?" Ray asked.

"No. Something from Jake and Nicole."

"What? Nicole finally got a speeding ticket?"

Pancake grunted. "She's immune to those."

"Apparently. So what is it?"

"Some emails and texts."

"Okay, I'll bite. What about them?"

They were seated in Longly Investigations de facto office. The round teak table on the deck of Ray's place, a stilted three-bedroom house on the sand in Gulf Shores. Pancake with his computer in front of him and the remnants of his lunch—actually only the waded bag that had held the four pulled pork sandwiches he had picked up at Captain Rocky's on his way over—one for Ray, three for him—near his right elbow. Ray, his computer also open, a can of Mountain Dew nearby.

"Jake called while I was on the way back with lunch," Pancake said. "Said he had some stuff he wanted me to track."

"Why?"

"Remember Nicole talking about her friend out in Orange County? The TV reporter?"

"Megan something? Right?"

"Megan Weatherly. Seems she has a rather intrusive fan. Sending a bunch of emails and texts. Acting more or less like a stalker. Some kind of weird anyway."

"I assume they have police in Newport Beach," Ray said.

"They do."

"Sounds like something they should handle." Ray waved a hand toward the stack of papers between them. "We need to finish our research on the case before us. We have a meeting with the clients tomorrow."

"I know. But the thing is that something don't smell right here."

"In what way?" Ray asked.

"First off, the sender of all the emails is one DevotedFan998877."

Ray laid aside the pages he had been reading. "Go on."

"It's a Gmail account. I looked into it but found zero personal info attached."

"Some folks do that."

"They do. Particularly if they want to stay off the radar."

"Or prefer privacy."

"Yeah, that, too. All the texts come from phones with 720 area codes. Denver area."

"Okay, so she has a devoted fan from Denver," Ray said. "Is there something in the messages that raises concern?"

"Somewhat. They do seem to escalate from nice friendly banter to something more needy. Someone who could indeed be a stalker. Which seems to be Nicole's take on it."

"She does have good instincts."

"Exactly. Anyway, Jake asked if I could track where they came from."

"Should be easy."

"Should be. All the texts were sent from several different locations. All in the Orange County area."

"So her Denver fan is in The OC?"

"Looks that way."

Ray leaned back, folded his hands over his abdomen. "That opens the door to several possibilities."

"You mean like he's traveled a thousand miles to be near her?"

"It crossed my mind."

"Mine, too."

"Or maybe he bought the phone in Denver while on vacation and he's actually from California," Ray said.

"Also possible. But here's the kicker. The messages come from four different phones. The IPs suggest they're all prepaid burners. AT&T is the carrier."

"People use those, too."

Pancake grunted. "Dealers and gangsters and pimps. And stalkers."

"Him using several burners does raise the stakes. Also means he won't be easy to ID."

"Nope. But I did find the place of purchase. In Denver."

"So call the store," Ray said.

"My next move."

Pancake stood, walked to the railing, and looked out over the beach as he made the call. Took a few minutes to convince the owner he was a legit P.I. and not some criminal type and finally got the info he needed. He returned to his seat.

"Anything?"

"Curious. A dozen phones. Purchased at one time. For cash. Under the name of Terry Zander. No address or contact info given. Guy said since it was a year ago; he has no independent recollection of the buyer." He shrugged. "Didn't suspect he would. So, now I need to find Mr. Zander."

"Don't take too long. We're under the gun with the case we're being paid for."

Pancake grunted again.

Over the next hour, Pancake rummaged around the internet, employed several of his tools, some anyone could purchase and others he had pilfered here and there from places that didn't allow pilfering. Not that that ever deterred him. In the end, he found that there were only three Terry or Terrance Zanders in the entire state of Colorado. One had an obituary from six months earlier; the other two alive and well. He tracked down three contact numbers—neither the number in question—and called them. The first was an eighty-two-year-old dude who lived in an assisted living facility and was more than a little crabby; the other a sixteen-year-old high school student who was mostly an asshole. In the end, neither seemed to be the purchaser of the dozen phones.

Ray had headed inside, made a few calls, and grabbed a fresh Dew. He returned, the can in one hand, a container of yogurt and a spoon in the other.

"That all you got to eat around here?" Pancake asked.

"There's some fruit on the kitchen counter."

"And?"

Ray shrugged. "Nothing in your culinary wheelhouse."

"Guess I better go shopping and restock your kitchen."

"Finish your research first."

"I don't work well when I'm hungry."

Ray sat. "You're always hungry. Besides, you just ate three sandwiches."

"That was then; this is now."

Ray spooned out a bite of yogurt. "I think I have some hot dogs in the freezer."

"Let me guess, turkey dogs?"

Ray smiled.

"That ain't a real hot dog."

"It's what I have."

Pancake headed to the kitchen and in fifteen minutes returned with a plate containing three dogs, each slathered with mustard. He ate one in three bites.

"Good?" Ray asked.

"Not bad. Not great. Expected since it ain't red meat."

"Should be enough to get you through the next couple of hours."

Pancake ate while he worked his computer. Finally, he leaned back, stretched. "Looks like I'm headed west in the morning."

"We have a meeting tomorrow."

Pancake smiled. "Which you don't really need me for."

Ray sighed. "Why do you need to go to California? I mean besides the blonds and bikinis."

"Well, there is that. But I got a bad feeling about this."

Ray finished his Dew and crushed the can. "Let's have it."

"We have a dude from Denver who's now in California. At least according to where he's sending stuff from. Uses multiple burner phones to send messages from various locations. Probably public places like coffee shops. Like he's hiding his identity and location. He's harassing a TV reporter. A very pretty one according to her online presence. Definite target for a stalker. His texts and emails show an escalation in his interest. Steadily becoming more personal, even demanding that she see him. Like his anger and frustration are mounting. That sort of thing."

"I agree it does sound a little sinister." Ray opened his hands. "Or he's merely an infatuated fan who has defective social skills."

"Could be. Not what I smell here though. Isn't finding folks like this what you pay me for?"

"I pay you to work on real cases."

"This is looking like one." Pancake stood and moved to the railing, leaning on it, and looked out over the Gulf for a full minute. He turned back to Ray. "Just doesn't feel like he's your run-of-the-mill fan or kinda, sorta, wimpy-ass stalker."

"Aren't *run of the mill* and *stalker* mutually exclusive?"

"You know what I mean," Pancake said. "Guy gets infatuated with someone, say like a movie star or a TV reporter or the girl across the classroom. He sends some not-so-cute emails, texts, phone calls. Then does something stupid like showing up at her home, causing trouble, does some damage. Some such. Then tries to deny it, acting all innocent. The cops track his texts, calls, and GPS and put him right at her door at the time in question. Handcuffs, jailhouse, the whole enchilada."

"This guy is different how?"

"He uses burners purchased three states away. Moves around to send his emails and texts. Very careful to not be trackable."

"Could be some married guy trying to get laid. Doesn't want the little woman to know about it. Picks up a handful of phones on a business trip and tries to woo the pretty girl on TV."

Pancake shrugged.

"But you don't believe that."

"Nope. According to Jake all his contacts have been through emails and texts. No calls. No personal appearances."

Ray rubbed one temple. "He's careful."

"Or maybe very clever."

"Which keeps him completely anonymous and could mean that he's dangerous."

"Now you're getting the picture." Pancake sat again, leaned back, folding his arms over his chest. "Which is why I'm headed west."

"What can you do there that you can't do here?"

"Boots on the ground is always best." He scratched one ear. "It's Jake, and Nicole, and Nicole's friend."

Ray considered that. "Okay. Get the research done today and I'll make do after that."

"Will do."

CHAPTER 9

FOR NICOLE, THE best restaurant in all of The OC was Rothschilds. She had told me this on more than a few occasions, and every time we visited, it was one of our first stops. After Charlie's Chili, of course. But that was breakfast, this was dinner.

We dressed up. Me in tan slacks, a white open-collar shirt, and a black sports coat; Nicole gray slacks and a black silk shirt. She looked magnificent. No surprise there.

We had time before our reservation so we decided to catch the sunset. One of The OC's best places for that wasn't far. A mere fifteen-minute drive south on Pacific Coast Highway, PCH, from Nicole's place plugged you into Corona del Mar, a quaint and very expensive Newport Beach neighborhood. It extended from PCH to the cliffs that overlooked the beaches and the Pacific. Thus its name. Corona del Mar means "Crown of the Sea." Driving, as we were doing, or walking along Ocean Boulevard offered elevated views that were spectacular, the sunsets breathtaking.

I found a parking space just beyond where Breakers Drive peeled off and dropped down to a row of even more expensive and truly oceanfront homes as well as the parking area for the Corona del Mar State Beach. We climbed out. I followed Nicole across a narrow, grassy, parklike stip to the cliff's edge. The sun hung low and painted the sky a fiery red-orange. The silhouette of Catalina Island was the only object that broke the crisp horizon line. Backlit, its humps and bumps looked like an elongated sea creature. Who knows, maybe the Loch Ness Monster was here on vacation.

"I love this place," Nicole said.

"It is special."

"Maybe we should buy one of the houses along here." She jerked her head over her shoulder toward the row of homes that lined Ocean Boulevard.

I laughed. "Have to win the Lotto first."

She hooked one arm with mine. "Or rob a bank."

"That, too."

I looped my arm around her and she rested her head against my chest. We stood quietly, watching the sun descend until it sank from sight, offering a parting wink. Not the famous green flash that was rarely, if ever, seen but pretty cool anyway.

"I'm starving," Nicole said. "Feed me."

We wound through the narrow streets and cozy homes of Corona del Mar and back up to PCH where we found an empty space only a half a block from the restaurant.

Rothschilds was a little slice of true European charm. A cozy bar and several even cozier rooms for dining. Antique tables, chairs, and a few hutches along the walls. Even the wall-mounted, gold-framed artwork looked old, as if one of the masters had painted them just for this place.

The hostess seated us at a four-top that looked out onto PCH. White tablecloths and a flower-filled vase in the table's center. We ordered a bottle of Napa Valley Cabernet and a plate of bruschetta for starters.

"So what's the latest with the filming?" I asked.

"All is still on schedule. Uncle Charles has the sound stages and the few locations we'll use all ready to go. As are all the techie guys."

"Techie guys?"

"You know. The lighting, sound, and film crews."

"The catering service?"

She laughed. "That's the only part you care about."

"Well, movie shoots are a bit boring. I need something to distract me."

"It won't be as good as this place," Nicole said.

"Is anything?"

"No. This is the best."

"Better than Captain Rocky's?"

"Not sure I'd go that far."

"Good answer." I smiled. "But I don't believe you."

She gave me a mock pout. "You've hurt my feelings."

"I doubt that. But lucky for you, or maybe I should say Uncle Charles, Pancake isn't here. Otherwise he'd have to double his catering budget."

Our waitress returned with the wine and bruschetta. While she went though the opening and pouring ceremony, she asked if we had any questions about the menu or if we needed more time. We didn't. Nicole ordered her usual, the fettuccine Romano, me, the lobster ravioli.

While we devoured the bruschetta, we talked about the party at Uncle Charles' place in the Malibu Colony. A private enclave where the roster of A-List actors, producers, and directors, as well as corporate moguls and rock stars, who either did or had lived there was staggering. Folks like Johnny Carson, Jack Nicholson, Tom Hanks, Paris Hilton, Eddie Van Halen, Steven Spielberg, and Sly Stallone, and from a bygone era, Bing Crosby, Clara Bow, Jack Warner, Gloria Swanson, and the list goes on. Money talks and massive money speaks loudly.

"Knowing Uncle Charles, it will be epic. Food, wine, and folks you see on TV and the big screen all the time."

"Not to mention your parents and Kirk Ford."

She nodded. "I'm curious about how Kirk is doing. That entire Kristi Guidry ordeal did a number on him. At least, that's what Uncle Charles said."

"I'd be surprised if it hadn't. But it sounds like he and the franchise survived."

"Yeah, I suppose. But I'm not sure you ever truly recover from something like that. The public outrage and scrutiny."

"Until the next *Space Quest* movie," I said. "Folks will line up to see it and all will be forgiven."

"Celebrity does trump all."

Boy, was that ever true. Back when I was a major-league pitcher, I had seen it many times. Hell, I had lived it. Booze and babes. An excess of each. In every town. Road trips were exhausting.

"If it gets that far," she said. "I guess a lot of it will depend on how the public accepts Kirk's return. *Murderwood* is the test case."

"No pressure though."

"No. None. I'm not worried at all."

"Liar."

She smiled. "Maybe a little."

The truth was that she had fretted over exactly that. As if she, and her movie, were the salvation, or death knell, for all of Hollywood. Silly, but perception was reality. We had talked about it a lot over the past month. I knew she felt the pressure, which on many levels was very real. Sometimes perception reflects reality. If the movie failed, if Kirk's fans abandoned him, Nicole would be crushed. No doubt about that. This was her big moment. To make it as a serious writer. To be accepted. For Uncle Charles, the stakes were measured in billions of dollars. I reassured her, and that did help, but didn't completely tamp down her anxiety.

"It'll be fine," I said. "Your movie will be a mega-hit and all of Tinsel Town will be indebted to you."

She reached over and clutched my hand. "You're the best."

"I am."

"Don't let it go to your head."

Our food arrived and we fell silent for a few minutes as we ate. Finally, Nicole spoke.

"What do you really think about the dude who's sending Megan all those emails and texts?" she asked.

"Not sure. Most likely, he's just a fan, but I have to admit some of them carry an uncomfortable undercurrent."

"That's my feeling." She took a bite of fettuccine. "God, I love this stuff."

"You get it every time."

"No one makes it like this anywhere else." She took a sip of wine. "I just keep remembering the stalkers I've had. At first, I felt good about the attention. You know, like someone thought I was good, or hot, or whatever. But each time it evolved into something else. Especially the really bad one." Another sip of wine. "I have the same feeling here."

"Hopefully Pancake can track the dude down and we can see just how dangerous he is."

"If anyone can, the big guy can."

A lot of truth to that. Pancake did know his way into the dark corners of the cyber world.

We finished our meal, shared a Linzer torte for dessert, paid the bill, and walked back to the car. The night was clear, warm, but with a slightly cool breeze.

"What do you want to do now?" I asked.

"You."

"No argument here."

As we drove back north on PCH, my cell chimed. Pancake.

I answered, placing it on speaker. "What's up?"

"I have something," he said.

"What?"

"Got a couple of other things to get into, to be sure, but I don't like it."

"Don't like what?" Nicole asked.

"It'll wait until I get there."

"What are you talking about?" I asked.

"I'm headed your way in the morning."

"I don't like the sound of that," Nicole said.

"Here I thought you'd be glad to see me, darling."

"I will. We both will. But it's that you feel the need to be here that's bothersome."

"It might be nothing," Pancake said.

"Or it might be something," Nicole replied.

"Maybe."

"Then tell us what's up," I said.

"Let's just say that I think this guy is indeed a stalker. Or is at least moving down that path. Feels to me he's not simply a casual fan but rather a more obsessive one."

"Based on what?" Nicole asked.

"The language he uses. The fact that his messages are becoming more personal, and aggressive. In the later ones he is pushing her for a face-to-face meeting."

"Which she has refused," I said.

"Something she should continue to do. Politely but firmly."

"Do you think he's dangerous?" Nicole asked.

"Don't know yet. From what you've said he hasn't physically confronted her. Shown up at her work or home. Anything like that. True?"

"That's right," Nicole said.

"We're early into this so it's hard to make a judgement on his state of mind yet. But, for sure, he's smart and careful to cover his tracks."

"So you haven't tracked him down yet?"

"Nope, but I'm getting there."

"What do we need to do?" Nicole asked.

"Sit tight. Keep an eye on Megan. Tell her to be aware and to not provoke him in any way."

"You're beginning to scare me," Nicole said.

"Don't be. But a healthy concern might be in order."

After Pancake hung up, Nicole called Megan, putting her iPhone on speaker.

"Are you at home?" Nicole asked.

"Yeah. All tucked in and reading a book."

"Make sure all your doors and windows are locked."

"Why?" Megan asked.

"Pancake found out some stuff about this guy. Not sure of the details but he asked me to tell you to be careful and aware."

"Why? What did he find?"

"He didn't say," Nicole said. "Not specifically. Except that this guy is clever and careful."

"What does that mean?"

"Just that," I said. "Pancake said you should be aware and be careful. Lock up and hunker down. He'll be here tomorrow and then we'll see what's what."

Megan sighed. "You're not helping my sleep here."

"Sorry. We thought you should know."

"I know. Thanks. I'll go check the doors and windows. Maybe pick another book to read. I don't think Dean Koontz is a good choice about now."

CHAPTER 10

LAST NIGHT, AFTER hanging up with Jake, Pancake had reached out to one of Ray's guys at the NSA. Dude named Graham Gordy. Deep into the cybersecurity world. Pancake had brought him up to speed on the problem he and Ray were facing. Well, him anyway. Ray was busy with the other case. "The real one," as Ray had said. Pancake told Gordy that he'd tracked the phones used for communication, all burners, to a store in Denver. He spoke with the store's owner but he had no memory of the guy. Yes, he had a security video system but it overwrote itself every thirty days. He confirmed the buyer had made a cash purchase of a dozen prepaid phones.

Graham had told him that the burners would be hard to track. In real time anyway. Particularly if the dude was using multiple devices. He added that he couldn't work on this at the shop but would do so on his setup at home, which is where he was at that time. Not as robust as the equipment he had access to at work, but good enough. Not to mention it would violate fewer federal laws than if he did it in-house. Regardless, he said he'd sniff around the dark web and see if anything was out there on the guy. He explained that sometimes a group of these stalker types would huddle in a cyber room and share notes. He suggested that Pancake give him a call the next morning before he jumped on the plane for California. So, after Pancake got through security at the Mobile airport, grabbed a couple of bacon, egg, and cheese biscuits from McDonald's, located his gate, and found a seat, he called.

"Anything?" Pancake asked.

"Not much," Gordy said. "He's definitely not using a VPN. None of the IP addresses associated with that phone lead down that road."

"What about the dark web?"

"Not a whiff. That would require he use a TOR browser, or something similar, and there's no evidence that he's done that. At least not from the phones in question. But he could have a laptop connected to the onion router and that would open up a whole other can of worms. That would take a lot of time and bandwidth to solve and even then it could be a dead end. Let me ask you, is this guy smart enough to rummage in that world?"

"Don't know yet. So far he seems to be lower key and lower tech."

"Good," Gordy said. "I take it that other than the emails and texts your client hasn't had other types of communication from him."

"Nope. Only the nineteen emails and forty-seven texts."

"No calls? Personal appearances?"

"None. Not yet anyway."

"*Yet* being the operative word," Gordy said.

"That's the concern. You know how some of these guys get frustrated, obsessed, and escalate."

"Unfortunately, I do. They all too often do so in a hurry. Some trigger and they go from zero to sixty in a heartbeat."

"Let's hope that doesn't happen here."

"What do you want me to do?"

"Sit tight right now. I don't have a lot yet but thought I'd ask you to take a look and see if I'd missed anything."

"You didn't. Burner phones, emails, texts. As you said, fairly low tech. Also, very effective for staying off the radar."

Wasn't that the truth. Simple, cheap, easy, and very effective. Pancake knew that even though these phones hooked into the internet and the cellular network just like any other phone, and that they had a unique identifying ISP number, not knowing who owns the device or whose hand it was in made identifying that person nearly impossible. That's why drug dealers and terrorists used them all the time.

"Thanks," Pancake said. "I'll let you know if I need anything else."

"I'll keep sniffing around a bit. See if he drops deeper into the cyber swamp."

"That's what I'd do," Pancake said.

A young lady, also a redhead, sat in the row across from him, placing her two carry-ons in the next seat. She smiled. He returned it.

"That's because you're smart," Gordy said. "This guy, like most of these miscreants, thinks he's invisible. It's always amazed me how many bad guys believe that once they put something out in cyberspace it evaporates and no breadcrumbs are left along the way. They're always shocked when we come down on them with reams of texts, calls, cyber traffic, GPS data. That kind of stuff is good for the soul." He laughed. "And keeps me employed."

"I truly appreciate this," Pancake said. "But, like I said, sit tight. I'll let you know if I need anything."

"You've tweaked my curiosity. I'll sniff around a little more. Don't get your hopes up but you just never know what snail trails are out there."

"Thanks. This guy just might turn out to be a big nothing."

"Let's hope," Graham said.

"Let's do."

CHAPTER 11

MEGAN LAY IN her bed, staring at the ceiling. Her head throbbed, felt fuzzy, and her entire body seemed to have stiffened in the night. Nothing wanted to move right. Like a bad hangover or as if she had spent the night doing rigorous Pilates, or maybe mud wrestling. From the looks of her covers, comforter half off the bed, sheet braided around her legs, probably the later.

More than once she had awakened with a feeling of being watched. Sure that she had heard the hiss of shoes sliding over the carpet, the squeak of a door hinge, or a bump against a wall. Certain she felt a cold draft, surely from an open door or window, or a warm breath on her neck. She would lie there, body tense, heart thumping against her chest, reaching out with all her senses, probing for some proof that what she had detected was real. The minutes ticked by while she berated herself for being so silly only to have the wave of fear reemerge. Twice she had slipped from bed and tiptoed through her condo, peering into closets, peeling back curtains to see what lurked in the darkness, and checking and rechecking the door locks. Only to chide herself for behaving like a paranoid fool or someone with compulsive OCD.

Get a grip, Megan.

More than once she had questioned her decision to take a first-floor unit. When she was looking, there were four available. One, a third-floor space, very similar to hers. But she didn't want to deal with stairs, or the elevator that was located at the far end. She had opted for convenience over safety. Now that seemed a shortsighted choice.

Even when she managed to drift off, the assault on her senses continued. Dreams of being trapped in a small, suffocating space, or being chased through—what?—jungle vines?—thick shrubbery?—something that clutched at her arms and legs, progressively limiting her movements as if she were encased in an invisible web.

Right now, she felt the urge to reinspect everything. Closets, doors, windows.

Quit being a ninnie.

She stretched her back, twisting from side to side, unwound her legs from the sheet, and sat up. Her feet rested on the carpeted floor as she massaged one temple. It didn't help.

She knew the source of her stress. The phone call last night from Nicole and Jake had gotten her brain all wound up and sparking.

They were completely overreacting to this. The guy was merely a fan. Awkward, sure, but still only a passionate fan. She had had many in the past. People who sent notes of praise to her or to the station. Folks who watched her telecasts religiously and truly liked what she did. Wasn't that one of the perks of the job? The feeling of being liked, even needed. Viewers trusted her. They knew she would thoroughly research her pieces and present only the verified facts. Like her recent report on the new construction projects at The Spectrum, or last month's piece on the county's vanishing strawberry fields, or her frequent very popular chats with local celebs or authors. She got fan mail all the time. So did many others at the station. Channel 16 had loyal viewers, no doubt.

So, this guy was simply a fan. Nothing more. To make him into something sinister was not very productive, and not fair to her, or to him.

She stood. Her legs wobbled and her balance betrayed her. She sat again. She sighed, clutched the bedside table, and lifted herself upright. Once she felt steady, she made her way to the bathroom.

The hot shower worked its magic as her tension ebbed and her headache dissolved. Clad in a robe and slippers, she shuffled her way to the kitchen and made a cup of Emeril's Big Easy in her Keurig coffee maker. She sat on her sofa and began reading through the notes she had made for her production meeting. All seemed in order.

She sat in front of her makeup mirror and examined her face. Skin slightly lax, eyes somewhat dark and baggy. Not too bad, at least not unfixable. A little extra makeup and she'd be good to go.

Once she got her war paint on, her hair worked into something that was no longer a rat's nest, and dressed in jeans, light-gray shirt, and navy blue jacket, she examined herself in the full-length mirror she had installed on the back of her bedroom door. She had looked better, but all in all not so bad.

Time to roll.

She stuffed everything she would need for the day into her shoulder bag and opened the door. A package flopped to the floor. It had obviously been leaning against her front door. Now she saw it was gift wrapped. White paper, red bow. Like the candy box.

Her heart rate ticked up.

She picked it up and retreated to her kitchen, placing it on the table. A small card was attached with a pledget of tape.

The card read:

For my one true love.

A small token of my love. Something exquisite for an exquisite lady. Perfect for our honeymoon.

Yours forever
Your future husband

She took an involuntary step back. What the hell?

She looked at the gift. Should she open it or back away? Was it some sort of explosive device or maybe filled with some toxic powder? She flashed on the ricin letters that had been sent to several politicians many years ago. Also, the two cops that had collapsed after opening a bag of fentanyl during a drug bust. Maybe there was a coiled snake inside.

Good lord, Megan. Shut your imagination down.

Curiosity finally won and she tore through the wrapping and removed the lid from the box. She folded back the pink tissue paper, revealing something black and silky. She lifted a camisole and then a pair of thong panties.

Her breath caught. Her head swiveled toward the door.

He had been here. At her home.

Were those the sounds she'd heard last night? The ones she had convinced herself were all in her head?

A chill rippled through her.

She frantically rummaged through her bag until she located her phone near the bottom.

CHAPTER 12

THE NEXT MORNING, Nicole and I were up early. Despite her keeping me up late. First by sitting out on her deck with a bottle of tequila where we watched a few late-night sailors cruise back into the harbor and then by, well, being Nicole.

Plus we were still hovering around Central time, not Pacific.

So, by seven, we were power walking down the bike path yet again. Much less painful than the Krav Maga classes we left behind in Gulf Shores, but still, after a night of tequila and Nicole, not all that easy. I had suggested a more leisurely pace, but Nicole murmured something that sounded like "Wimp" and we were off. Halfway back from The Wedge, my legs hurt, my head ached, and I wanted to sit and watch the waves. Mommy, can I have a recess?

But Nicole charged on and I followed. To Charlie's Chili. Apparently, she hadn't yet had her fill of chili cheese omelets. Me either, apparently. I woofed mine along with three cups of coffee. By the time we left and headed back to Nicole's condo, the cobwebs in my head shredded. I felt almost human again.

It was eight thirty.

"What time is Pancake's flight getting in?" she asked.

"Around three. He said he'd text when he hit the tarmac."

"Are we picking him up or is he grabbing a rental?"

"We're his rental."

"We might need a bigger car then." She laughed.

"I think the Range Rover can handle him."

As we entered Nicole's condo, her cell buzzed. It was Megan. Nicole mostly listened then said, "We're on the way. Half hour, tops."

"What is it?" I asked after she disconnected the call.

"Something's happened."

"To Megan?"

"No, not that. But she received a package and she's upset."

"What was in it? A severed head or something?"

"You watch too much TV."

Actually, I didn't, but she made her point.

"She said we had to see it."

We took a quick shower, together, but no play time, dressed, and headed up Newport Boulevard toward Megan's place.

She lived in an upscale condo project near South Coast Plaza off Sunflower Avenue in Costa Mesa. Mature palm trees lined the paver entry drive that ended at a circle that spun around a flower-enveloped fountain. Eight buildings, each three floors and containing a dozen units, were arrayed around two community pools. Large, with ample deck space for sunbathing, a SoCal necessity, and a row of open cabanas along one side of each. More palms, red and pink bougainvillea, and flowering shrubs added a touch of class.

We found Megan's place toward the back, first floor. Nicole rang the buzzer.

I expected to see swollen eyes, tearstained cheeks, disheveled hair, maybe pajamas. Not even close. She was obviously dressed for work. Her hair and makeup were model perfect, but stress lines hung near the corners of her eyes and mouth.

"Thanks for coming," Megan said. She held the door for us to enter. "I'm sorry to be such a bother."

"You're not," Nicole said.

"What happened?" I asked.

She sighed. "Maybe I'm overreacting and simply being a big baby. But it spooked me."

"What?" Nicole asked.

She led us to the kitchen. A gift box sat on the table, its tissue folded open, black lingerie exposed. She lifted the thong with one finger. "This."

"He sent this?"

"No. He left it leaning against my door."

"Oh," Nicole said. Now worry lines emerged on her forehead. "He was here?"

"Apparently." She glanced toward her front door. "All night I heard—I don't know what I heard—footsteps, bumps and creaks, even breath sounds." She gave a headshake. "Didn't sleep worth a damn."

"What's this?" I asked, lifting the small envelope.

"The card that was attached."

I tugged the card out, unfolded it and read it, tilting it toward Nicole.

"This has officially reached creepy," I said.

"And dangerous," Nicole added. "My guy, the really bad one, sent me all sorts of lingerie. Even a box of condoms." She glanced at me. "In case I had sex with someone besides him. He said he knew all actresses were whores so figured I might need them. To stay clean and pure for him."

"Good Lord," Megan said.

This was part of the story I'd never heard. Disturbing didn't cover it. Made me wonder about my gender.

"He and the Lord didn't have even a passing acquaintance," Nicole said.

"Is this as bad as I think it is?" Megan asked.

"It's definitely an escalation," I said. "Much more personal, and creepier than creepy."

"Do you have any idea what time he might have left it?" Nicole asked.

"No. Like I said, I heard things all night. Bumps and scrapes and footsteps." She shrugged. "My imagination was definitely in overdrive. I convinced myself it was in my head, or maybe the wind. After I found the package leaning against my door, I had this image of me checking the lock last night and him standing just on the other side." Her lips trembled. "Freaked me out that I could've been that close to him."

Nicole hugged her. "Honey, I'm so sorry that this is happening."

"I'm glad you're here. Thanks for coming."

"We're here now, so relax." Nicole pushed Megan back and looked at her. "Before we get all wound up, let's wait for Pancake to get here. He knows all about this stuff."

"When will that be?"

"This afternoon," Nicole said. "We're picking him up."

"Then we can all get together and try to make some sense of this," I said.

Megan sighed. "At least I get to meet the mysterious Pancake."

"He's not that mysterious," I said. "What you see is what you get."

"I feel like I know him already. Nicole has talked about him a lot."

"There's a lot to say. Also a lot of Pancake."

Silence fell for a good half a minute.

"Should we go to the police?" Nicole asked.

"And say what?" Megan said. "That some dude sent me some underwear?"

"Also, he's been stalking you with unwanted emails," Nicole said. "And, oh by the way, came to your door."

"I'm sure they have more important things to deal with."

"Do they? Maybe you can at least get a restraining order."

"Against who? John Doe Number One?"

That was true, I thought. Without a name, I'm not sure you can get a TRO, Temporary Restraining Order. Since there had been no overt threat, there likely wasn't anything the police could, or would, do. Maybe if he had fired a round through her window or kicked her door in, but words in a bunch of emails? Words that really weren't very threatening. I didn't see them getting all amped up. Or even very interested.

"Let's wait until Pancake gets here," I said. "Get his take. He has good instincts on things like this."

"You're coming to stay with us," Nicole said.

"No." Megan shook her head. "I'm not going to have some freak run me out of my home."

"Humor me," Nicole said. "I'd feel much better."

"I'll be fine."

Nicole touched her arm. "After another sleepless night? Hearing things?"

Megan seemed to consider that, but then shook her head. "No. I'll be fine."

"With us, Jake will be there to protect you."

"Me?" I said. "You're the queen of Krav Maga."

Megan smiled. "You guys still doing that?"

I shrugged. "Unfortunately."

"He whines a lot but he actually loves it."

No, I didn't. For me, the only silver lining was seeing Nicole in her gym outfit. Sort of like elastic body paint. That and knowing that my girlfriend can kick the hell out of yours. So there.

"Besides," Nicole continued, "we'll have Pancake."

"I appreciate it," Megan said. "I know you're concerned. I love you for that. But I have a life to live and a few squirrely emails aren't going to prevent that."

"Don't forget the undies he left at your door," I said.

"How could I?"

"It proves he knows where you live," Nicole said.

"I know."

"So come stay with us."

"I'll think about it." Megan checked her watch. "But right now, I need to get to the studio."

"Okay." Nicole nodded toward me. "We'll follow you."

"Why?"

"He was here," I said. "Might still be in the area. Watching and waiting."

"In broad daylight? Why?"

"To see you in person," Nicole said. "In the flesh and up close."

Megan glanced toward the window. The curtains were closed.

"My guy," Nicole said, "had taken over a thousand pictures of me and dozens of videos. Home, the studio, shopping, the gym. He followed me everywhere for nearly a year. The entire time I was clueless. Until he stepped forward, came out of the shadows, and began to approach me directly, I never knew he existed."

"This is crazy," Megan said.

"It is," I said. "That's why we're following you to work and why you won't leave work until we pick up Pancake and come back by."

"Okay." Megan grabbed her purse and shoulder bag from her sofa. "Let's get rolling."

CHAPTER 13

IT'S HARD TO miss Pancake. Sort of like picking out a rhino running with a herd of gazelles. Today was no exception. As I rolled the Range Rover into the Arrivals area of John Wayne Airport, some traffic but at least it moved, and pulled to the curb outside baggage claim, there he was. His red hair a beacon over the heads of the other passengers. He stood next to the bronze statue of The Duke himself. I had read the statue was nine feet tall. Pancake looked bigger.

He had one hand on a rolling suitcase and the other clamping his phone to his ear. His computer bag hung over one shoulder. He saw us and dragged his suitcase our way. After tossing it in the back he climbed in the left rear seat, the car tilting that way as he settled in. He ended his call and shoved his phone in one pocket.

"How was your flight?" Nicole asked.

"Long and boring. The cuisine sucked."

"Doesn't it always?"

Pancake grunted. "I need food."

Of course he did.

I pulled into traffic and followed the stream toward the airport exit. "What would you like?"

"Something big."

"There's a Jersey Mike's near here," Nicole said.

"Drive faster."

I did. Sort of. Not Nicole-fast but I did push the speed limit as best I could in traffic. The sub shop was on Sunflower Avenue, very near Megan's condo. We grabbed Pancake a pair of twelve-inch subs, one Italian and the other meatball. I then did a spin through Megan's complex and cruised by her condo. Everything looked quiet, and I didn't see any strangers around. Not that I expected to.

"What's this?" Pancake asked, napkining sauce from his chin.

"This's where Megan lives," Nicole said.

Pancake scanned the area. "Nice. Clean. Upscale."

"It is." Nicole twisted in her seat to more directly face Pancake. "The guy, the one stalking her, left a package at her door this morning."

Pancake stopped chewing for a beat. "She didn't see him, I take it?"

"Nope. It was there when she was leaving for work."

"What was in it?" Pancake asked. "A severed head?"

"Good Lord, you and Jake think alike."

Pancake grunted. "Jake doesn't think all that much."

This was my best friend talking.

"But he's cute so he can get by on his looks," Nicole said.

Now my girlfriend chimes in. All I needed was for Ray to be here and add his own special dig and the chorus would be complete. A full-house backfield of comedians. I didn't engage, letting them play out their little game of verbal badminton with me as the shuttlecock.

"Story of his life." Pancake shoved the last of the meatball sub in his mouth and spoke around it. "So, what was in it?"

"Lingerie. Plus a card that said it was for their honeymoon."

"That the first time he hand-delivered anything?"

"Yes," Nicole said. "Megan said he had sent flowers and candy a few times, but each of those was delivered."

"He's closing the distance," Pancake said. "Beginning to step out of the shadows."

"That doesn't sound good," Nicole said.

"It isn't and it is. It means he's becoming more aggressive but also means he's exposing himself. Never underestimate the power of luck. Or for some citizen to witness, even prevent, some crime."

"I'll go for prevent," Nicole said.

"Better not to wait for him to slip up," Pancake said. "Better to go after him."

"How?" I asked.

"Unfortunately, that'll be easier said than done. It looks like he's using a series of prepaid burner phones. If he stuck with one it'd be hard enough, but rotating them makes it almost impossible to track. Actually a clever move on his part."

"You're saying those prepaid phones can't be traced?" Nicole said.

"Not like a regular phone for sure. We can grab call logs and such. See who he called, when, and for how long. Even track the general area where the call came from by seeing which cell towers were used. But those rigs don't typically have GPS so pinpointing his location in real time is out the window."

"He still has to buy the phones," I said. "That's an exposure."

"He does." Now Pancake was into the Italian sub. "If the buyer's stupid enough to give up a credit card or his real name, that creates a viable trail. But, if he's smart and buys it anonymously, for cash, and gives a fake name, then there's no trail to him."

"Which this guy did, I suspect."

"He did. He purchased a dozen phones a year ago in Denver."

"Denver?" Nicole asked. "Do you think he's in Denver? That this is all long distance?"

"Nope. His emails and texts are sent locally. Besides, he wouldn't be able to leave lingerie at her door if he was in Denver," Pancake said.

Nicole shrugged. "True."

"The IPs he's been using for the emails are here in Orange County."

"IP," I said. "I've heard of that. It's those little number things in emails. Right?"

"Yeah. Little number things."

"Okay, codes, whatever."

"IP address stands for internet protocol address. Every machine has its own. Computers, phones, any device that uses the internet. It's more or less the device's ID or address in the cyber world. Then a Wi-Fi hot spot, say a coffee shop or a public Wi-Fi system, has a router and it too has an IP address. When you log on to one of those, your computer or phone will be given a temporary IP. That's done through what's called a DHCP, or Dynamic Host Configuration Protocol."

"Can you dumb this down?" I asked.

"For you? Sure."

Did I say Pancake was my BFF? He was also a couple of other things but I refrained from pointing that out.

He continued. "All that gibberish means that we can track his device through his carrier. In this case AT&T. Get a general location through the cell towers, and when he jumps on the internet to send emails, we can locate the router that the email was sent through. Doing that in real time isn't easy so all the information gathered is past history. He would've moved on to another spot. It looks like this guy's using places like coffee shops and public Wi-Fi setups to connect."

"It still sounds like a lot of information," Nicole said.

"Not enough though," Pancake said. "Not what we need. It only tells us where he's been, not where he is."

"So what now?" Nicole asked.

"Unfortunately, right now we're swimming in dark water. We need to get below the surface."

"Doesn't sound like it's going to be easy," Nicole said.

"It won't. I spoke with my guy earlier. Actually, Ray's guy. He lives in the cyber world. I wanted to make sure I was on the right track. He said I was, so there is that."

"This guy?" I asked. "He's going to help?"

"Right now he's laying back. But if we need him, he's ready to jump in. Problem is he can't use his work computers so he's doing it from home on his own time. So if we have to bring him in, that might slow things down some."

"Who is he?" I asked. "FBI? CIA?"

Pancake grunted. "He might be a fourteen-year-old with a laptop."

"Who has a job where he can't use his work computer?" I asked.

"You're smarter than you look."

Not sure if that was a compliment or not but I let it ride. "So which is it?" I asked.

"Right idea, wrong letters."

"NSA."

Pancake grunted.

"Wait a minute," Nicole said. "If you and Ray reached out to someone at the NSA, this is a big deal. Is that what you're saying?"

"Maybe, maybe not. But you know me. Never make a fight a slappy fight. Make it a war. Haul out the nuclear weapons early and end it quickly. *Deguello.*"

"Which means?" Nicole asked.

"It's a ZZ Top album," I said. "Actually, the best Top album."

"It was also the battle cry by Santa Ana's men at the Alamo. It means take no prisoners, give no quarter. A fight to the death."

"Isn't that a little dramatic?" Nicole asked.

"It is until it isn't," Pancake said. "Then it's real."

CHAPTER 14

AFTER ENSCONCING PANCAKE in one of Nicole's guest rooms, we had an hour to kill before heading over to the studio to chat with Megan, who was apparently in a production meeting right now. Pancake and I poured some Makers Mark over ice and settled in the comfy chairs on the deck. A warm breeze flowed up the ship channel. In the boat slot directly below, a shirtless guy in frayed jeans hosed off a sailboat. It appeared to be forty-two or so feet long and fairly new. White with a dark-blue waterline.

"Nice place," Pancake said.

"It is. Nicole and I were talking last night about us not coming here often enough."

"You're a busy boy. With a restaurant to run and all."

Pancake's way of jabbing me. I actually did mostly nothing as far as Captain Rocky's was concerned, leaving that to my manager, Carla Martinez. Which reminded me, I should call her and see if all was smooth. The truth was I'd hear if things weren't. Or maybe not. More likely she would handle it, and I'd hear about it when I got back. Plus, I didn't want to have her bitch at me about dragging Pancake off to California. Which, in my defense, I didn't. He came of his own accord. She probably wouldn't see it that way. She always missed her mornings with the Big Guy when he was away. Missed sitting on the deck watching him devour free breakfast burritos. I think he sort of fed her mothering instincts.

Nicole joined us, glass of red wine in her hand. She walked to the railing and looked down.

"Hey, Jimmy. How's it going?" Nicole said.

"Nicole. I didn't know you were here."

"Just for a couple of weeks."

He stepped off the boat, shut off the water flow, and began looping the hose.

Nicole waved a hand toward us. "I don't think you've met Jake yet. Or Pancake."

"Hello." He gave a brief nod. "Pancake? Can't say I've heard that one before."

"Me either," Pancake said.

"This is Jimmy Fabrick," Nicole said. "He rents my boat slip."

"It's a lifesaver. Finding a slip in Newport Beach, Dana Point, or really anywhere around here isn't easy. I was down in Dana Point for a while, but the guy I rented from sold the space." He hung the coiled hose on the metal hook that protruded from a post near the bow. "Nicole was kind enough to rent me the space."

"Which makes you the lifesaver," Nicole said. "Since I don't have a boat."

He glanced at his watch. "Got to run. Nice meeting you." He snatched up the green tee shirt that lay on the pier and tugged it on as he wiggled on a pair of sandals.

"See you again, I'm sure," I said.

He headed up the boardwalk. Nicole sat next to me.

"I never knew you had a boat slip," I said.

"I tied up the lease when I purchased the condo. Those things are like gold around here. The rent it commands more than covers my lease fees."

"Smart move," Pancake said.

"It was. It is."

"What's Ray up to?" I asked Pancake.

"Busy being Ray. He's buried his teeth into some big-money lawsuit in Montgomery. One partner taking on another."

"Those can be tricky."

"This one's like a nasty divorce. The two partners might've been able to work things out but the wives are at war to the point that dissolving the partnership is the only solution."

"Ah, the life of a P.I."

"You got that right." He took a slug of his drink. "We're doing some financial snooping to make sure all the funds are where they should be and are fairly divided." He smiled. "Right now that's Ray's problem. Me? I'm enjoying the warm California air and a good bourbon."

"Bet Ray's happy you bolted."

"Happy isn't the word I'd choose. But he's okay with it. Once I explained my concerns."

"You really are bothered by this guy, aren't you?" Nicole asked.

"I am."

"Which makes me uncomfortable. If he spooks you, I'm really worried."

Pancake grunted, swirled the ice in his bourbon.

"What is it exactly? I get that he's using untraceable phones and sending a bunch of messages and presents and stuff and that he's sounded more creepy lately. From past history, I know that can blossom into trouble. But I sense something else is bothering you?"

Pancake gazed up the row of boats, gathering his thoughts. "Let me ask you this. Does Megan have any intentions of meeting with this guy? At any time?"

"No. Definitely not."

He nodded. "That's where the rubber meets the road."

"Meaning?"

"I agree. She shouldn't meet this guy. At least not alone."

"She won't."

He sighed. "Maybe, if she's lucky, the guy will get bored, or latch on to someone else, and all this will evaporate."

"But you don't believe that," I said.

"Could happen. But these guys, these stalker types, expect to fulfill their fantasies. Achieve the pipe dream that the target will fall in love with them and they'll live happily ever after. At least that's the script they create."

"And if not?" Nicole said. "If she rejects him completely?"

"That's where it can get testy. He might grow frustrated, angry, vindictive, and so on to downright dangerous." Another slug of bourbon. "No one likes to have their dreams dashed. Particularly someone who is a born loser."

"We don't know anything about him. How do you know he's a loser?"

"If he was cool, and charming, and actually had a chance to win her heart, he wouldn't be doing this." Another headshake. "These types aren't adept at relationships. That's why they stalk anonymously. Weren't the guys who harassed you at the end of the day losers?" Pancake asked.

"I get your point," Nicole said.

"But it's really more than that. Her rejection, or anyone's rejection, only underlines the stalker's own feelings of inadequacy. He goes out, sees happy couples, beautiful people having fun. Something he might never have experienced. Or did and it ended badly. Either way, it stokes his own pathology. Why can't he get the girl? Only feeds his dark nature."

"You make him sound like a monster," Nicole said.

"Not yet. But he could be headed that way."

"You think?" I asked.

"What really bothers me is that he hasn't called and spoken directly with her. He hasn't simply walked up to her and introduced himself. He hasn't hand-delivered the flowers or the candy. Even the lingerie was done on the sly."

"Isn't that a good thing?" Nicole asked.

"You'd think. But to me it says he has something to hide. He needs to stay in the shadows, out of sight."

"And?" I asked, sensing there was more to this line of thinking.

"Maybe his agenda isn't to show her he's the guy for her. That they should ride off into the sunset and live happily ever after. Maybe he gets his kicks by inflicting terror on her. If that's his goal, then staying murky and unknown makes the fear more intense. A faceless monster is always scarier than the one you know."

"Like the troll under the bridge," I said.

Pancake nodded. "The creature under the bed."

Nicole seemed to consider that. She leaned forward and rested her forearms on her knees, hands clasped. "I have to agree. The ones I attracted were always known to me. They contacted me. Showed up at unexpected times. That was scary enough, but it never crossed my mind that that was actually better than not knowing who was following me."

"Paul Simon wrote a song about it," Pancake said. "Life is black and white but our imaginations are Kodachrome."

"Do you really believe that?" Nicole asked. "That this is all terror tactics and not some ploy to grab her attention?"

"He's got her attention alright," I said.

"True, but you know what I mean."

"Not sure what I believe yet," Pancake said. "We're too early in this to create a coherent image of this dude. But, based on what little I've seen, I think that's possible."

Silence fell for a full minute, then Nicole said, "Megan doesn't deserve this."

"No one deserves this," I said.

"So we have to find him," Nicole said. "Before he does something stupid."

"You mean like leaving lingerie at her door?" I asked.

"Or worse."

"It's the *worse* we have to worry about," Pancake said.

I saw tears collect in Nicole's eyes.

"I hate this shit," she said.

"Look," Pancake said. "He might be benign. Merely a green fly buzzing around and annoying. But if he's not, we need to dissuade him from pursuing this agenda. And the way to do that is to know who he is and explain things. Face-to-face. Then we'll know who and what he really is."

"Wouldn't that only anger him more?"

Pancake made a fist, relaxed it. "Depends on the nature of the explanation."

Pancake was gifted at explanations. He actually enjoyed them. I'd seen it before. I flashed on a drug dealer named Jimmy Walker, aka Rag Man. Pancake had explained things to him in an alleyway off Decatur in the French Quarter. Literally tossed him about twenty feet. Got his attention to say the least.

"It's time for Megan's broadcast," Nicole said. "Let's go in and watch it, then we can head over to the studio."

CHAPTER 15

As I drove up Newport Boulevard toward Channel 16, I asked Pancake, "How do you want to handle this?"

"As far as?" he asked.

"What are you going to tell Megan about what we were discussing?"

"Right now, I don't see a reason to lay too much on her. That was all speculation and possibilities. We don't know exactly what type of creature we're dealing with yet. No need to raise her angst until we do."

"Doesn't she need to know how dangerous this guy could be?" Nicole asked. "Personally, I don't think she's taking this seriously enough. Maybe increasing her angst is the right answer."

Pancake seemed to consider that. "Let's play it by ear."

When Nicole, Pancake, and I entered the Channel 16 studio complex, receptionist Phyllis P had her phone to one ear. She flashed a smile and, while continuing her conversation, pointed toward the hallway, meaning we should go on back. Only two of the studios were in use. One looked like an infomercial of some type. In the main studio, the one Megan used for her broadcasts, two news reporters sat behind a desk, the Channel 16 logo on the front as well as on the two mics before them. Each wore the same blue blazer, smiled, and stared directly into the cameras.

We rolled on past and found Megan was in the quad office where we had met before. She sat before her computer; her email program open. She was using a tissue to swipe the remnants of her studio makeup from her ears and hairline. Abby sat to her left, facing her computer, screen open to what appeared to be a news site. She was reading an online article about beach pollution in Huntington Beach.

Megan looked up. "Hey."

Abby spun her chair toward us. "Hey," she echoed Megan.

"We saw your broadcast," Nicole said. "Good one."

"Yeah, I thought so, too. We give updates on local farmers markets a few times a year. You know me and farmers markets. Love my veggies." She stood, looked at Pancake. "You must be the infamous Pancake."

"I am," Pancake said. "Famous and infamous."

"This is Megan," Nicole said.

Pancake gave her a hug. "You're even prettier in person."

She laughed. "And I just took my makeup off."

"Don't need it."

"This is Abby," Nicole said.

Pancake nodded to her. "Another pretty lady."

Abby smiled. "You are the charmer, aren't you?"

Pancake gave a slight head bow. "That's me. Charming and all that."

We rolled chairs away from the empty desks and sat.

"So you're the cavalry?" Megan said to Pancake.

Pancake grinned. "You might say."

"Anything new?" Nicole asked Megan.

"Looks like he sent another email while I was on the air." She opened it. It read:

"Your show was excellent. Made me hungry. And not just for fresh fruits and vegetables. You are so incredibly beautiful. Big

*news. I have something very important for you. Check your
email frequently. It'll be coming soon."*

Pancake had rolled his chair closer to the screen and nudged up next
to Megan. He studied the note. "What do you think?" He glanced
toward Megan.

"What do you think?" Megan asked.

"I do have some thoughts on this, on everything, but you first. I
want to know how you feel about this."

Okay, so Pancake opted for plan B. Talk about the options.

Megan hesitated, her brow furrowed, then she said, "Okay. I find
this one a little more bothersome than many of the others. The 'something important' carries a lot of possibilities. The ones rattling in
my head aren't all pleasant. Of course, the whole 'hungry' thing is
disturbing." Her gaze fell to the floor. "How does it make me feel?"
She looked up. "Scared. Vulnerable."

"Oh, sorry."

The voice came from behind us. I turned to see a young man, maybe
late twenties, khakis, green and brown plaid shirt, untucked, a stack
of pages in one hand. Short and what you might call pudgy, he wore
round, black-rimmed glasses that made him look smart. Like an owl.
I expected to see a pocket protector and a slide rule in his shirt pocket.

"I didn't know you were in a meeting," he said.

"No problem," Megan said. "We were just talking." She looked at
us. "This is Darren. He's our researcher extraordinaire. I, for sure,
couldn't do a single show without his help."

"She says that all the time," Darren said. He glanced down, rolled
one shoe on its side. He looked like a schoolboy before the principal.
"But the truth is that she'd do just fine without me." He gave a head
bob, another glance at the floor. Then extended the pages toward her.
"Here's what I have so far on the summer beach events."

"I'll take those," Abby said, extending her arm. "I'm putting that story together right now."

Darren passed the pages to her. He gave another half nod, said, "Back at it," and left the room.

"I'd say you have another fan," Nicole said.

"What?" Megan asked. "Oh no. Darren's just a friend."

"Not sure he sees it that way."

"Based on?"

"Body language. The way he looks at you." Nicole smiled. "It's sweet."

"Told you," Abby said.

Megan rolled her eyes. "Don't start that again. Abby has been harping on that since she got here."

"Because it's obvious," Abby said. "Apparently to everyone but you." She laughed. "He has a crush on you."

"Get real."

"I'm afraid I agree with Abby and Nicole," I said. "He does look smitten."

"It just dawned on me," Abby said. "Do you think Darren could be the one sending the messages and presents?"

"No," Megan said. "No way."

"How do you know?" Pancake asked.

"Because it's not possible. He's so . . . nice. Shy and polite." She motioned toward her computer. "Darren would never send this kind of stuff."

Pancake spun toward her. He clasped her hands in his. Hers disappeared. "Earlier, we were talking about you feeling scared and vulnerable. Why? Other than the words, why do you feel scared?"

Another hesitation. "Because I don't know who he is. Where he is. What he has in mind. Does he want to screw me? Marry me? Harm me? What?"

Pancake gave a slow nod. "Exactly. We have no idea who it is. Could be anyone."

Megan nodded but said nothing.

Pancake continued. "We have no clear picture of his intentions. Unrequited puppy love that will fade, or something stronger, more demanding."

"Now that's scary."

"Unfortunately, it's the truth," Pancake said. "We simply don't know. It could be someone who has never met you. Only seen you on TV. Or someone closer. Like Darren."

"It's not Darren," Megan said.

"He does know a lot about you," I said. "All your contact info, where you live."

Megan glanced toward the door. She seemed to be searching for a response. Her email program dinged.

It was from him, the stalker. She opened it. We all gathered around and read.

"A glorious day. A milestone. A threshold even. My heart is filled with love for you and I want to make you my wife. To that end, I now formally ask you to marry me. For better, or worse, til death do us part. I've already planned the honeymoon. In Mexico. Followed by a lifetime of love. Don't forget to pack your gift."

Megan's breath caught.

"Open the attachment," I said.

"What? Oh, I didn't even see it."

She opened it. A single page. A marriage contract. Her name filled in, his blank.

"This is getting crazier," Megan said. "I need to do something to put an end to this."

"Answer him," Pancake said.

"What?"

"Tell him you're flattered. Tell him you aren't saying no but that you think you should meet. Spend some time with each other. That you can't agree to something as special as marriage with someone you don't know."

"I thought you said she shouldn't meet with him," I said.

"I said she shouldn't meet him alone. *Alone* being the operative word. With us there, it's a different story." He looked at the computer screen again. Nodded toward it. "The truth is, he just might have given us a pathway."

"What?" Megan asked.

"Send the reply. Ask for a place and time to meet."

"You sure?" Megan asked.

"The shortest path between two points is a straight line. This could be that." He shrugged. "If he takes the bait."

"Do you think he will?" Megan asked.

"Depends on his true agenda. If he really wants to meet you and show you what a swell guy he is, then he might. If his plan is to continue terrorizing you, probably not."

"Unless he wants to get me alone where he can do something to me."

Pancake smiled. "That's what I'm here for."

CHAPTER 16

IT WAS ELEVEN p.m. A documentary on Ted Bundy droned from the TV. This one peppered with interviews with the ever-charming Ted. Strange to see him talking so calmly, his classic smirk front and center. Cool dude when all was said and done.

The half-full bottle of Grey Goose sat on the coffee table. He picked it up. "More?" he asked.

"Sure. Why not. We've come this far."

He refilled both glasses, then pointed at the TV. "There's a dude who understood terror."

"Got to see it up close and personal. Last breath sort of stuff."

"Like you haven't?"

"True." A sip of vodka. "You've got to hand it to Bundy. He did it right. Kidnapping, terrorizing his victims for hours if not days, before killing them. Heady stuff. Not like that coward Berkowitz. What a slug. Shooting someone from ten feet isn't the same as actually feeling them struggle in your hands while you watch their life slip away. I mean, Ted had a front-row seat to the raw terror and saw in their eyes the final resignation that fate had come calling."

"Aren't we waxing poetic tonight?"

"It's the vodka talking."

"What does the vodka say about our next step?"

"Her reply is a trap, of course. No way a meet with her will happen. For sure, not on her terms and at her chosen location. Besides, it's too early for that. I want to play some more. This's merely a ploy to expose us."

"It is. How do you want to respond to her request?"

"Let me work on it. I'll come up with something by morning."

"Surely you have some ideas?"

"I do. Just need to think about the right words and tone. All I know for sure is that it will show indignation and anger. It's time to up the ante and make the threats more real."

"Sounds delicious."

"It will be."

"Of that, I'm sure." He drained his glass. "More?"

"Sure."

CHAPTER 17

THE NEXT MORNING, Megan, Abby, and Darren huddled before Megan's computer. A video of fierce waves crashing at The Wedge played on the screen. When it finished, Megan rolled her chair back.

"I like that one best," Megan said.

"Me, too," Abby added.

They had watched a dozen beach scene films. Huntington Beach surfers, Laguna Beach sunbathers, Newport Beach strollers, and more surfers at Trestles near the San Onofre nuclear plant, one of The OC's most famous wave-riding spots.

"Maybe frame the story with this one," Darren said. "The images of The Wedge are powerful and will be a good intro and outro." He glanced at Megan. "That's my thought anyway."

Megan nodded. "I agree. You found all of these in our archives?"

"I did. We actually have a pretty large collection of similar videos. I selected these, but if you want to see others, I can have them in no time."

"No. I think we have plenty to work with here. Now, Abby and I need to get the script put together and we'll be ready to get into production."

"We have time," Abby said. "This isn't going to run until next month. I do have much of the script written already. At least the preliminary version. It'll still need your magic touch."

"Magic?" Megan raised an eyebrow. "Does that make me the good witch or the bad witch?"

"Definitely the good one," Darren said. He blushed.

Megan buried her smile. Mostly. "Good job with this. Management will be thrilled we have all the footage we need. Saves the money of a film crew."

"Well," Darren said, standing. "I better get back to it."

"Thanks," Megan said. "Excellent work."

He nodded, turned to leave.

Megan's email program dinged. She spun toward her screen and opened it.

Abby scooted up next to her. "It's from him."

"Who?" Darren asked.

"Her boyfriend," Abby said. "Or should I say fiancé?"

Darren looked confused. "What? Fiancé?"

"Abby's simply poking fun at me."

"This is the guy who's been sending the flowers and candy?" Darren asked.

"The same."

"I thought he was just some fan."

"More than that," Abby said. "He's a creep."

"Well, tell him to send more candy." Darren laughed, patted his stomach, and left the room.

Megan felt a pang of guilt. She hadn't kept Darren in the loop on any of this. He, of course, knew about the flowers and the candy that came to the station but she had mostly concealed the emails and texts. Only Abby knew about them. So, why had she kept Darren in the dark? He was a friend, and a coworker, and they were together every day.

She flashed on what Nicole and Jake—Abby too—had said about Darren having a crush on her. Was that even true? Did she subconsciously sense his infatuation and that made her keep him at arm's length? She still couldn't see it, but were all three of them right about this and she was wandering around clueless? It wouldn't be the first time. She remembered back in high school when a popular boy had a thing for her. He was too shy to say anything and she had no inkling he was interested. She definitely felt the same about him, but in the end, nothing ever happened and like the proverbial ships in the night they each went their separate ways. She hadn't learned about it until years later when she reconnected with a classmate and she told her of his infatuation.

But the major part of her reluctance was that she felt embarrassed. Not the right word but it was at least something akin to that. Maybe awkward or self-conscious would fit better. Regardless, she didn't want Darren, or anyone at the studio for that matter, to look at her—what? Differently? Another part was that she didn't want to air her laundry in the workplace. Angst among the staff, or worse the management and the owners, could create difficulties for her. No one wanted problem employees even if the troubles weren't of their own making.

She'd seen it before. Many years ago, when she was at another station, one of her coworkers had had boyfriend problems. She brought them to work on her back every day. Her constant mood swings and crying jags made things uncomfortable and it definitely affected her performance. She ultimately "found other employment." A euphemism for being fired.

The truth was that only Abby knew what was really going on and Megan preferred to keep it that way.

Megan scrolled down to the body of the email. They read:

"Why do you mock me, demean me, and treat me like a gutter dog? I love you. Deeply, completely, forever. I know that deep down you feel the same way, yet you refuse my proposal. You've

crushed my heart, my very soul. Maybe I was wrong about you.
Maybe you are the gutter dweller. I beg you to reconsider. But
know this—YOU ARE MINE. If I can't have you, no one will.
Not now. Not ever."

The words blurred as tears collected in her eyes. She sniffed.

"This is not good," Abby said.

"Not good? It's downright frightening."

"Terrifying might be a better word."

Megan knuckled a tear from the corner of one eye. "I need to call Nicole."

"What's happening?" Nicole asked when she answered.

"I got his reply," Megan said.

"Oh?"

"It's bad. Very bad."

"Tell me."

"Better that you see it. Can you come?"

"We'll be there in twenty minutes."

After she ended the call, Abby hugged her. "I'm so sorry."

Megan was near breaking down but she caught herself. No, she thought, don't let him win. Don't make a scene.

"Thanks," Megan said as she broke the embrace. "I will not, will not, will not let him do this to me."

Abby clasped both of Megan's hands. "What can I do?"

"You're doing it. You're here and right now I need that."

She saw tears collect in Abby's eyes.

"God, I hate this," Abby said. "Brings back too many memories."

"I'm sorry," Megan said. "I don't want any of this to fall on you."

"Too late." Abby wiped her eyes. "But you're strong, and I'm here. We'll get through this."

Megan sighed. "Will we?"

"We will."

A warm wave of relief enveloped Megan when Nicole, Jake, and Pancake appeared. She stood, hugged Nicole, and let it all out. Tears flowed and her shoulders lurched.

"It's okay," Nicole said. "We're here now."

"I'm so scared."

"Show us," Pancake said.

Megan motioned toward her computer. Pancake sat, read the note.

"He's declared himself," Pancake said. "Now we know what we're dealing with."

"Which is?" Megan asked.

"He's deranged, obsessed, and based on this note a little more unhinged."

"Dangerous?" Megan asked.

Pancake nodded. "Could be."

Megan swiped tears from her eyes. "What now?"

Pancake stood, paced the room, head down, deep in thought. As if no one else existed. He stopped. "Not sure. Except we have to find him."

"How?" I asked.

"That's the trick. I'll call my guy. See what he can do on his end."

"The NSA guy?" Nicole asked.

"NSA?" Abby asked. "Are you talking about THE NSA?"

"Yeah," Pancake said.

"How do you do that?"

"Ray," Jake said. "My father. Pancake, too. They have connections no one knows about."

"Can he help?" Megan asked.

"Hopefully."

"Shouldn't we go to the police?" Megan asked.

"Doubt they can help," Pancake said.

"Why would you think that?"

"They have rules and laws to abide. Things that put handcuffs on them instead of the bad guys. We don't. We—me, Ray, my guy—have access to things they don't. Places they can't go."

"That's true," Jake said. "But I agree with Megan. I think it would be smart to at least have an official report on file if nothing else."

"It's the *nothing else* that's the problem," Pancake said. "If he finds out we've involved the police, he might melt down."

"What does that mean?" Megan asked.

"Look, I don't want to scare you," Pancake began.

"Too late for that. I'm beyond scared. So tell me and don't sugar-coat it."

"Okay." Pancake glanced toward the window. "He could become aggressive. Do something crazy like show up with a gun. Here, at your home, on the street. Anywhere. Go out in a blaze of glory, so to speak."

"Are you serious?" Megan asked.

"As serious as a heart attack. These guys are often hanging by a thread. This email suggests he just might be getting there. Pressure mounts as his obsessions are thwarted. He goes to condition red, and anything is possible."

"Jesus," Megan said. "This is a waking nightmare."

"How would he know we went to the police?" Jake asked.

"Lots of ways. We don't know him. Don't know who he is, where he is, or what he is. Hell, he could be a cop."

That dropped the room into silence. The tension palpable.

"Still," Megan said. "I'd feel better if we talked with the Newport Police."

Pancake nodded. "Okay. Let me call Ray. See if he knows someone over there we can trust."

"Trust?" Abby asked. "We can't trust the police?"

"Not always all of them." Pancake looked at Megan. "We don't know all the players over there. Who we might be able to work with. I don't want you to simply walk in and get some flunky who doesn't have a clue. Or doesn't give a rat's ass and lacks even a sliver of discretion."

"Okay," Megan said. "Make your call. But then let's talk with the police at the very least."

"Want me to go with you?" Abby asked. "For moral support."

Megan considered that. "I don't want to overwhelm them with people. Maybe it's better if we go. Besides, you have more work to do on the script."

"That makes sense. I do have a few ideas for making it snappier."

Megan smiled. "We like snappy."

CHAPTER 18

No shock here but Ray knew a guy who knew a guy who knew a woman. Claire Mills. A detective with the Newport Beach PD. According to Ray's guy, someone in the FBI's LA office, she was experienced, tough, and took no prisoners. Took Ray all of twenty minutes to uncover all this and get the ball rolling.

The result was that Pancake called her, had a brief chat, and set up a meeting. Fortunately, she was in her office "pushing papers around" and said we could drop by at any time. Which was now.

The Newport Beach Police Department, like everything else in Newport Beach, looked expensive. Bright, modern, encased in clean white stucco, and with a palm-tree-framed entrance. Looked more like a spa or a library than a cop shop. The sign above the door dispelled any confusion. It read: POLICE DEPARTMENT in large black lettering.

Good thing the city had wads of cash as the facility sat on a wallet-emptying patch of dirt near the corner of Jamboree Drive and Santa Barbara Road. Only a nine iron from two golf courses—the Back Bay Golf Club and the uber-exclusive Big Canyon Country Club. Oh, and maybe a strong three iron from Fashion Island, one of the top-grossing shopping centers in the world. Mostly outdoor, arranged in a palm-treed circle, and populated with high-end shops and restaurants—no fast food here, thank you.

You could almost smell the money and for sure could see it in the bright white Bentley convertible that rolled by as we ascended the front steps. We stopped and watched the white car disappear around the curve in the road.

"Buy me one of those, daddy," Nicole said.

"Since your movie's going to be a major hit, you can buy me one," I said.

"Deal."

Just like that I was getting a new Bentley. Probably not. Not that Nicole's movie wouldn't rake it in, I was sure of that, but rather that I wouldn't know what to do with a car like that if I had one. I liked my '65 Mustang much better.

Since there were four of us, a uniformed officer ferried a couple of extra chairs into Lieutenant Claire Mills' office and we all sat. Introductions followed.

Mills looked to be late thirties, stocky, muscular, no stranger to the gym. Her hair was short and sandy blond, eyes brown, and her face stern, which contrasted with her friendly smile.

"It's not often I get a call from the FBI's Regional Director."

"Like I told you on the phone," Pancake said. "That's Ray's doing. He's the one that owns our firm, Longly Investigations. He's also Jake's father."

"I see. Well, he must have some pull somewhere along the line."

"Comes from his military days," I said.

"What branch?"

"Marines. But most of his time was spent elsewhere."

Mills smiled, her head nodding slightly. "Got it. My brother also spent a considerable slice of his career 'elsewhere.'" She turned to Megan. "I know you. I watch your show as often as I can."

"Thanks."

"You do a good job. So good I hear you've picked up some unwanted baggage."

"More like a steamer trunk, it seems."

Mills offered a sympathetic smile. "Tell me about it."

Megan nodded toward Pancake. "He might do a better job."

Pancake proceeded to lay it all out. The emails, texts, gifts, leaving one at Megan's doorstep, the escalating treats in his communications. He handed Mills a copy of the emails and texts. He had circled the problematic ones with a red marker. We waited while she scanned them.

She placed the pages on her desktop and leaned back. "I agree. You've got a bad actor here. A least it feels that way. But, and this is a big but, though these are definitely disconcerting, even somewhat threatening, there's no overt threat here."

"Feels overt to me," Megan said.

"I know it does. As it should. But it doesn't rise to the level that I can put any resources on it."

"Why not?" Nicole asked.

"The truth? I wish I could. I don't like the sound of this guy. Hell, I don't like these stalker-types in any form. Makes me want to take a swing at them." She smiled, shrugged.

I liked her. I also agreed with her. I'd like to take a Louisville Slugger to this guy, too.

"Unfortunately, the truth is that we get this kind of stuff around here all the time. You know? California, the land of the nutjobs. So we can't track every one of them. Not until there is a real, tangible, direct threat."

"I guessed as much," Pancake said.

"That's because you understand the rules. The restrictions. Another cold hard truth is that everyone, even this miscreant, has rights. Free speech, free communication, that kind of thing. He can send all the letters and emails and texts he wants. Until he makes a real, credible threat, that is. Then we can come in." She glanced at Megan. "It's all BS. If I had my way I'd run this guy down with my SUV." She smiled. "Maybe worse. But, sadly, I can't do any of that."

"I sort of understand," Megan said. "But part of me doesn't."

"That's because it's a very gray area. A balancing act between protecting and overstepping. There's no right answer."

"So what do you suggest we do?" I asked.

"I will open a file. A complaint, if you will. That will at least create a record. If we can ID the guy, I'll personally go have a chat with him. In fact, I'd love to. I'll also talk with my guys over in the cyber division and see if they have any tricks."

"I appreciate it," Megan said. "This is getting scary."

"I know," Mills said. "I truly wish I could do more, but I promise, I'll do everything I can." She opened her hands toward Megan. "In the meantime, be diligent and aware. Stay close to friends. Don't go out alone."

"Sort of like house arrest, I guess," Megan said.

"Not quite that but do use common sense."

"She's going to stay with me," Nicole said. "I tried to get her to before and she refused, but now we'll kidnap her if we have to."

"That's a felony," Mills said. She smiled. "But we'd probably let it slide."

"Jake and Pancake are staying at my place too. So it'll be like a slumber party."

"If you make s'mores," Mills said, "I'll drop by."

"S'mores sound good," Pancake said.

Of course they did.

Mills actually walked us outside. As we exited, a gleaming yellow Lamborghini rolled by. Maybe Nicole would buy me one of those instead of the Bentley. A Lambo I could get behind.

"I know this is frustrating," Mills said to Megan. "I know you hoped we could swoop in and whack this dude in the head. No doubt he needs it. But I want you to know that I take this personally. I'll keep my finger on it. I'll talk with our tech guys and see what I can get done. Sort of off the books since I can't do it officially."

"Thanks," Megan said.

"I imagine Pancake here—I love that name, by the way—has a few tricks up his sleeve too."

"A few."

"Just don't break the law."

Pancake tossed her a mock-surprised look. "*Moi?* Wouldn't dream of it."

Mills laughed. "Yeah. That's what I thought."

CHAPTER 19

THIS ALSO WILL come as no shock—Pancake was hungry. He said so before we made it out of the Newport PD parking lot. I guess he'd forgotten about the two sandwiches he had woofed down—what? A couple of hours ago?

When Nicole learned that Pancake was coming, she had insisted on stocking the fridge. Her take was that a hungry Pancake would be intolerable. I told her Pancake, at least chronologically, was an adult and could fend for himself. She countered with why would I want to roll the dice with Pancake becoming hypoglycemic? She had a point.

So, off to Gelson's Market where we filled five bags with—well—everything. At least I got some oatmeal.

Back to Pancake's sandwich. A Dagwood. This triple-decker deal is a massive sandwich anyway and when Pancake hammers it together it becomes a sight to behold. Like twin towers. Each with three slices of bread; layers of meats like salami, ham, pepperoni, turkey, and bologna; more layers of cheese, in this case cheddar, provolone, Swiss, and smoked gouda; banana and pepperoni peppers, and a few jalapeños; lettuce, tomato, and red onion; all slathered with mayo and mustard. Did I mention he ate two of them?

Anyway, he was hungry so we headed back north on PCH then onto Newport Boulevard. Pancake worked his phone and decided we should go to Burger Lounge, just off Newport on 17th Street. I knew better than to argue, so five minutes later we were placing our orders at the counter. We found a table along one wall. Pancake said he needed to make a call, got up, and walked outside.

Megan's phone buzzed. She mostly listened, then said, "You hungry?" A pause. "Great. We're having lunch at Burger Lounge. Bring it with you." Pause. "Yeah, that's the one. I'll order you a burger."

She slid her phone into her purse. "That was Abby. He sent another flower box."

"Maybe trying to make up," Nicole said. "After this morning's email."

Pancake returned. Megan told him of the new gift.

"Maybe trying to kiss and make up," Pancake said.

"That's what I thought," Nicole said.

"Great minds run in the same small circles, darlin'."

"All that geniusness aside, this isn't bad news," I said.

"I'd rather he just go away," Megan said.

"I know, but at least he's still communicating."

"Exactly," Pancake said. "My fear was that he would stop reaching out and we'd have no idea what he was up to. Or maybe, more importantly, his state of mind. The more he communicates, the better the chance he'll slip up."

"I guess that's true," Megan said. "I just wish he'd get hit by a garbage truck."

"Or Pancake," Nicole said.

"Same thing actually," I said.

"You're funny," Pancake said. "Both of you."

"We try."

"Anyway, back to the issue at hand, the call I made was to my guy. Told him it was time to dig deeper."

"Can he?" Megan asked. "Find this guy?"

"Not going to be easy but he has a few tricks. Access to certain databases, search and tracking algorithms, that sort of thing."

Our burgers came and we dug in. They were hot, juicy, and excellent.

Abby came in, a long white box tucked beneath one arm. "Here you go." She handed it to Megan.

Inside. A single white lily.

"The funeral flower," I said.

"What?" Megan asked.

"Lilies. They're for funerals."

Megan sighed. "Great. Just freaking great."

"Guess our hopes that this was an apology doesn't hold up," Nicole said.

"Nope." Pancake wiped grease from his chin with a napkin. "It's a message for sure. Sort of an exclamation point to his last missive. The silver lining is that he hasn't gone silent."

"Not a message I want to receive," Megan said.

"It's what these guys do. They thrive on generating fear. The power that gives them. Your fear is his drug. That's what he needs."

I had a thought. Yes, I do have those from time to time. Some of them were damn good. Like this one, I hoped. "Can I ask something?"

Pancake grunted.

"If he feeds on fear, wouldn't he want to experience it? Be able to actually feel it?"

Pancake nodded.

"So why not show up? Why not go to Megan's office, or her home? See her up close?"

"That would expose him," Nicole said.

"He's apparently not ready for that," Pancake said.

"I don't want to see him," Megan said. "Ever. Unless he's behind bars."

"Okay," I said. "Maybe not face-to-face but why not call? He's sending all these scary messages and gifts, like this one. But he can't see her reaction. Only guess at it. Maybe get a hint of it whenever she responds. If he called, he could experience it firsthand."

I noticed Abby seemed uncomfortable. Fidgety, gaze down toward her lap.

"What is it?" I asked her.

She looked up. "Nothing."

"It's something. What is it?"

The stress lines around her eyes and lips deepened. "I don't like this. It reminds me of the guy that glommed on to me. He called all the time. Showed up way too often."

"Mine, too," Nicole said. "He seemed to always know where I was."

Abby wound her napkin into a knot. "Yeah. He even sent me photos of me out doing normal stuff. Like he was following me. Which, I guess he was."

"I don't want to talk to him," Megan said. "The emails and texts are enough, thank you."

"That's my point," I said. "You're sitting here all wound up and scared, yet he experiences none of that. It's like his work, for lack of a better term, goes unrewarded. Like Pancake said, your fear is his drug. He'd want to savor it."

"Unless he's nearby," Nicole said.

Megan's head swiveled. She seemed to examine everyone in sight. "You guys aren't helping me here."

"Relax," I said. "You're safe here. You have Pancake and Nicole to protect you."

"What about you?"

"I could throw my burger at him." I smiled. A feeble attempt to tamp down her angst, but I saw no sign that it worked. "That would at least distract him so Nicole could Krav Maga him into submission, and Pancake could garbage truck him."

Megan smiled. "I love you guys. Without you I'd be going insane about now."

"When we leave here," Nicole said, "we're going to go by your place and pack what you need. You're moving in with me." Megan started to protest but Nicole continued. "It's not open for discussion."

"But aren't you leaving tomorrow? Going up to Malibu?"

"So are you."

"I can't do that."

"You can and you will."

"What's in Malibu?" Abby asked.

"My uncle's place," Nicole said.

"Her uncle is Charles Balfour, the big producer," Megan said.

"Really?" Abby asked. "He's a huge deal."

"He has a house in The Colony," Nicole said. "Right on the beach."

"I can't crash your party," Megan said. "Or your uncle's home."

"Trust me, he'll be fine with it. Besides, you can finally meet my parents."

"As an added bonus," I said, "Kirk Ford will be there."

"You've got to be kidding," Abby said. "Kirk Ford? Wow."

"Come too," Nicole said. "You'd enjoy it."

"Oh. No, I couldn't."

"What?" I asked. "You have something better to do?"

Abby smiled. "Better than that? Not now. Maybe not ever."

"Then it's settled. I'll call Uncle Charles and let him know."

Abby glanced at Megan, then back to Nicole. "I don't know. I'd feel like a gate crasher."

"Exactly," Megan said.

"The house is seven thousand square feet and has a dozen bedrooms. All suites. I think he has plenty of room for you."

"It is tempting," Megan said.

"Listen," Nicole said. "With all this going on, I think it would be good to get away. Even just for one day. Get away from this guy and clear your head." She shrugged. "Both of you."

Megan sighed, then nodded. "It would be a welcome break from this clown."

"He can still send emails and texts," Abby said.

Megan raised one shoulder. "True. But I won't have to look over my shoulder and wonder if he's following me."

"So, it's a done deal," Nicole said.

Abby and Megan exchanged a glance, then each of them nodded.

"What's the party for?" Abby asked.

"Me," Nicole said. She laughed. "And Kirk."

"It's to celebrate the upcoming production of Nicole's new screenplay," I said. "Her uncle is the executive producer and Kirk is the star."

"Amazing," Abby said. "Megan told me you were out here to film a movie, but I never imagined it was something like that. That is so way cool."

"Uncle Charles has invited a ton of big-name producers, directors, and actors. Not to mention his neighbors who I'm sure will wander in. All on the A-list."

Abby looked starstruck. "I don't have anything to wear to something like that."

Nicole laughed. "You have a swimsuit, don't you? Did I mention it sits right on the beach? And he has a massive pool. It'll be fun and wild. Uncle Charles never does anything that isn't over the top."

CHAPTER 20

I HAD AN hour to kill before we rolled north toward Malibu. Since it was only an overnight trip and not much would be needed, I had tossed a few things into a small bag and was good to go. Nicole stalked around doing the same. Megan, who had reluctantly moved in the night before, had disappeared into her room to get squared away for the trip.

I found Pancake on the deck, his computer in his lap. I took the chair next to him.

"You good to go?" I asked.

He gave me a look. The one that said of course he was. One thing about Pancake is that he was never late, and never unprepared.

"What are you doing?" I asked.

"Looking into Darren Slater. Megan's researcher."

"You thinking he could be the one doing this?"

"He's close. He knows her schedule, her contact info, probably where she lives." He worked the keyboard. "Toss into the soup the fact that he has a crush on her."

"Those do sometimes turn into obsessions."

"They do."

"So?" I asked. "Anything?"

"Nada. He has no criminal record, a solid work history, and he's been at the station a few years. He graduated from UCI with an

English Lit degree and then taught high school briefly before this current gig. No red flags. Nothing very exciting."

"Aren't the quiet ones the ones you have to watch out for?" I asked.

"That makes you two safe," Nicole said as she stepped onto the deck. "But then looks are deceiving." She leaned on the rail facing us. "What are you doing?" she asked Pancake.

"Looking at that Darren dude."

"Better not let Megan know."

"Let me know what?" Megan stood in the open slider, rolling up the sleeves of the untucked yellow shirt she wore. That and a pair of white shorts.

"Nicole's just being a drama queen," Pancake said. "I'm checking out Darren, your research guy."

"Darren? Why?"

Pancake ran through it—he was close, had knowledge, and a crush.

"No way," Megan said. "I told you that. Darren's as sweet as anyone I've ever known."

"Sure looks that way," Pancake said. "But since we're churning the water and not getting anywhere, everybody is fair game."

"Let me guess," Megan said, "you found nothing."

"Not a ripple."

"You about ready?" Nicole asked.

Megan nodded. "Yeah. What time are we leaving?"

"Ten," I said. I glanced at my watch. "Did you hear from Abby?"

"She's on the way. I'll finish up my hair and I'm good to go." She disappeared toward her room.

"Want to sit?" I asked Nicole.

"You offering me your chair?"

"My lap."

"Don't want to scare the neighbors."

"I'll behave."

She laughed. "No, you won't. Besides, I think that seat's taken. By Maryanne."

Took me a few seconds then I retrieved the name. "Flight attendant Maryanne?"

"She has dibs."

"Flight attendant?" Pancake said. "One of my favorite flavors."

"You're a pig," Nicole said.

"Proudly."

"Well, dear old Maryanne has the hots for Jake."

"Everybody does," I said, proud of myself for the snappy comeback.

"Not me," Pancake said. "I see you more as a pain in the ass."

The doorbell buzzed. I heard Megan open it and Abby come in.

We decided that we could all drive up in the Range Rover. Maybe a little tight but not as tight as parking in The Malibu Colony. We left a little before ten and actually made good time. LA traffic is never light but at least today it moved on. We made it to Uncle Charles' place by noon.

A black Porche convertible, top down exposing a rich gray interior, sat in the drive. I parked next to it and we climbed out.

Nicole had said his home was magnificent, but that didn't come close to covering it. Nicole pushed open one of the two huge carved-wooden entry doors, which led us into a cavernous foyer and then an even more cavernous room. Open concept on steroids. A giant living room, kitchen, dining room with twenty-foot ceilings. The far wall was all glass panels, the ones that slide into one another and merged outside and inside into a single space. Beyond a massive infinity pool, a party-sized bubbling jacuzzi, the beach, and the Pacific, calm and flat today.

To my left, caterers were already busy setting up the dining area for serving. The living area held two deeply cushioned sofas and several comfy-looking chairs. Uncle Charles and Nicole's parents, Bob and

Connie Jamison, sat on the sofas talking. They all stood when we came in.

Nicole hugged everyone and then introduced Megan, Abby, and Pancake. I shook hands with Bob and Uncle Charles and hugged Connie.

"So good to see you again," I said.

Connie took a step back and looked me up and down. "Is Nicole not feeding you enough?" She laughed. "Actually, you look great."

"She feeds me just fine. Except she ends up eating it all."

"Been that way her whole life," Bob said. He wrapped an arm around Nicole and pulled her against his side.

"Just trying to keep up with Pancake," Nicole said.

"Fool's errand," I said.

Pancake grunted.

"Please," Uncle Charles said. "Relax. Make yourselves at home."

"We were having some lemonade," Connie said. "Any takers?"

"Maybe later," Nicole said. "I want to show Megan and Abby around."

"Wow, just wow," Megan said, her gaze swiveling around, taking in the entire room. "I've never seen any place like this."

"My humble abode," Uncle Charles said.

"Thank you for inviting us," Abby said. "Even though we feel like we're crashing the party."

"No, no. It's my pleasure. I'm glad you could make it."

A woman who looked to be in charge of the catering crew motioned to Uncle Charles.

"Looks like I'm needed," he said. "The guests will begin trickling in around four or so. In the meantime, enjoy." He walked away.

"Is that who I think it is?" Nicole asked. She motioned toward the pool deck.

It was. Kirk Ford. He had been sitting in a lounge chair, back to us, facing the ocean, phone to his ear. Now he stood, slipped the phone into the pocket of his shorts, and waved. He wore a black tee shirt and cap, each with the "Space Quest" logo front and center.

We walked out onto the deck. Nicole hugged him and then introduced Megan and Abby, who each now had that starstruck, deer-in-headlights look. Kirk did that to people. Particularly women.

"You two look great," Kirk said to Nicole and me. "I take it all is well."

"It is," I said. "What about you?"

"Couldn't be better." He glanced at Nicole. "Now that she's hired me to be in her movie."

"That was Uncle Charles."

"He might sign the checks, but I know the idea was all yours." Nicole shrugged.

"I think you have a winner on your hands," I said. "Not that I'm an expert in any of this, but I read the script. It's excellent."

"It is," Kirk said. "Grabbed me from the first scene."

"What's it about?" Abby asked.

"It's called *Murderwood*," Kirk said.

"It's a riff on a true Hollywood mystery," Nicole said. "A never-solved case."

"I get to play the hero detective." Kirk laughed.

"Sort of like *Space Quest*?" Megan asked. "Which, by the way, I'm a huge fan."

"Love to hear that. No, this is about as far from that as possible. It's a dark story."

"Nicole wrote it," I said. "Would you expect less?"

She punched my arm. I've got to learn to disconnect my mouth from my brain. Boy, how many times have I told myself that over the years? Pancake and Ray, too. Probably too late for that but I made a mental note to work on it. Maybe I should count to ten before speaking. That seemed long so maybe just to three, or two. Change is hard.

"It's going to test my acting chops," Kirk said.

"You'll be outstanding," Nicole said. "That's why I wanted you for the part."

"I'll do my best to live up to your expectations."

I started to say something like good luck with that. That I tried all the time and still stuck my foot in my mouth. Or did something that resulted in her punching me. Instead, I said nothing. See, I'm getting better already.

"Let's get everything out of the car," Nicole said, "and settle Megan and Abby in their rooms. Then let's take a walk on the beach."

"I'm all over that," Abby said.

CHAPTER 21

I WATCHED NICOLE, Megan, Abby, and Kirk stroll up the beach, near the waterline. Nicole wore an orange bikini, not much to it, but it did the job. If revealing a lot of flesh was its purpose. My, my. Megan and Abby chose more modest suits.

I sat at an umbrella-shaded table near the pool with Pancake, Bob, and Connie. The catering crew brought out lemonade and chips and salsa. They also found the time to whip up a giant ham and cheese sandwich for Pancake. He busied himself devouring it.

They say that if you want to know how people will age, look at their parents. Not sure I buy that. Rather I prayed it wasn't true. I didn't want to be Ray. But if that's true, Nicole's future looked bright. Her mom was basically a twenty-year-older version of her. Lean, fit, blond, and with the same deeply blue eyes. Connie's were even bluer, if that was possible. From the few other times I had been around her, she had the same smart-ass attitude as Nicole.

Uncle Charles had the same good looks and trim build as his sister, Connie. The family had good genes.

Bob, also lean, fit, and tanned, had darker hair, which he kept cut short. Quieter and more soft spoken than Connie, and very smart. I sensed that from the first time I met him. He and Connie were successful producers, writers, directors, the whole enchilada. I figured that Bob was the brains behind their success but that Connie was the straw that stirred the drink. A good combo. Sort of like the Arnaz duo—Lucy and Desi. Except that Bob and Connie, each with the looks to be movie stars, had chosen to work their magic behind the lens.

I saw some of each of them in Nicole. Beauty, brains, and an attitude. Heavy on the attitude at times.

"What's new with you guys?" I asked.

"Lots of stuff," Connie said. "We have a few too many irons in the fire right now. Several productions we're working on."

"But this one, Nicole's project, has pushed those aside for the time being," Bob said.

"A lot is riding on this," Connie said. "Nicole's first big project. Kirk's rehabilitation with his fans." She shoved her hair back. "Not to mention the salvaging of *Space Quest*."

"Nicole has felt the pressure," I said. "Not that she'd ever admit it, but I see it."

"I do too," Connie said. "She appears a little tired." She looked at me. "But I thought maybe that was your fault." She laughed.

See? Just like Nicole.

"It is," Pancake said. "They're like a pair of rabbits."

Connie laughed again. "I like you. Nicole has told me a lot about you and it's about time I got to meet the mysterious Pancake."

"Not much of a mystery," I said. "He's exactly what he looks to be."

"What? Hungry?"

Pancake grunted. "My body's a temple and it needs feeding."

"Want another sandwich?" Connie asked.

"Wouldn't turn it down."

She waved to one of the crew, motioned him to make another sandwich. He nodded and smiled.

"Megan and Abby seem nice," Bob said.

"They are." I looked at him. "I assumed you guys had met Megan before."

"No," Connie said. "Nicole was going to bring her up once, maybe a couple of years ago, but something came up with her work."

"She's a TV reporter, isn't she?" Bob asked.

"Yeah. She's good at it."

Bob nodded, said nothing. Glanced out toward the water. Then, "What's the story on this guy that's bothering her?"

I laid out the chronology of what had happened so far and what we knew about him. Which wasn't much.

"He sounds like he could be dangerous," Bob said.

"Could be," Pancake said. "Sure starting to smell that way."

"Any idea who it is?" Connie asked.

"Nope," Pancake said. "Not even a clue."

"I hate this crap," Connie said. She reached over and took Bob's hand, lacing her fingers with his. "Resurrects all those memories of what Nicole went through." She took a sip of lemonade. "It was a horrible time. Notes, and gifts, and phone calls, and showing up everywhere she went. Nicole was beside herself. She couldn't sleep and became wary of people and of going out anywhere. Not like her at all."

"The only silver lining," Bob said, "was that she knew who he was. Which of course ultimately led to his day in court. It didn't go well for him."

"We hired a private investigator," Connie said. "Like you guys. We were able to build a solid case against him."

"Sort of stalked the stalker?" I said.

"Exactly. We had him dead to rights. We knew where he was and what he was doing."

"To say that the judge was impressed would be an understatement," Bob said. "We had pictures, videos, phone and text records, even recorded all his calls. No chance for him to deny any of it." He sighed. "I can't even imagine what it would be like not knowing who was doing it."

"It does add an extra layer of fear," I said.

"I see that," Connie said. "Not knowing if it's a total stranger or someone right next to you. Someone you know or work with."

"How are you going to find him?" Bob asked.

I glanced at Pancake.

"I've got a few things working," Pancake said. "But the truth is that since he's using anonymously purchased and apparently rotating burner phones, finding him will be close to impossible. Unless, until, he steps out of the shadows, reveals himself, and does something stupid."

"Does something?" Connie asked.

"It's the *something* that's the problem," Pancake said. "Hopefully he'll show up, drop to a knee, and ask for her hand in marriage." He tapped the tabletop with an index finger. "Not appear with a weapon of some sort."

"So it's not possible to track a burner phone?" Bob asked.

"Not impossible but not easy. We can, of course, find where it was purchased—which we did. That didn't help. These purchases are always made under a fake name so unless you have security video from the store, the purchase info won't help. Many of these stores don't have such systems and even if they do they get erased every two to thirty days. Like in this case. We can track where it's used. Where he logs into Wi-Fi to send messages. Mostly after the fact so this isn't often helpful. Since these devices don't typically have a GPS function, locating him in real time doesn't happen."

"Poor girl," Connie said. "No one should have to go through this."

Hard to argue with that. The minor little stalker types I had had, mainly girls who wouldn't take "so long it's been nice," as a final answer, were merely annoyances. Not scary at all. Or maybe I misread the entire thing. At least none of them ever shot at me or boiled a rabbit on my stove. There was this one girl who tossed a pair of jogging shoes I had left at her condo up onto my porch. Middle of the night since I found them early the next morning. I remembered I had felt uncomfortable that she had been on my property. Not afraid, or concerned, just uncomfortable. I couldn't imagine what Megan must be going through.

"What's your next move?" Bob asked.

"I got a few ideas," Pancake said. "Maybe a way to smoke him out. Still researching a couple of things. We'll get on this as soon as we get back tomorrow."

"Good," Connie said. "In the meantime, let's have a fun day."

Sounded like a plan to me.

CHAPTER 22

NICOLE, MEGAN, ABBY, and Kirk descended the steps to the beach. They angled across the sand to the water's edge where the sand was firmer and headed north. They walked four abreast with Abby hanging as close to Kirk as she could without climbing in his knee-length bathing trunks. Nicole guessed she'd actually like to do just that. Knowing Kirk, it wouldn't be rejected. He rarely passed up an opportunity. Any opportunity.

Most people ignored them, only a few stopping, pointing their way, whispering to each other.

"Looks like you have some fans," Megan said.

"Better here than most places," Kirk said. "Folks in The Colony, even those who visit here, aren't as starstruck as most. Or maybe because there are so many movie stars, and rock icons, and TV folks here that they can't focus on anyone."

"I suspect all the attention can get tedious," Megan said.

"It can. In LA, I don't think I've ever completed a meal without signing a bunch of autographs."

"I bet it can get crazy," Abby said.

"It can. But, you know, all those folks buy tickets. They pay for everything I have. So part of me is grateful." He waved to a couple of kids, boy and girl, early teens, who called his name from the deck of a modern white stucco and glass mansion. "That's Shane and Willa Cuthbert. Good kids. Their parents are fairly heavyweight producers."

"My, they've grown," Nicole said. "I met them years ago. When they were maybe five or so. At Uncle Charles' place."

"Have you had any crazy ones?" Abby asked. "Fans?"

"Sure. Unavoidable. But you know what? Every time I feel like complaining about the loonies, I remind myself that I'm not Elvis."

"Elvis?"

"Oh, yeah. Talk about a prisoner in a gilded cage. He couldn't go out in public. He was so recognizable and his fans were certifiably insane. They would've ripped his clothes off."

"I guess that's true," Megan said.

"It was. Think about it. He couldn't go out to dinner, or a movie, or to the grocery store. It would've been chaos on steroids. So he had everything brought to him and watched movies at home."

"A big price for stardom," Megan said.

"What about you?" Abby asked Kirk. "You're definitely recognizable. Have you had any really scary stalkers?"

"Of course. Most are simply overzealous fans, but some got a little too aggressive. You know, not just sending notes and gifts, but making a scene at the studio or when I'm out somewhere. Or climbing the fence to my home."

"Really?"

He laughed. "Once I found a pair of naked teenage girls in my swimming pool. Drunk, splashing around, hollering. They weren't too happy the Beverley Hills PD showed up." He laughed. "I didn't press charges. They seemed like nice young ladies. Of course, my attorney filed a restraining order against them to prevent a repeat performance."

"Smart move," Nicole said.

"You know what the most concerning part was? That I was home alone with two underage and under-clothed girls in my pool. They could have alleged anything. Two against one. The courts and the tabloids would have shredded me. Reminded me of the movie. *Wild Things.*"

"Oh yeah," Megan said. "Neve Campbell and Denise Richards."

"And Kevin Bacon and Matt Dillon," Abby added. "Good movie."

"It was. That movie actually crossed my mind. That's why I stayed inside with the door locked until the police showed up."

"But did you have any that really scared you?" Abby asked. "You know, physically?"

"Sure. I've had my house broken into, my car damaged, even had a girl attack me on Rodeo Drive. She said I had been ignoring her and that she wouldn't be taken for granted." He gave a headshake. "I had no idea who she was but later found she had sent a series of letters over several months. Each professing her love. A couple asking for me to marry her."

"Let me guess," Nicole, said. "You never saw her letters. Your people who handle that sort of stuff sent her polite responses and a thanks for being a fan?"

"Exactly."

"Then I had one that painted my door with chicken blood."

"What?" Megan asked.

"Funny now. It wasn't then. Turned out she was a follower of voo-doo and was blessing my home and blocking evil spirits."

"That's crazy."

"Actually, she was completely sane, just a voodoo priestess. She was simply protecting me."

"Another restraining order?" Nicole asked.

"Yeah. That makes twenty-four and counting."

"Twenty-four?" Megan asked. "Here I am worried about one."

"Nicole told me about it. What's the story?"

Megan sighed. "Some guy, I don't know who, has been sending emails and texts and gifts. Most are benign but some have an edge."

"More than an edge," Abby said. "Not to mention he left lingerie at your front door."

"Hmmm," Kirk said.

"What?" Megan asked.

"All I can tell you, from personal experience and from what I've learned from a few experts in this arena, is that as long as they send notes and gifts and stay at arm's length they aren't usually a threat. Once they start showing up at your home or work or on the street, wherever, that changes things. That type of behavior elevates the danger factor. A P.I. I once hired called it 'closing the gap.' That seemed a good description to me."

Megan looked at him. "I don't want to hear that."

"You have to. Remember, it's better to overreact than underreact."

"That's what I've been telling her," Abby said. "But she's stubborn."

"We did go to the police," Megan said. "Not that they can do anything. He hasn't really done anything overtly threatening."

Kirk nodded. "Always the problem. Which ones to ignore and which to go full protection with. My guys, the ones that go with me to events, keep digital files of photos and whatever else they can put together on the ones that could be a problem. Costs me a fortune."

"I suspect so," Nicole said.

"You have no idea. Home alarm systems, armed guards, security checks of hotels and venues. It's a huge drain." He sighed. "But at least here, in The Colony, I can give them the day off and enjoy the beach."

CHAPTER 23

A-LIST. A-LIST. A-LIST. B movie scream queen. A-list. Hollywood icon. Multiple Academy Award winner. Rock star. A-list. Producer with a long list of scandals. Director who made last year's number one blockbuster. A-list.

I scanned the room, taking inventory. Everyone was beautiful. Perfect teeth, perfect hair, perfect skin. Most of the women showed a lot of it.

Uncle Charles knew how to throw a party and who to invite. Plus the connections and clout to do so. One couple flew in from "our place" in Grand Cayman. The lead singer of an always-on-the-charts rock group flew in from Switzerland with his painfully thin, glassy-eyed, over-amped super-model girlfriend. I figured she controlled her weight with a combination of coke and meth. Seemed to work as she had graced the cover of every fashion magazine known and probably raked in more money than her rock star boyfriend.

Others came from New York, Paris, and of course Beverly Hills and other high-dollar neighborhoods in LA. Some were his neighbors and simply strolled down the beach. The latest Hollywood power couple arrived by Uber. Consciously showing their disdain for conspicuous consumption. Well, except for the gold and diamonds that draped her neck and swayed from her ears. I mean, you can only take this austerity stuff so far.

Nicole's director, Lee Goldberg, came. Tall, handsome, and gregarious. A much sought-after director who dropped everything and immediately jumped on board when Charles Balfour called. Did I say Uncle Charles had clout? Goldberg had had a series of hits and I suspected adding him to the team greatly assured the success of *Murderwood*. Right now he huddled, sipped champagne, and shared laughs with a pair of other industry heavyweights.

Then there was Kirk Ford. Speaking of assuring success. If the public forgave him, that is. I was sure they would. Hollywood and scandal being interchangeable words.

But among all these power brokers, there was no doubt that Kirk and Nicole were the costars of Uncle Charles' little soiree. Nicole to introduce her to the Hollywood elites she didn't already know, make her name known as a serious screenwriter, and Kirk to celebrate his return to the big screen. Show that he was alive, well, out of jail, and ready to snatch up the reins of the *Space Quest* franchise once again.

Kirk was in his element. He sat in the jacuzzi, a young starlet on each side. I noticed these two were different from the pair I had seen earlier. Was there a rotation involved? A schedule? A sign-up sheet?

Nicole and Megan sat on the opposite side of the jacuzzi, legs dangling in the water. Abby lay on a lounge chair, soaking up some sun, and chatting with a young actress who spoke more with her hands than anything else.

The sun hung low, sunset still an hour or so away, and its glow painted the sky, the water, the deck, everything with a warm, yellow-orange hue. Seemed Uncle Charles had even arranged for the lighting to be perfect. He was a producer, after all.

I stood near the catered spread, munching on a small crab cake with perfect remoulade sauce. Pancake refilled his plate—for the third time—prime rib, grilled lobster bites, and a dozen boiled shrimp.

"Pretty good grub," he said.

"Sure is," I said.

"Lots of it, too."

"They knew you were coming."

One of the catering staff walked up. The young lady who had earlier brought Pancake his sandwiches. "Need anything?" she asked.

"What else do you have?"

"Lots more of the same. Plus we have some lobster quesadillas and shrimp tacos coming. Oh, and some incredible crab-fried rice."

"Sounds good." Pancake gave her a look. "What's your name?"

"Carrie."

"Nice to meet you. I'm Pancake. This is Jake."

She smiled, seemed to register the names, but never looked at me. She stared at Pancake. "Pancake? That's not your real name, is it?"

"It is now. My mom named me Tommy but everyone calls me Pancake."

"I like it."

"Me too."

"If you want to go outside and enjoy the sun, I'll come find you when the new items come out. Or bring you anything you need."

Again, her focus never left the big guy.

"Cool. But I think I've found my spot."

She laughed. "Save some room though. We have some fabulous desserts coming."

"I got room."

"Looks that way." She blushed. "Sorry. That didn't come out right."

"Sure it did," Pancake said. He patted his abdomen. "This thing doesn't ever fill up."

"He's telling the truth," I said. "He could demolish this entire table. Literally. He's just being polite."

"That's me. Mr. Polite."

. P. LYLE

"I'm glad I don't have to grocery-shop for you," she said. "I'd need a bigger car."

"That's why he has a massive truck," I said.

"I'll go check on the quesadillas. You'll love them." She headed toward the kitchen area.

"She likes you," I said.

"Of course she does. All women do."

"Probably your modesty."

"That's part of it."

"And the rest?"

"I'm handsome, charming, suave, and debonaire."

"Don't forget dripping with humility."

"That, too."

Nicole and Megan walked up. They now wore swimsuit coverlets. Megan's white terrycloth, Nicole's thin black mesh that hid nothing.

"Did Pancake leave us anything?" Nicole asked.

"Some," I said. "Just watch out for the gnaw marks."

"He's funny," Pancake said. "He really is."

"One of his many charming qualities," Nicole said.

"See," I said to Pancake. "You're not the only one who's charming."

"I'm just better at it."

Carrie appeared with a tray of quesadillas and tacos. We each took a taco. Pancake three, plus a couple of quesadillas. She smiled, held his gaze a few extra seconds, and then weaved through the crowd in the living area, extending the offerings to each. Abby, coming in from the sun, intercepted her, grabbing a napkin and a taco. She continued our way.

"Having fun?" I asked.

"This is all so amazing. I mean, this house. The people I've met. Unbelievable."

"Uncle Charles does throw a good party," Nicole said.

We managed to crowbar Pancake from the spread and gathered at one of the shaded outdoor tables. We ate. The consensus was that the food was over the top good.

Megan's phone dinged an incoming text. She removed her phone from her jacket pocket and read the message. Her breath caught; her face paled.

"What is it?" I asked.

"Him." She handed me the phone.

I read:

"Why do you treat me this way? I professed my love and put my heart out there. I asked you to marry me. This is your reply? You run off to Malibu with the beautiful people? Are you fucking some actor? Maybe Kirk Ford?"

I showed the text to Nicole, Pancake, and Abby.

"How did he know where you are?" Abby asked.

"I don't know."

"Who else knows where you were going?" I asked.

She considered that for a beat. "My station manager. Darren." She looked at me. "He knows."

"I see."

"It's not Darren," Megan said. "There is no way."

"Are those the only two who knew?" Pancake asked.

She seemed to think for a beat and then nodded. "Yes."

"Also Jimmy Fabrick," Nicole said.

"The guy who rents your boat slip?" I asked.

"Yeah. He was there this morning. I introduced him to Megan. He asked what we were up to. I told him we were headed to Malibu for a party."

"Anything there?" I asked.

"With Jimmy? No. He just met Megan this morning. How could it be him?"

"Maybe he saw her on TV," Pancake said. "Which is how we think this guy latched on to Megan in the first place. Built his obsession from her image."

"Does that make any sense?" Nicole asked. "What are the odds? The guy who parks his boat at my place somehow becomes infatuated with a friend? No way he could know Megan and I were friends. Or even knew each other."

"It does stretch the limits of probability," Pancake said.

"Stretches?" Nicole asked. "It breaks them. I mean, life is full of serendipity, but this? It doesn't pass the probability, or even believability, test."

Megan's phone chimed again. She looked at it, her brow furrowed as she studied the screen, then her eyes popped wide and she dropped the phone on the table.

I picked it up. A photo. Of Megan, Nicole, Abby, and Kirk Ford. Walking down the beach. Just a few hours ago.

Another text chime:

"Are you fucking him?
ARE YOU FUCKING HIM?"

CHAPTER 24

"THIS IS VERY upsetting," Connie said. She handed Megan's phone back to her. "It brings back too many memories of what Nicole went through."

It was the next morning. Megan had showed Connie and Bob and Uncle Charles the photo and the texts she had received last night.

"This is worse," Nicole said. "I knew who my douchebag was. I could recognize him every time I saw him. Which meant I knew where to point the police."

"Yes, but until he sent all the photos and videos he had taken of you, you had no idea he was following you everywhere you went. That his obsession ran that deep."

"True. But when he did send them, I knew who they were from. He certainly made no mystery of who he was and what he wanted." She reached over, grabbed Megan's hand. "Megan has no idea who this is."

We—Nicole, Pancake, Megan, Abby, Bob, Connie, and Uncle Charles—were seated at the dining room table, having just finished a wonderful breakfast. No remnants of last night's party remained, everything restored to its pristine perfection. Except there was no sun. The typical morning marine layer had settled a gray cap over everything. Wouldn't last long. By midmorning the sun would reappear and SoCal perfection would be restored.

Not so Megan. The sun's appearance would not return her world to anything resembling normal.

I watched her fold into herself. Head down, shoulders forward, she suddenly seemed tired and frayed. I was sure her nerves were in even worse condition. Hell, mine were sparking pretty good.

"Trust me," Megan said. "I've been racking my brain to come up with something. Anything or anyone." She wound her napkin around one finger. "After that—" she nodded toward her phone—"I stayed awake all night."

"Me, too," Uncle Charles said. "At least until the wee hours. I have security cameras around the house. Some face the beach, of course. I thought I might see someone taking the photo. But the beach is full of people, even here in The Colony. Public access and all."

I had read somewhere that that had been a point of contention many years ago. The folks in The Colony felt that the beach was their private backyard. I suspected that fell in line with what they paid for their homes. You'd think twenty or more million would buy you a beach. But in California, the beaches are public domain. So, the residents had to create paths between a few of the houses that led down to the sand.

"Lots of sunbathers, strollers, surfers, even folks taking photos of the ocean and the houses. But I didn't see anyone focused on you guys. Or anyone acting odd in any way. At least not right here in the range of my cameras."

"I can't believe you did that," Megan said. Her eyes glistened with tears.

"You're a guest in my home. You're a friend of Nicole's. You're a special young lady. I take this personally. It's an invasion of privacy. Mine, yours, everyone's."

"Still, that was so nice of you to do."

"I'll tell you right now, I'll do more. Whatever it takes."

Megan nodded, fought back tears.

"What are we going to do?" Nicole asked.

"Get more aggressive," Pancake said. "This little stunt proves he has access to you in real time. To your comings and goings. That means there's a digital trail; we just need to find it."

"How?" Bob asked.

"When we get back to The OC, I'll give Ray a call and see what we can come up with."

"If anyone can, you two can," Nicole said.

Pancake shrugged, opened his palms.

"I have an idea," I said.

"This'll be good," Pancake said.

I scanned the faces around the table. "See what I have to put up with?"

"Poor, poor Jake," Pancake said.

Nicole ruffled my hair. "He has a good idea rattling around in that pretty head every now and then."

"I had a couple last night," I said.

"That you did." She smiled. "Very good ideas."

"You started it."

"You were available. What's a girl supposed to do?"

"Glad I could be there for you, and available."

"You make me so proud," Connie said. "Proof that you're indeed my daughter." She gave me a raised eyebrow and a wicked smile. "Apple—tree."

See? I told you. Connie was simply a slightly older version of Nicole.

"Okay, enough of *Animal Planet*," Pancake said. "What was your big idea?"

"Maybe we should do a one-eighty. You've been keeping this guy at arm's length. Why not reel him in?"

"I'm listening," Pancake said.

"Why not send him a reply? One that says how sorry she is? How she didn't realize the depth of his love. That she hasn't been very fair to him. That they should meet. See if there's a future for them."

"Do you think he'll fall for that?" Abby asked. "After all that's happened?"

"I don't know," I said. "It was just a thought."

"I like it," Pancake said. "Let me think on it. See what we can come up with."

The doorbell rang.

"Wonder who that is?" Uncle Charles said. He stood. "I don't get many Sunday morning visitors." He walked toward the door.

My thinking was that someone had left a purse or cell phone and was returning to get it. Or maybe a pair of panties. The party had gotten pretty wild. I did remember a few bare breasts in the jacuzzi late last night. Most rubbing up against Kirk.

Uncle Charles returned, a white flower box in his hand. "I thought it might be for Nicole," he said. "But it says it's for Megan."

I saw Megan stiffen. "Me?"

He handed it to her. She fingernailed the tape and opened it. Inside were twelve roses. Dead, brown, crinkled. She caught her breath. A card fell out. She opened it.

It read:

"Dead flowers for a dead girl. I can take your mocking only so long. You will be mine or you will be no ones."

"He was here?" Megan said. Her pupils now black with fear. "Right outside the door?"

Uncle Charles worked his iPhone. He brought up the security camera out front. Scrolled back and found what he was looking for. He pressed PLAY. We watched.

A kid. He placed the box against the door, pressed the buzzer, hopped on his bicycle, turned left, and rode out of view.

"Let's go," I said to Pancake.

CHAPTER 25

"He went that way," Pancake said.

I was driving the Range Rover, Pancake shotgun. I turned west down Malibu Colony Road. The kid was nowhere in sight. We rolled past the backside of the seamless row of mansions. All seemed quiet, no one out and about, then we saw a kid on a bike, coming our way, my side of the road. Not the dude we were looking for but rather a girl with short blond hair and a yellow bathing suit. I stopped, lowered my window.

"Excuse me," I said.

She jerked to a halt and gave us a suspicious look.

"Did you see a kid on a bike come by?" I asked.

She stared but said nothing.

"Longish light brown hair, baggy gray shorts, light blue tee shirt."

"Why?"

"No time to explain, but if you saw him, it would help."

"Is he in trouble?"

"No. We need to ask him something though."

She hesitated. "Yeah. I know him. His name's Sean." She jerked her head. "He was headed that way."

"Any idea where he's going?"

"Probably down to the parking lot to hook up with Danny and Chris. They like to do wheelies and stupid stuff down there."

"Which lot?"

"On around the corner on Malibu Road."

"Thanks," I said.

She took off.

"That's good intel," Pancake said.

"Unless she calls the cops to report a couple of strange dudes asking about kids."

Pancake grunted. "There is that."

We continued and quickly approached the road's intersection with Malibu Road.

"There," Pancake said. He pointed.

The kid swung right, hugging the shoulder, pumping the peddles of his bike. We followed. A half a block later, he wheeled into a parking lot where a couple of other kids straddled bikes and waited. They appeared to be twelve or so. I eased up near the trio and came to a stop. They gave us questioning looks.

"Sean?" I asked.

He stared at me but said nothing. Probably deciding whether to run or not. Pancake and I stepped from the car.

"Can I ask you something?" I said.

"How do you know my name?"

I pasted on my friendliest smile. "The young lady on the bicycle told us."

"Marsha?"

"She didn't say. Yellow bathing suit."

"Yeah, that's her."

I scanned the other two boys. "You guys must be Danny and Chris."

"She tell you that, too?" one of them asked.

"She did."

"She talks too much."

I tossed him another one of my smiles and lowered my voice as if we were co-conspirators. "Girls usually do."

The three boys laughed as if we were now teammates in the locker room, snickering about the mysteries of the opposite sex. Boy, if they only knew what was headed their way. In a year or two their attitude would do a one-eighty and some cute girl with bright eyes and a big smile and evolving body parts would turn their brains into oatmeal. Voice of experience here.

"They sure do," Sean said.

"I want to ask you about the flowers you just delivered."

"I didn't do anything."

"You're not in trouble," Pancake said. "We simply want to know who you delivered them for."

"Why?" He worked the brake levers on the bike's handlebars. Made me wonder if he was getting ready to bolt. If so, the next question could be critical to him making that decision. How much to tell him? The truth, the whole truth, or something else? I opted for the later.

"They were beautiful," I said. "The lady who got them was impressed. But there was no sender's name. She wants to know who to thank."

He seemed to relax, no longer fidgeting with the brakes. "I don't know who he was. Never seen him before."

"How'd you get elected to deliver them?" Pancake asked.

"I got here a little early to hook up with Danny and Chris. This dude comes up and asks if I'll deliver a present for him. I told him no, that I was busy. He offered me forty bucks."

"So you took it?"

"Sure." He nodded toward his friends. "Means we can have pizza later."

"What did this guy say?"

"Said he had something for a friend and he wanted it to be a surprise." He shrugged. "So, I said okay." He patted his pants pocket. "Forty bucks is forty bucks."

"He gave you the address?" I asked.

"Yeah."

"He write it down or anything?"

"No. Just told me. I live a few doors down so I knew where it was."

"This guy?" Pancake asked. "What'd he look like?"

"A dude. A regular guy."

"How tall?" I asked.

"Shorter than you. More like my dad's height. Five-eleven I guess."

"Weight? Was he thin? Fat? Muscular?"

"More muscular." He looked at Pancake. "Not nearly as big as you but he looked pretty fit."

"What was he wearing?" Pancake asked.

"Jeans and a tee shirt. Sort of purple or brown. Something like that."

"Maroon?" I asked.

"Yeah. That's probably the best word for it."

"How old would you think?"

"Not real old but some older. I'd guess thirty or something like that."

Only a twelve-year-old would think thirty was older. But then he'd likely think that forties was ancient. That would be Sean's "real old." So I felt the guy's age was probably just as Sean suspected, late twenties to early thirties.

"Hair, eyes?"

"He had both."

The trio giggled.

"Good one," I said. "You guys should have your own TV show."

"We're working on it," Chris said.

Of course they were. Everyone around here was working on developing a TV show, a movie, a YouTube channel, anything to get their image out there. I guess you could say most had already made it or they'd live elsewhere. The Colony wasn't for those who didn't make the cut.

"So, what color were they?" I asked.

"Brown hair. It was cut fairly short. I don't remember his eye color."

"What about his car?" Pancake asked.

"Didn't see one." He pointed across the street to several buildings and a road that angled off Malibu Road. "He walked from over there somewhere. I didn't see a car."

"Okay. So he gave you the box, an address, and forty bucks. What happened then?"

"He headed back across the street and I took off to deliver the package."

"Did you see him again?" Pancake asked.

"Nope. Never before and never since."

"Anything else that you remember about him?"

"He had cool sunglasses. Sort of bronze-colored wraparounds."

We asked a few more questions but gathered no useful information. The truth was, the kid didn't know much else. But he had helped a lot and to me seemed to possess excellent recall. I mentioned that to Pancake as we drove away.

"He did. Now we have a picture to work with."

That was true. Five-eleven, sort of muscular, late twenties or so, short brown hair, and cool sunglasses. At least cool to Sean. Problem was that his description fit countless thousands of dudes in SoCal.

CHAPTER 26

WHILE WE ORGANIZED our bags in the Range Rover's rear compartment, Pancake called Ray and brought him up to date. We said our goodbyes, thanking Uncle Charles and telling him, Bob, and Connie we'd see them at the studios in a couple of weeks when the filming began.

While Uncle Charles hugged Nicole, he said, "I'll have a surprise for you when I next see you."

"What?"

"If I told you it wouldn't be a surprise."

"That's not fair," Nicole said. "To tease me that way."

Uncle Charles released his embrace and laughed. "Trust me. You'll love it."

Nicole tried to pout but it wouldn't stick. A smile broke out, then to Connie she said, "Mom, your brother is being a brat."

"He was born a brat."

Then we were off. As we left The Colony and merged into the always heavy traffic on PCH, Pancake elaborated on the kid's description of the dude who sent the flowers.

"That could be almost anyone," Nicole said.

"At least it clears Darren," Megan said. "He's nothing like that. Not that he ever needed clearing."

"Clears your boat dude, too," I said to Nicole.

"Jimmy Fabrick?" Nicole said. "He never needed clearing either."

"I don't know. He seems like a shady character to me."

"Are you jealous?" Megan asked.

"Jake doesn't do jealous," Nicole said. "He's just messing with me."

I caught her gaze in the rearview mirror. Smiled.

She thumped the back of my head. "He also knows he'll pay for it later."

"I love it when a plan comes together," I said.

"Will someone throw water on these two?" Pancake said.

That got a laugh from everyone, but then we rode in silence for a good thirty minutes. Like everyone had turned inward, probably thinking about all that had transpired in the past twelve hours or so. The photo, the flowers, the mysterious dude who had had them delivered. Finally, we reached Santa Monica and merged onto I-10 East. The traffic thinned, somewhat, and I picked up speed.

"I have a question," Abby said. "What if the guy hired someone else to do the dead flowers deal? I mean, this is a long way from Orange County."

"I've been thinking on that," Pancake said. "Flowers hand-delivered to Megan's door in Costa Mesa, and now here in Malibu."

"It's doable," I said. "Not that far apart. At least distance-wise."

Pancake grunted.

"You don't think so?" I asked.

"Actually, I do. Stalking like this is always personal. He wouldn't want to share it with someone else."

"Seems risky," Abby said.

"It is. But that's part of the thrill. Anything that causes Megan stress and grief, he'd want to do himself. Want to be close. Sense the fear."

"But he did pass it to a kid to deliver?" Megan said.

"Practical," Pancake said. "Didn't want to expose himself."

"But he did. To a kid."

"Yeah, but not on Uncle Charles' video system."

"How would he know that he had one?" Megan asked.

"Common sense," Pancake said. "Bet there isn't a single home in The Colony that doesn't have a pretty robust security system."

"I suppose that's true," Megan said. "But if he wanted to feel the thrill, or sense the fear as you say, he still didn't. He wasn't present when I freaked over the dead flowers."

Pancake sighed. "That's what's been bothering me. He keeps everything at arm's length as if he's afraid to get too near you. Like he wants to feel it, experience it firsthand, but he's afraid to let that happen."

I merged onto I-405 where the traffic thickened. A couple of cholos rolled by, their Toyota lowered so much that it looked like a sled, and the base from a sound system that probably cost more than the car cranked up to the point that it threatened to crack the concrete. Maybe even rev up the San Andreas Fault.

"Cyber stalkers do that," I said. "They work their mischief online."

"True. But they usually don't creep up to your door either. Or expose themselves to a third party, like a kid on a bicycle. They live in that internet world of electrons and think if they stay there, they'll never be found. Hell, many of them are far away from the victim. Sometimes different states, or countries. They get off on the fear and terror in the victim's replies."

"But I haven't really replied," Megan said. "Except to respectively decline his advances and offers of marriage."

I glanced at Pancake. "You said earlier that you might have a plan to draw him out. Maybe change the narrative. Any thoughts?"

"I'm working on it."

We soon entered The OC, the airport a few miles ahead on the right, South Coast Plaza on the left.

"Can we stop by my place for a second?" Megan asked. "I need to pick up some fresh clothes."

"No problem," I said.

"Cool," Abby said. "I've never seen your place. Can I come in and take a peek?"

"Sure."

"I hear it's pretty cool."

"From who?" Megan asked.

"Darren."

"Yeah. He's been there a couple of times." Megan caught my gaze in the rearview mirror. "To pick up some work stuff and no, he's not the stalker."

"I didn't say anything," I said.

"But you thought it."

I shrugged.

"You've got to quit doing that, Jake," Nicole said.

"Doing what?"

"Thinking."

I can't win. In fact, I'm not even in the race. As my grandfather often said, "Sometimes you're the windshield and sometimes you're the bug."

CHAPTER 27

I PULLED INTO The Oasis, Megan's condo project, and found an empty slot near the front door of her unit. A couple walked by, pushing a stroller, but otherwise all was quiet and peaceful. Megan had picked a pleasant place to call home. Even if this psycho had forced her to flee. Her reflection in the rearview mirror clearly showed the toll this was taking on her. I really wanted to deliver a baseball bat to this creep's melon. Better yet, turn Pancake loose on him. That I'd love to see.

"I still can't believe I've been run out of my own home," Megan said.

"It's just temporary," Nicole said.

"Define *temporary*. Haven't some of these stalking things gone on for years?"

"Don't dwell on that kind of thing," Nicole said. "Let's get you some clothes and then go from there."

"Worst case," Pancake said, "we'll beef up your security so you can return."

"How?"

"Cameras, better door and window security, maybe a weapon or two."

"I don't like guns."

Pancake grunted. "You will. Nothing quite like them in a pinch." He looked over his shoulder. "It probably won't come to that, but if it does, I'll teach you everything you need to know."

"Handguns are scary. I might shoot myself."

"They're only scary until you get used to them. Then they're comforting."

Megan gave a headshake. "There's an oxymoron. Guns and comforting."

"I wouldn't get you a handgun anyway," Pancake said. "Better to have a shotgun."

"Why?"

"A pistol requires more skill. Easy to miss a barn when you're hyped up or scared. A shotgun is autofocus. Point and shoot."

"You can always repaint and re-carpet," I said.

"This is such a pleasant conversation," Megan said.

Nicole pushed open her rear car door and she and Abby stepped out. "Let's go get your stuff."

"We're all going," I said.

"Why?" Megan asked. "I'm only going to grab a couple of things."

"Pancake and I'll check it out first."

"What? You don't think he's here, do you?"

"No way to know until we know," Pancake said.

We all piled out and climbed the four steps to Megan's front door. She worked the lock and pushed the door open. Pancake took the lead; I followed. But he only made it a couple of steps before he jerked to a stop. I couldn't see past the big guy, but my senses jumped to the redline. What did he see? What could make Pancake screech to a halt? I'd seen three-hundred-pound defensive linemen fail at that. Hell, even a brick wall once. He ran right through it.

He moved forward and now I saw what had grabbed his attention. I heard Megan gasp behind me.

Her living room was cool, classy, well appointed, and had a soaring ceiling. Behind the sofa a blank white wall was no longer blank. The bright-red, spray-painted graffiti seemed almost three-dimensional. As if the words lifted from the background and jumped right in your face.

DO NOT DISRESPECT ME WHORE

"He was here? In my home?" Megan began to shake as if she were a pinged tuning fork. She staggered back, wavered.

Nicole hugged her from behind, enveloping her in her arms. "It's okay."

"No, it's not. It'll never be okay."

Pancake and I made our way from room to room, making sure no one was still inside. Other than the message on the wall, everything appeared undisturbed, normal.

When we returned to the living room. Megan sat on the sofa, her face in her hands. Nicole sat next to her, one arm around her shoulders.

Abby stood, giving the red words a wide-eyed stare. "This is unbelievable."

Megan looked up. "I'm scared shitless right now."

"You should be," Abby said. "This is exactly what I was afraid of. He's getting crazier, and a lot more dangerous."

Hard to argue with that. This dude was diabolical and very busy. Photos and flowers and angry messages in Malibu and now this. Talking about angry messages. His choice of red made the words almost an audible scream.

Megan finally got her head sorted out and called the police. They said wait outside and not to touch anything. Mostly, that's what happened. Megan did grab some clothes. She feared that if they locked her place down she wouldn't have what she needed for work the next day. Or would it be longer? She packed a small suitcase, and once that was stacked on the others in the Range Rover, we waited on her porch.

Pancake called Ray and told him the story. They chatted for a few minutes more. When Pancake hung up, he said, "Ray's coming."

"He is?" I asked.

"That's what he said."

"When?"

"As soon as he gets a flight. He'll probably grab a red-eye."

"Why does he feel the need to be here?" Nicole asked.

"Said if push comes to shove, we might need more firepower."

So very Ray. Saddle up and ride into the fray. The disturbing part was the question: Would we need more firepower? Was this that type of situation? I had to admit that virtually every time I did any work for Ray, and I guess this had morphed into that on some level, it turned into a shooting gallery. Did Ray simply attract that type of chaos, or was that what every P.I. dealt with? Part of me was sure Ray was a magnet for violence. Probably not a fair assessment but there it was. A more charitable view would be that violence and Ray weren't strangers.

But wasn't this simply a stalker? Not a mafioso or criminal kingpin or leader of a biker gang or Mexican cartel thugs or anything that would need a massive response? Okay, so he did send threatening messages, and follow Megan to Malibu, and invade her home. Maybe Ray's concerns were spot on. Or maybe, this was simply a matter of identifying the dude and calling the police.

Which reminded me.

I called Detective Claire Mills. Even though it was Sunday, she had said for us to call her directly, anytime, if we had more information. I suspected this qualified.

Two uniformed officers arrived and got the story from a shaken Megan before entering and once again clearing the condo. One of them stepped outside and said they had called the crime scene crew in for photos and fingerprints.

Then he asked, "Did any of you call Lieutenant Mills?"

"I did," I said.

He nodded, glanced around. He seemed almost annoyed. I suspected the last thing he wanted was someone leaning on him or looking over his shoulder. Maybe especially Mills. She seemed like a tough, no-nonsense cop, and probably demanded perfection from those around her.

"We had talked to her about Megan's stalker," I said. "She said we should call her directly if anything changed." I waved a hand toward the front door. "I thought this would qualify."

He nodded, sighed, obviously resigned to the fact that I had made his day a tad more difficult. But this wasn't a simple break-in and property damage issue. This was a stalker. One that was becoming progressively intrusive and probably truly dangerous. So, bottom line, I didn't feel too sorry for him.

Mills arrived fifteen minutes later. The CSI types rolled up right behind her. After she said hello to us, and said she'd be back in a minute, she followed the uniforms and the techs inside to get a tour of the scene. Five minutes later, she exited and joined us where we stood near our vehicle.

"You okay?" she asked Megan.

"No. Not close."

"It's really scary," Abby said. She stood next to Megan, one hand on Megan's arm. "Someone invading your privacy like this. Writing those awful words."

"It is," Mills said. "But then, this might be the break we need."

"What does that mean?" Megan asked.

"Looks like he came in through the pool area. The sliding doors in your den were not locked and seem to be a little off track."

"They were locked when I left. I'm sure they were. I always check them." She sighed. "Lately even more than usual."

"Pretty easy to jimmy open. No way to relock them once outside. Or take the time to do it anyway."

"That makes sense, I guess."

"He also took down a pair of pictures from the wall so he could do his artsy thing." She gave a weak smile. "Maybe he left some prints in those areas. The doors and the frames."

"You think so?" Megan asked.

"The thing about evidence, it's either present or it's not. So I'd go with fifty-fifty."

An hour and a half later, the police and crime scene folks had finished working the scene. We thanked Detective Mills for coming. Part of the job was her take. She also said she would now open an official file on the stalking and get her cyber guys cranked up. She added that she would keep us updated and that we should call if anything else came up.

We watched the uniforms, the crime scene van, and Mills drive away. It was like the air hissed out of Megan. That post hyper flagging. She suddenly seemed frail, pale, and exhausted.

Abby took her hands in hers. "Is there anything I can do?"

"I don't know what," Megan said. "Except make this movie stop."

CHAPTER 28

"How'd you get inside?"

"It wasn't difficult. Those sliders are flimsy. A screwdriver did the trick."

"You sure no one saw you?"

"As sure as I can be. I waited and watched. For a couple of hours at least. That place shuts down pretty early so by midnight it was like a cemetery."

"Interesting choice of words."

"There were lots of trees and shrubs around and the lighting wasn't the best so I had plenty of shadows to use. Didn't see a soul." He leaned back on the sofa, arms stretched across the back. "Her unit was perfect. It was way toward the back and had a great little fenced patio and yard space. It was surrounded by a four-foot fence and even more shrubs. Once I hopped over that, I was invisible." He smiled. "It was delicious."

"Wish I could've been with you."

"You were busy."

"Still."

"Truth is that I could have invaded any of those places. It's amazing how naive and trusting people are."

"Getting into her place is the money shot."

"So far. Lots more to come though."

"True. I wonder how well she'll sleep tonight?"

"Not well, I imagine."

A nod. "For sure this will ramp up the stress. Someone breaking into your domain, the one place you should feel safe, and now all of a sudden you don't." A headshake. "I really love this shit."

"I know you do. Me, too."

"I can almost see her right now. Lying in bed, staring at the ceiling, and wondering if this will ever end."

"Not to mention the ceiling she's staring at isn't her own. Not now that she's left her place and is staying with friends."

"Yeah, like that'll save her."

A shrug. "Nothing can save her. Moving out simply collapsed her world further and added more pressure."

"She'll definitely feel displaced and off balance."

"Which only ramps up the terror." A smile. "Talk about delicious."

CHAPTER 29

I AWOKE, ON my stomach, pillow over my head. I rolled over but found no Nicole. Sunlight illuminated the curtain. What time was it? Then the aromas of bacon, toast, and coffee wafted my way. My grumbling stomach tugged me out of bed. I hit the head, washed my face, and brushed my teeth. I needed a shower and a shave but that could wait. Jeans, tee shirt, barefoot, I headed toward the kitchen.

Pancake had two skillets going. One sizzled with bacon, the other held a mound of scrambled eggs. A stack of toasted bagels sat on the table.

Nicole stood by the sink, wearing one of my shirts, pouring orange juice into four glasses. She turned when she heard me. "Good morning. Did you get enough beauty sleep?"

"Why didn't you wake me?"

"You seemed too comfy to disturb."

"How long have you been up?"

"Long enough to be Pancake's sous chef."

She handed me a glass of OJ and I took a gulp. "Good." I nodded toward the stove. "Where'd all this come from?"

"I found Pancake swinging on the fridge door when I got up."

"She didn't have shit," he said.

"We bought you a bunch of stuff," I said.

He grunted. "Already ate it."

"We went to the store. Got this and Pancake has busied himself ever since."

"Smells good," I said.

"Sure does." Megan walked in. "I like this B&B."

"How'd you sleep?" I asked.

Megan rubbed one eye. "Actually, not bad, all things considered. I'd expected another night of wrestling the pillow and bedsheets, but I guess I was exhausted."

"You do look refreshed," Nicole said.

"Yeah, except for makeup and dealing with this rat's nest." She fingered her hair.

Pancake pointed a spatula at her. "You look mighty fine, darlin'."

"You must have low standards."

"He doesn't," Nicole said. "I can vouch for him in that department."

"Everyone grab a seat," Pancake said. "Grub's ready."

It was even better than it smelled. No surprise there. The big guy knew his way around the kitchen. Always did. Growing up, both of his parents worked long hours so unless he wanted to exist on peanut butter and crackers, he needed to know how to cook. He learned quickly. It was that old necessity and invention deal.

Megan settled her coffee cup on the table. "I spent a lot of time last night thinking about how this guy knows so much about me. Not just where I work and where I live, as disturbing as that is, but he knew I was going to Malibu. Hell, I didn't even know until a day before. How'd he know that?"

"That's one of things I'm still looking into," Pancake said. "But it comes down to either he has access to your communications or he's following you." He shoved an entire piece of bacon in his mouth. "Maybe both."

Megan sighed. "I'm not sure which is more concerning."

"He's definitely not afraid to travel," I said. "He was in Malibu Saturday afternoon when he snapped that photo of you guys on the beach. He was also there yesterday morning when he had the flowers delivered. In between, he must've been here, breaking into your condo and painting the walls."

"Ain't that far," Pancake said. "Couple of hours. He likely came back down late at night and then back up very early. Not much traffic between midnight and five a.m."

I nodded. "If he followed us, he'd know our vehicle. If it was still at Uncle Charles' at midnight, the odds would be that we were staying over. Which meant that Megan wouldn't be home. No chance of him being surprised while doing his work."

"Then back up for this morning's performance," Pancake said.

I stood and began collecting the empty dishes. I avoided Pancake's as he was still flashing a knife and fork and devouring the remaining eggs.

"What's on your plate today?" Nicole asked Megan.

"Eggs and bacon." She smiled. "Or at least it was." She patted her belly. "I can't believe I ate so much."

"At least you haven't lost your sense of humor," Nicole said.

"Got to find humor where you can." She took a sip of coffee. "I actually have a fairly short day today. Abby and I have to complete a couple of scripts, and get to work on a piece we're doing next month. But I don't have an on-camera live thing today, which is good since I don't think they make enough makeup to prevent me from frightening the viewers." She again fingered her hair. "I should finish early. Maybe around three."

"How's Abby working out?" Nicole asked.

"Very well, actually. I've never had an intern so I wasn't sure what to expect. I guess I thought it would be a time and energy drain with all the teaching and mentoring. Abby wasn't all that experienced in this business in the beginning but she's learned quickly. She has good insights and, most importantly, writes well."

"She seems nice."

"She's been a shoulder to lean on." She looked at Nicole. "Now I have you for that also." Tears collected in her eyes. "All of you."

"That's what we're here for," I said.

"We'll get this guy," Pancake said.

"How?" Megan asked. "He seems like a puff of smoke."

Pancake grunted. "Smoke leaves behind a soot trail and we'll find it."

"I like that analogy."

"I'm a freaking poet," Pancake said.

"Dirty limericks don't count," I said.

"Sure, they do." He indicated the plate of remaining eggs and bacon. "Anybody want more?"

We all shook our heads.

"Good." He scraped every tidbit onto his plate.

"What time do you need to head to the studio?" I asked Megan.

She glanced at her watch. "Maybe an hour."

"Okay." I stood. "Guess I better go shower and shave. Then we'll follow you to work."

"Seems overkill, but okay."

"Let us know when you get ready to leave and we'll come follow you back here."

"It'll be daylight. I'll be okay."

"You'll be okay because we'll be following you," Nicole said.

"I feel like a third grader being walked to school."

"Until this is over, you are," Pancake said.

Megan drained her coffee cup. "Still seems a bit much."

"You have car insurance, don't you?" I asked.

"Sure."

"You don't need it until you need it. Consider us an insurance policy."

CHAPTER 30

RAY HAD INDEED taken the red-eye and called around ten a.m., saying he would grab a rental car and head our way. Earlier, Nicole and I had followed Megan to work, stopped by the store to get Pancake more food, and Ray a case of Mountain Dew, his only addiction. Now, we sat out on her deck, watching Jimmy Fabrick wash down the sides of his boat. One of those tasks that watching's much better than doing. Of course, I felt that way about most things. Like running my restaurant. That's what I had Carla for. Which reminded me to make another mental note to call her. The last one, a couple of days ago, apparently slipped my mind.

Through the open slider, I could hear Pancake at the kitchen table, hammering away on his keyboard. When I went inside to get us more coffee, I asked him how it was going. He never looked up, only grunted. Meant it was somewhere between something and nothing. With Pancake you just never knew. I was smart enough not to dig deeper, so I refilled our cups and returned to the deck.

"How's it going in there?" Nicole asked.

"He grunted at me."

"Hmmm. A good grunt or a bad one?"

I shrugged. "I can never tell the difference."

"Maybe he's hungry."

"He's always hungry."

"Should I check?"

"He knows how to use the fridge."

"True." She cradled her cup in her hands and took a sip. "I hope he finds something."

"In the fridge?"

She gave me a look. "No. Out in the cyber world."

"He will."

"Let's hope. If it was up to me, I wouldn't know where to look, or even where to start."

"He has his ways."

A young lady came down the walkway and stopped at Jimmy's sailboat. She wore a bathing suit beneath a coverlet, a large canvas bag over one shoulder, all shaded by a floppy, broad-brimmed hat.

"Looks like Jimmy has a first mate," I said.

"He often does. I think he has a bevy of them."

"Bevy. I like that word."

"You would."

Jimmy and his mate quickly got everything settled, cranked up the small trolling engine, and backed away from the slip. The clear sky and light wind made for a perfect day for lazy sailing.

Ray arrived before eleven. Since Nicole's three bedrooms were filled with Nicole and me, Pancake, and Megan, Ray said the couch would be fine. If it got too claustrophobic for everyone, he and Pancake could move to a hotel.

"It'll be fun," Nicole said. "Like a sleepover."

After Nicole showed him around, Ray dropped in a chair at the kitchen table across from Pancake. Nicole and I joined them.

"Anything new?" Ray asked.

"Maybe."

"Want to share it?"

"Not quite yet. Need to check out a couple of things first, but everything's looking promising."

"A hint."

Pancake closed his laptop. "This just might not be his first rodeo." He stood. "Now let's go grab some lunch."

Of course.

"Better idea," Nicole said. "There's a good rib joint near here. Jake and I'll go pick up some and you guys can stay here and keep at it."

"Ribs work." Pancake sat and reopened his laptop.

"I thought they might,"

"That's 'cause you know me too well, darlin'."

Nicole called and ordered ribs, pulled pork, and hot links along with a ton of sides, and off we went to pick them up. It took all of a half hour. While we ate, Pancake unfolded his research.

"I started out looking at celebrity stalkers in the US. Amazingly, there're more than you might think. Hundreds that led to investigations, convictions, and the like. Probably thousands of others that never made it that far."

"Lot's of sick souls out there," Nicole said.

Pancake forked a wad of coleslaw in his mouth and spoke around it. "I then looked at TV personalities. I took all the Hollywood-types out of the equation. Still more than you want to know." He gnawed a rib.

"Why eliminate them?" I asked. "The movie folks?"

"These guys, these stalkers, tend to focus on a single person or a single type. Often it's a one-off, but some do become serial stalkers and jump from victim to victim. Much like serial killers."

"Serial killers?" Nicole asked.

Pancake nodded. "Not a big leap. A stalker who latches onto a single person, say a teacher, a classmate, a neighbor, or someone they know at work or socially, tends to focus solely on that person. The drama plays out between the two of them."

"Sort of a one-woman man?" Nicole asked.

"Yeah, that works," Pancake said. "Anyway, they either ultimately back off or the law gets involved. Or they do something more dramatic."

"Like kill the woman?" I asked

"Exactly. Or her lover or husband or someone close who he perceives is blocking her from accepting him as her one true love. Either way, that often ends things. Either the focus of his obsession is dead or he's in prison or dead himself. Done deal." A bite of hot link. "If they're still free and roaming around, some will then move on to another target. Often one that is similar in appearance, in occupation, in whatever stirs his chili."

"That makes sense," I said.

"My thinking is that this guy's done this before."

"Based on?" Ray asked.

"His MO. He uses a series of burner phones and stays completely off the radar. To me that means he's methodical and not some out-of-contol, obsessed, lovesick puppy who fell in love with the face on TV and got all frantic and drooly."

"Is *drooly* a word?" Nicole asked.

"It is now." Pancake bounced his eyebrows. "Anyway, to me, his methods and caution could also imply some experience in this arena."

"Does that make him more or less dangerous?" Nicole asked.

"Good question. The answer is, I don't know. From what I've seen, I don't read him as someone who's likely to go all postal as would a more frantic or disturbed dude. He seems more careful and thoughtful than that. Even his threats have been somewhat controlled."

"He goes back and forth. One text professes love and the other makes threats."

Pancake nodded. "But even the threats seem well controlled. Planned, if you will. Not the frenzied ramblings of someone who is truly disturbed."

"I don't know," Nicole said. "They seem scary to me."

"They are. They're intended to be. That's the game plan. So far, at least."

"What does that mean?"

Pancake shrugged. "That we don't know his endgame. What his ultimate plan is."

"Not very comforting," Nicole said.

"No, it's not. So far, he hasn't physically confronted Megan. Either to harm her or to beg her to give him the chance to show her that he's the one for her. He tracks her, follows her, and has even invaded her space. In a well-populated condo project. A risky move, but still, he's never stepped up and confronted her face-to-face."

"That's a good thing," I said.

"No doubt. This guy knows what he's doing and he hasn't made any mistakes. Makes me think this is very well orchestrated and that he's been there, done that."

"So he's a serial stalker," I said. Not really a question.

Pancake shrugged. "Let's hope he isn't or doesn't evolve into a serial killer. Too often these obsessions end in murder."

"You're just filled with pleasant thoughts," Nicole said.

"Is what it is."

"Let's get back to what you've uncovered," Ray said.

"I then looked into TV personalities in smaller markets. Like here with Megan. I found a passel of them. A disturbing number actually. There's a whole tribe of obsessed dudes out there. Or to give them the benefit of the doubt, lovesick hombres. I've culled out those that are closer to home. Meaning the West Coast area."

"Why West Coast only?" Nicole asked.

"Comfort. Knowledge of the area. Predators have a preferred domain, a hunting ground, so that's where I started. The Rockies and west. He bought the phones he's using in Denver so I used that as the dividing line. For now anyway. I also narrowed my search to only the past two years. Since this guy is active, I don't think he would have a lot of down time. I figured that more recent events was the best place to start." He shrugged. "Of course, that is if he's done this before and I'm not overreading things here."

"You're not," Ray said. "I like this line of reasoning."

"That's what you pay me for." Pancake raised an eyebrow. "Not enough though." He shrugged. "Anyway, I found twenty-seven cases."

"That many?" I asked.

Pancake nodded. "Just now getting into them, but I suspect I'll stumble on a few more. I'd bet most of them will be minor. Facebook and social media stuff with no police involvement. Next I'll weed those out and focus on those that are more egregious."

"You're thinking the guy who's harassing Megan is the egregious type?" Nicole asked.

"If he's not then there's less urgency in this. An annoyance is just that, and no big deal, but I'm more concerned by those that cross the line."

"Sounds like you have a lot more to do," I said.

"I do. As soon as I finish lunch, I'll dive back in." He attacked another rib.

CHAPTER 31

NICOLE AND I had little to do. Pancake and Ray busied themselves at the dining table, each buried in cyberspace, and Megan was at the studio. We cleaned the kitchen—after extracting the leftovers from Pancake. Wasn't easy but Nicole convinced him that the odor was getting a little stifling and that the meats would stay fresher in the fridge and that if he wanted any more, she would reheat it for him. He took two more ribs and a hot link and let her have her way. Of course, the fridge was only five feet away so he could keep an eye on it, and raid it at will.

Nicole and I grabbed some coffee and sat on her deck. I slid down in the chair and propped my bare feet on the top of the railing. This was my idea of work.

"What do you think about what Pancake said?" Nicole asked. "That this guy has done this before?"

While we cleaned the kitchen, I had mentally run through everything he had said. A lot to digest. I tried to twist it and look at it from various angles, hoping to somehow make sense of all of it. No easy task as everything seemed to have a multitude of moving parts and unknown facts.

I agreed with Pancake's take that this dude was methodical, careful, and not all squirrely. Twisted for sure but not frantic. To me, that didn't guarantee that the fuse hadn't been lit and that he wasn't on the verge of exploding into violence. It's possible that his ultimate plan included such a flame-out. Hadn't the careful, deliberate Ted Bundy done just that at Florida State University?

It's odd, but all this reminded me of a house fire Pancake and I had witnessed as kids. I think we were eight. The fire broke out a couple of blocks from where we lived so we pumped our bikes in that direction. The flames shot out of windows and the fire ate its way through the roof. The firemen released arcs of water over everything, which created massive clouds of steam. Then with cracks and creaks, the roof collapsed, followed by an explosion of flames. We were across the street, straddling our bikes on the sidewalk, yet the heat wave hit us like someone had opened a hot oven. Even the firemen took a step back. Then, just like that, it was over. As if the fire had taken its final breath before dying.

Part of me felt that with this guy we might be dealing with a smoldering house fire, the final outcome yet to be determined. As if calm and methodical could take a hard left into crazy and chaos in a heartbeat.

The question that hung out there was what did this guy want? What was his finish line? Murder? Rape and murder? Simply scaring the hell out of a vulnerable woman? I was rooting for the latter, but the truth was we had no idea.

I remembered talking with an FBI agent once. A friend of Ray's. Couldn't recall his name right now, but he was an expert in serial predators and had worked on a couple of task forces that tracked active serial killers. He had said at one point that the irony of his job was that the more murders the killer performed, the better it was for law enforcement. More data points, more chances to leave behind the one clue that would end the terror. So he found himself in the uncomfortable position of hoping the killings would end while wishing they had just one more. The one that left breadcrumbs right to the killer's door.

It felt like we were there with Megan's stalker. As long as he stayed at arm's length, didn't expose himself, kept using burner phones, kept everything electronic, we might never find him. Then we'd be left with him getting bored or finding another target or whatever. Of course, if he did simply fade away, Megan would have to live with an undercurrent of fear that he could reappear at any time. That would be a slowly simmering hell.

I told Nicole of my thoughts, ending with, "Which means that if he has left a trail of other victims and if Pancake can find them, we will have more pieces of the puzzle. Maybe enough to ID the guy."

She sat quietly for a couple of minutes, considering everything. Finally, she said, "Let's jump in the shower."

"What? After what I just said you want to have sex?"

"No. I want us to scrub up and get over to the studio."

"Why?"

"I need to see Megan. Make sure she's okay."

"She is. She's with people."

"Humor me."

We showered, no fun stuff though, dressed, and headed toward the studio. We left Ray and Pancake doing what they do.

It was three thirty when we entered Channel 16. We found Megan, Abby, and Darren Slater in the conference room across from their offices, huddled around the long table, going over an array of orange grove photographs. Megan looked up.

"What are you guys doing here?" Concern wrinkled her brow.

"We wanted to watch your show live," I said.

"Jake was bored," Nicole added. "If I don't keep him busy, he gets in trouble."

I thought of better ways to keep me occupied but refrained from voicing them. Part of my ongoing efforts to disconnect my brain from my mouth.

Megan laughed. "Well, I'm glad you came. Want some coffee?"

We declined.

"Well, I need some. Abby?"

"That would be great."

A Keurig coffee maker sat on a small table in one corner. Megan loaded a pod and waited while the machine did its thing.

"I keep meaning to get one of these for home," Megan said.

"Me, too," Abby said.

"I'm sure someone around here carries them."

"I know a couple of places," Abby said. "I'll check it out and see where we can get the best price."

"You don't need to do that," Megan said.

"No problem. Besides, isn't my job here to do research?" She smiled.

"What's all this?" Nicole asked. She pointed toward the tabletop.

"Going over some images. Trying to decide which ones to use in the show."

Now she spread out even more grove photos. Some bright and colorful, others black and white, definitely older. "The piece is on how the orange groves that littered Orange County are mostly gone and replaced by houses and strip malls."

"I never knew there were so many orchards around here back then," Abby said. "I'm sorry I never saw it."

"Before our time," Megan said. "Go back thirty or forty years and Orange County was mostly a farming community." Megan tapped two images—one older, the other more recent. "Let's go with these two."

"I agree," Abby said.

"You got it." Darren scooped up all the pictures, nodded to us, and left the room.

"Anything new?" Megan asked.

I hadn't noticed this morning, probably because everyone was just getting up and hadn't really awakened for the day, but Megan appeared even more tired and worn. Deeper lines of stress infiltrated the corners of her eyes and mouth.

"Ray's here," I said. "He and Pancake are hard at it."

"Ray?" Abby asked. "That's your father, right?"

I nodded.

"He's a bulldog," Nicole said. "Between him and Pancake, they'll find this guy."

"If he's findable," Megan said.

"He seems like a ghost," Abby said.

"He's not," I said. "Sooner or later, he'll make a mistake."

Megan's lips tightened, narrowed. "I'll go with sooner."

"She got more emails today," Abby said.

"What did he say?" Nicole asked.

"Depends. Some were professing endless love, others were nastier."

We headed to the office area. Megan settled in her chair and pulled her phone from her pocket. She worked it and then handed it to Nicole. I read over her shoulder.

The messages were a mixed bag. There were apologies where he said things like:

I'm so sorry I caused you any discomfort. I only meant to let you know how painful it is that we aren't together.

You speak to my soul. We were truly meant for each other.

And then others:

You mock me and don't take my love seriously.

You rejected my marriage proposal. My offer to make you happy for the remainder of your life. By so doing, you crushed my very being.

You are the whore of the earth.

"Then there's this one," Megan said. She opened a text. "I answered this one. Here's the thread."

Him: *I offered you my heart and my soul and you rejected me.*

Megan: *I didn't. Truly I didn't. It's just that how can you expect me to commit to someone I've never met?*

Him: *Can't you feel my love and devotion? Feel how deeply I care for you?*

Megan: *I do. Let's meet for a drink or dinner. You name the time and place.*

Him: *We will meet. Soon. I alone will decide the time and place.*

Megan: *OK. When?*

The thread ended.

"I never heard back," Megan said.
"Forward those to me," Nicole said. "I'll send them on to Pancake and Ray."
She did. "Now what?"

"You do your show," I said. "Let us work on finding this guy."

"Before he does something," Abby said. She laid a hand on Megan's arm. "Something awful."

"So far he's kept his distance," Nicole said.

"Really?" Abby said. "He left flowers at her door. He followed her to Malibu. He damaged her condo." She raised her jaw. "That doesn't seem very far away to me."

She had a point.

CHAPTER 32

"THIS'S TAKING ITS toll on her," Abby said, her voice lowered to a whisper.

"I know," Nicole said, also a whisper. "I wish I knew what to do. Or even what to say."

We were standing in the shadows near the back of the studio. Well away from the producer who flanked one of the two cameramen. The stress that ate Megan was obvious. Her usual welcoming smile and energetic eyes, even her hair, had lost their sparkle. She looked worn and haggard; her voice was weak and she stumbled over a couple of the words that scrolled at her from the teleprompter. Though definitely off her game, she struggled and fought her way through her story until it wrapped and moved on to a prerecorded package. Relief fell over her. She unhooked her lapel mic and headed our way. Her producer intercepted her near where we stood.

"Good piece," he said.

"No. I screwed it up."

He hugged her. "It's not as bad as you think." He pushed her back and looked at her. "You'll see. Now go get some rest."

She nodded. "Thanks."

We moved back to the office area. The show continued on the monitor in one corner.

"You did good," I said.

"It was awful. I felt like I had oatmeal for brains."

"Let's get out of here," I said.

"Sounds good."

"I'll ride with you," Nicole said. "Jake can follow us."

"I've got some errands to run." Abby grabbed her purse. "I'll walk out with you guys."

I headed to the public parking out front. I climbed in the Range Rover, cranked it up, and waited for them to ascend from the underground employee parking area. Seemed to take a while. Or maybe I was simply anxious to get back to Nicole's place and see what Pancake and Ray had uncovered. If anything.

Nicole ran up the ramp, head on a swivel. She gave me a frantic "come on" wave. I shut the engine down, jumped out, and hurried in her direction.

"What is it?"

She didn't reply but rather turned and scampered back down the slope. I followed.

Megan and Abby stood next to Megan's car. At first all looked normal, then I saw the tears that streaked Megan's face. That's when I noticed her rear tires. Both were flat.

"He was here," Megan said.

Abby hugged her. Megan's shoulders lurched with sobs. "It's okay. Take a breath."

I walked around the car. All four tires showed deep slashes through the side walls. What the hell? I turned and scanned the other half dozen cars, looking for signs of someone, but saw nothing. No real place to hide down here. Except one of the cars. I did a tour of each, but found them empty, tires intact.

I made two calls. To Pancake and then to Detective Claire Mills. The cavalry was en route.

While we waited, we attempted to console and calm Megan. With some success but truly tamping down her fear was impossible.

I understood. This guy had invaded everything. Her cyber world, her home, and now her workplace. Worse, this time he had employed a weapon. A knife, no doubt. But the worst part was that he had invaded her head. Wormed his way inside and left a snail-trail of fear.

Fifteen minutes later, Ray and Pancake drove down the ramp, followed by Mills, and a police cruiser, two uniforms inside. I introduced her and Ray.

Mills listened carefully, asked a few questions, as Megan went through the story. Nicole and I added what we knew, which wasn't much. She then inspected the damaged tries.

"We'll take the car over to our impound lot," Mills said. "Get the forensic guys to give a look." She turned to the two uniforms. "Canvas the locals and see if anyone saw anything and check out any area security cameras. There must be a few around here." She sighed. "Who knows? We might get lucky."

Once we got back to Nicole's, the decision was to walk over to The Cannery for food and drinks. Lots of drinks. Especially Megan who seemed to need to get hammered. Two hours later: mission accomplished. Back in the condo, Megan thanked each of us, with hugs and a few more tears, then disappeared into her room. Hopefully, for some much-needed sleep, but I doubted she'd get much.

CHAPTER 33

I WOKE UP the next morning, feeling like it would be a good day. Not sure why. Seemed like just another day. Sunlight pressed against the curtain. Nicole lay wrapped in a sheet like a taquito, her back to me. I laced my fingers behind my head and stared at the ceiling fan that spun overhead.

Why did I feel this would be a good day? Based on the past two days I couldn't see any rational explanation for it. Actually, the opposite.

Megan's stalker had basically dismantled her life. The constant stream of emails and texts, the invasion of her privacy and safety. Her home, Malibu, her condo, now her car. This guy was like swamp fog. He seeped into her life, every nook and cranny. No place left untouched. Well, except for Megan herself. And that could easily be in the offing.

Not much to be optimistic about there. Yet, that feeling that we were on the threshold of something big was unshakeable.

Nicole stirred, stretched, rolled my way, the sheet unfurling from her body. She pressed against me.

"What are you doing?" she asked.

"Thinking."

"Didn't I tell you not to do that?"

"You did. Many times"

"Yet, you persist."

I fiddled with her hair. "That's me. A rebel all the way."

"What are you thinking about?"

"You."

"Liar."

"I was. But also, I have a feeling this will be a good day."

"We could use one but why do you think so?"

I rolled her way, our heads now resting on one pillow, facing each other. "Not sure. I know Ray and Pancake were up late last night. I could hear them talking and clicking keyboards. If they spend that much time on anything, something good usually comes from it."

"Let's hope." She stifled a yawn. "What's that I smell?"

I had noticed it also. Bacon. "I suspect Pancake's up and hungry."

"Not a newsflash."

We rolled out of bed, took a quick shower, and got ready for the day. I slipped on jeans and a dark green tee; Nicole white slacks and a tangerine shell top. I loved that color on her. With her blond hair it made her look like a Dreamsicle. I've always had a thing for Dreamsicles.

Pancake had yet again hammered out a massive breakfast. Everyone ate too much. Well, except for Pancake. Too much food wasn't possible in his world. I noticed that Megan ate little. The wear and tear progressively apparent on her face and her slumped shoulders. I tried to keep things light, but failed miserably. Megan was not consolable. Even Pancake assuring her that he and Ray had made some progress didn't seem to help.

"Jake thinks this is going to be a good day," Nicole said.

"How so?" Ray asked.

"I don't know," I said. "Just a feeling. But I figured you guys must have uncovered something last night. Lord knows you were at it until way late."

"Did we interfere with your beauty sleep?" Pancake asked.

"No. But maybe Nicole's."

"She don't need it," Pancake said. "You do."

"What'd you find?" Nicole asked.

That's when Detective Mills called. She had something we needed to see.

"What is it?" I asked.

"Better if you take a look," she said.

*   *   *

Next stop the Newport PD.

Mills had apparently located a pair of witnesses. Definitely a good thing. But then maybe not.

"One young lady said she saw a guy walking near the station around three or so. She said he looked 'suspicious,' whatever that means. Described him as short and stocky and he walked with a slight limp. He had on cargo shorts—she thinks they were tan—and a yellow tee shirt. Sound familiar?"

Megan shook her head. "No."

"Didn't think so," Mills said. "He apparently was a half a block away, walking down Church Street toward Broadway. We haven't been able to locate him or any other witnesses who saw him."

"The other witness?" Ray asked.

"This one might be more viable. A guy sitting in a coffee shop, working on his laptop, waiting for a business associate to show up, saw a guy walk past. He was on the opposite side of the street, moving away from the TV studio and toward Orange Avenue. He said he disappeared into the neighborhood."

I knew that area. Right around the studio were several other businesses, but a block away, to the east, a neighborhood that extended all the way to the Back Bay rose up. Densely packed homes, most costing more than you'd think. SoCal property always made you shake your head. Particularly in The OC. Homes that would go for a couple of hundred K back in Gulf Shores fetched seven figures here. Made no sense, but that's the way it was.

"The witness said he was dressed in jeans and a dark blue or black tee. Carried a small backpack over one shoulder. He guessed he was maybe six feet and looked to be fit."

"What made him stand out?" I asked.

"The guy said he seemed to be in a hurry. Not running or anything like that but moving along. Also, he kept looking back over his shoulder."

"Did anyone else see this guy?" Pancake asked.

"Not that we've found yet. But here is what I wanted to show you." She picked up her iPad. "We scoured the area for security cameras and found a few but none that was very helpful. Except for maybe this one."

She tapped an icon and a grainy video played. The camera aimed up 19th Street and appeared to be maybe a block away. Channel 16 visible on the left. A figure came around the side of the building and turned away from the camera, toward the neighborhood. He did indeed glance back a couple of times, but at that distance and with the image being of poor quality, his face was never visible.

"As you can see," Mills said. "He more or less fits the description coffee-shop dude gave us. Tall enough, dark shirt, looks like a backpack, and he's walking quickly."

"Any way to enlarge or enhance this?" Pancake asked.

Mills shook her head. "My computer guys tried. This video was grabbed from the service station on the corner. The equipment is about a century old so the quality sucks. This is really all we have."

Which wasn't much. All you could really decipher from the fourteen seconds he was in frame was that he was tallish and carried a backpack. No other features were evident. Which meant this could fit hundreds of dudes in the area. Literally. Was this our guy? Maybe. He was in the right place anyway.

"What time was this?" I asked.

"Time stamp shows it was three fifteen."

That was maybe fifteen minutes before Nicole and I arrived at the studio. Were we that close to crossing his path? If this was the guy, the answer was yes.

Mills replayed the video a couple of times, the screen angled toward Megan. "Any familiarity here?"

Megan examined it, brow furrowed. She gave a headshake. "No. Doesn't look like anyone I now."

"I figured." She shut down the iPad. "Too far away and poor quality. Not enough to make an ID, or even create a useful description, but that's all we have."

"Not exactly nothing," Pancake said. "Dude looked to be six feet or so, and fit, like your witness said."

"If that's him," I said. "Could just be a random person."

Ray nodded. "We don't know exactly when Megan's tires were slashed. Could have been much earlier or later than this video."

"That's why I was hoping Megan might recognize him."

"Sorry," she said. "No one comes to mind."

"I didn't think it would." Mills scratched the back of one hand. "Sorry to drag you down here, but I had to take a chance."

"No worry," Megan said. "Anything to catch this guy."

"The good news," Mills said, "is that you can have your car back. We've finished with it." She shrugged. "Found nothing of interest. Looks like he simply slashed the tires and walked away."

Next stop, the police impound lot where we arranged to have Megan's car trailered to a nearby tire store. Took another hour to get the tires replaced. We headed back to Nicole's.

CHAPTER 34

BACK AT THE condo, Nicole and I waited for Megan to get ready and gather her materials for work, then followed her to the studio. I was happy to see that the station had hired a guy to guard the place, including the underground parking area. He looked like a high school kid but it turned out he was in college, taking a semester off to make some tuition money. He wasn't armed, but did he really need to be? I looked at him as more of a scarecrow than anything else. His mere presence might deter the stalker.

Not that I thought the guy would return for an encore. He had done his damage and delivered his message. More or less a hit-and-run. Time to move on. To what was the question. To think I had foolishly believed this was going to be a good day.

But in all fairness, none of what we had learned today was bad news. We had a description of sorts and an image of—someone. Not sure it was our guy but it was at least possible, which was more than we had yesterday.

Nicole and I swung by Jersey Mike's and picked up sandwiches. Two extra-large for Pancake, of course. I knew better than to return empty-handed. Besides, I was getting hungry, too. After lunch, Nicole and I sat on her deck, reading, enjoying another perfect day in paradise. Ray and Pancake hung at the kitchen table doing Ray and Pancake stuff.

I almost felt guilty loafing while they worked. But the truth was that me and computers weren't on a first-name basis so what could I do? Except stay out of the way, and hang with Nicole. Why wouldn't I?

An hour later, Pancake stuck his head out the door. "Got something."

We hustled inside and sat at the table.

Pancake explained. "Of those twenty-seven cases I told you about, most proved to be nothing. Nuisances more than anything else. Nothing really to them. But I found six cases of small station TV reporters who were stalked aggressively enough to reach law enforcement's radar. Each involved emails and texts and gifts, it seems. Of those, four were solved. Two with restraining orders and the guy seemed to have given up and moved on. Two with jail time. One got two years plus three more on proby. The other, fifteen years. He physically attacked his victim."

"I take it he's still locked up?" I asked.

"He is. It's the other two cases that I found interesting. From what I could determine, each of the victims was stalked electronically for several months. The first, nearly a year ago near Salt Lake City. Dana Roderick, twenty-nine, the social reporter for a small Christian station. She was stalked for several months and ultimately murdered."

"Really?" Nicole asked.

"Yep. Case never solved."

"How was she killed?" Ray asked.

"The reports say she was strangled. Apparently, she was abducted from a mall and her body was found a couple of days later along a deserted roadside several miles outside of Salt Lake."

"Strangling is usually personal," Ray said.

Pancake gave a half nod. "Totally."

"You think this might be the dude harassing Megan?" Nicole asked.

"Don't know. I'm just saying it has some similar elements."

"The other case?" I asked.

"Tiffany Cole. Worked at a small station in Henderson, Nevada. Similar to Megan, she's very pretty and did mostly human-interest stories. Apparently, her stalker harassed her for a few months until about six months ago when she bolted. Moved away, fell off the radar, and disappeared. Not like a missing person but rather it seems she left the area and evaporated from social media."

"I don't like this," Nicole said. "None of it."

"Not much to like," Pancake said.

"What's next?" I asked.

"A couple of phone calls."

Pancake put his cell on speaker and dialed the Henderson station, saying we might want to start with the more recent of the two. Unfortunately, the station manager was in a meeting so Pancake said he'd call back. He then tapped in the Salt Lake City station's number. The manager, Scott Hartman, was available. Pancake introduced himself, Longly Investigations, and each of us, ending by telling Hartman that the call was on speaker. He then explained the reason for the call.

Hartman hesitated before responding. "You think this guy might be related to your situation?"

"Could be. We did find more than a few similarities."

"This was a year ago," Hartman said, "but I remember it like yesterday. Dana was a very special young lady. She had been with us for four years. Good at what she did. Her work was always top notch and she was so engaging. Our viewers loved her. She had such a bright future." An audible sigh. "Then this guy crashed into her life."

"Tell us about it."

"She had a huge following so she got notes and gifts and things like that not infrequently. This guy started out just like any other fan. Nothing alarming at first, but then it morphed into something else. The messages became more aggressive. He accused her of ignoring and offending him, of not taking their love seriously. Amazingly, that's how he saw all this. A love story. Dana changed in many ways. She was scared all the time, always looking over her shoulder, not trusting anyone."

"Did she have any idea who might be doing it?" I asked.

"None. Lord knows she fretted over it. She considered just about everyone she'd ever known. It got so bad that she couldn't sleep, lost weight, and was worn out and tired all the time. Her work suffered considerably."

"You mentioned gifts," Nicole said. "What kinds of things did he send?"

"At first they were the usual things. Flowers, boxes of candy. Then the gifts became more disturbing."

"Such as?" Ray asked.

"Dead flowers, boxes of crushed cookies, even a dead mouse."

"Really?" Nicole asked.

"Yeah. That one threw her for a loop. I tried to convince her to go to the police, but she was reluctant. Then the very next day a box of beautiful yellow roses arrived here, along with a marriage proposal."

I glanced at Ray, then Nicole.

"This is more or less what we have going on here," Pancake said. "A similar escalation."

"Then tell your young lady to take all this very seriously." He sighed. "Which I guess she is if you guys are involved."

"Any physical confrontations or overt invasions of her life?" I asked.

"Oh, yes," Hartman said. "He painted graffiti on her garage door. Words like 'bitch' and 'whore' and the like. Bright red. I can still see it. He also punctured a couple of her car tires."

This was becoming officially eerie. The MO of this guy and our guy seemed to be in lockstep. Hundreds of miles and a year apart, yet they seemed to follow the same script. I had to admit, Pancake just might have hit the jackpot. He always had a knack for reading between the lines, and this was all that and more. To extract this case from all the others—hell, to even find all the others—was a major bit of mental gymnastics and cyber sleuthing. He was a freaking Sherlock sometimes.

"So he never actually confronted her?" Pancake asked. "Face-to-face?"

"Not until that day." He sighed. "The irony was that I had convinced her to bring in the cops and she had agreed to do so. She was going in to report it the next day."

"What happened?" I asked.

"She was at one of our larger malls. He apparently took her from the parking deck. Her car was found unlocked and her purse sitting on the passenger's seat. The police said it was like she was prepping to get in. But she never did."

"Did the police ever suspect anyone?" I asked.

"No. At least that's what I was told. As far as I could tell they did a good job. Pulled out all the stops, but in the end, it was never solved."

"Do you remember who led the investigation?" Ray asked.

"Sure. Detective Roberto Gomez. He's a real bulldog. I think his failure to solve it hurt him as much as it did all of us here at the station."

"Anything else that you can think of?" Pancake asked.

A long ,slow exhale. "I don't know the details but I do know she had been tortured before he killed her. The cops held all that close to the vest. They didn't want to let the public know that part."

"Not an unusual move," Ray said. "Helps filter out the nuts and also with the interrogation of any suspects."

"The worst part?" Hartman said. "She was dumped along a rural road. Like someone might discard a soda can. I still can't get over that."

CHAPTER 35

I CHECKED MY watch. Still fifteen minutes before Richard McCluskey, the station manager in Henderson, would conclude his meeting. While we waited, Pancake tracked down the number for Detective Roberto Gomez in Salt Lake City and called.

Once Gomez was on the line, Pancake told him who was present on the call and explained who we were and what we were doing.

"You're thinking the guy here might be the guy there?" Gomez asked.

"Not sure," Ray said. "Right now, we're scrambling."

"I hear you. For your sake, I hope it isn't. But for my sake, I hope it is. This is the one that got away. Still eats at me."

"I'd be surprised if it didn't. Anything you can tell us might help."

"I suspect you already know she had picked up a stalker. She never made contact with us about it, but her boss said she was planning to. Too bad she didn't. Anyway, she was abducted from a mall not far from where I'm sitting right now. Disappeared without a trace. Until an older couple saw something on the side of the road literally out in the middle of nowhere. They stopped to see and found her. That was two days later."

"I understand she was strangled," I said.

"That's true. He did other things, too. During those two days, she'd been bound and tortured."

Nicole stiffened. I reached over and grabbed her hand.

"In what way?" I asked.

"She had bruising and abrasions of her wrists and ankles, indicating that she'd been bound. Based on the nature of the bruises, I suspect with ropes. She was tased. Multiple times. She showed evidence of burns over her chest, back, legs. Looked like they were from cigarettes."

Nicole's palms were now cold and damp. Mine too.

"As bad as that was, it seemed as though she was struck with some instrument. Likely a ball-peen hammer. Broken fingers and toes, one arm, lower leg."

"Really?" I asked.

"Sure enough. To make all that worse, the coroner said all these wounds, the hammer blows and the burns, were inflicted over a couple of days."

I couldn't get my head around this. It was too much. I thought Billy Wayne Baker was a bad dude. I mean, he was a quiet, soft-spoken guy, but he did rape and murder women. But this guy? He made Billy Wayne look like a wussy.

Gomez wasn't finished. "He also repeatedly strangled her over the two days she was captive."

"The bruise patterns?" Ray asked.

"Exactly. The ME said it appeared that the ligature marks were of varying age. Like she was choked out over and over." He sighed. "The coroner ultimately signed out the cause of death as ligature strangulation but he couldn't be completely sure. When she was found, she had a plastic bag over her head, secured at the neck with duct tape." He sighed. "Don't know where these guys come from, but they aren't part of my humanity."

I flashed on something I'd read, many years ago about the BTK killer. Dennis Rader. BTK stood for his methods: bind, torture, kill.

What I remembered was that he would do this. Strangle, or use a plastic bag, to render his victims unconscious then let them revive only to do it all again. Sometimes for hours. It seemed that Dana Roderick had gone through this and more for days.

"I've seen it before," Ray said. "You're right. These guys aren't part of anyone's humanity and shouldn't be allowed to breathe."

"I like your thinking," Gomez said.

"Did your investigation uncover any leads?" I asked.

"Unfortunately not. We looked into Dana Roderick's life. Other than this stalker, we found nothing unusual. Very nice young lady. A good reporter and her coworkers loved her. Her boss, too."

"Yeah," Pancake said. "We talked to him."

"Good guy. He was crushed. We looked at all her friends and coworkers and even a couple guys she had dated in the past. At the time of the murder she wasn't involved with anyone. In the end, we found no one to implicate except this unknown stalker. Which of course was the obvious choice from the beginning. We tracked all the emails and texts she received. Over a nearly four-month period. They came from several burners. I think four different ones, if I remember correctly."

"Did you find out where they were purchased?" Pancake asked.

"Sure did. A couple of months earlier in Denver. Small mom-and-pop shop with no security cameras. He paid cash."

Bingo. There it was. The connection. Cell phones from Denver.

"Let me guess," I said. "He purchased a dozen phones."

A hesitation, then Gomez said, "Yeah. How'd you know?"

"We have the same situation here," Pancake said. "The phones he's using, several of them, were from Denver. I spoke with the store owner. The buyer used the name Terry Zander."

"Oh, Lord," Gomez said. "That's exactly what we discovered. We couldn't find any Terry Zander that fit this guy."

"I didn't either," Pancake said.

"I'd say my guy has relocated to your area. I mean, what are the odds?"

Exactly. The odds were incalculable.

"Things are starting to smell that way," Pancake said.

"I hate those phones," Gomez said. "No way to track them. Makes it more or less a dead end. Left us with only the crime scene to analyze. Our forensic team's pretty good, but they found nothing. Not on, in, or near her car or at the dump site. Not a single print, or hair, or fiber, or anything. We analyzed the security videos from the mall and the parking deck. The mall cameras showed nothing unusual. We did find Dana going in and out of several stores. Seemed to be a normal shopping trip. She didn't buy anything though. We saw no one following her or anything like that. But I doubt the guy came inside. More likely he waited in the deck. The parking structure had three entrance/exit ramps and each had a camera set up. We went through hours of video, looking for single males driving in or out in the several hours before and after she was seen on the mall cameras."

"Big job," Pancake said.

"It was. We identified eighty-something cars of interest. As I said, single males. We tracked them all down over the next few weeks but none were viable for this."

"Anything else we can use?" Ray asked.

"That's about it." He hesitated. "I hope you have a line on him. I truly do. He needs to be found. Everything I saw told me Dana Roderick was a wonderful young lady and she suffered greatly before he killed her."

The weight of that settled over me. Nicole had a death grip on my hand. I glanced at her. She seemed paler than before. Was she thinking the same as me? That one of her stalkers could have been carved from the same mold?

CHAPTER 36

AFTER HANGING UP with Detective Gomez, Pancake and Ray began hammering away at their computers. Each making notes on the conversation. The grunt work of the P.I. world. Recording everything was an obsession for both of them and an important part of the job. One of the many reasons I actively avoided having anything to do with Ray's business.

Yet, once again, here I was in Ray's domain. Memo to self—get better at tap dancing away.

Nicole worked her iPhone and Pancake and Ray seemed to carry on with the click-click-clicking for an hour. More likely three minutes but too long for me to sit still. All I could do was play with the salt shaker. For a minute anyway. Nicole plucked it from my hand and placed it on the table out of reach, tossing me a scowl. Like I was acting up in class. It was a look I had garnered many times during my school years. I had to admire their concentration. All three of them. It seemed intense and unwavering.

I never had that kind of focus. Not in school for sure. Not even on the mound when I pitched big-league ball. Deciding where to place a slider or a cutting fastball was a snap. That, for some unknown reason, came easy to me. Even in Little League. So, when the catcher went through all his hand and finger gyrations, indicating he wanted a breaking ball low on the outside corner, part of my brain recorded that data, and I adjusted my grip, the seam location, and the arm angle I would use as well as the speed I'd cut loose that little packet of leather. Those calculations required no thinking or processing. It all seemed automatic. Which was good since my brain was usually elsewhere. Maybe I would think about next week's travel to New York and my favorite watering holes in the city. Or about the vintage Mustang I had just purchased and that sat in my garage in Gulf Shores and how I wished I was in it motoring down the coast. Or maybe I would consider the blond beauty in the fourth row just left of home plate and try to figure out a way to meet her after the game. So, focus wasn't my thing. But I did record a lot of strikeouts.

Finally, thankfully, Ray and Pancake simultaneously closed their laptops. I had witnessed this before. It was as if their brains were wired together. Or more likely the Ray-virus had infected Pancake. They were in sync in a way that would create envy among the Radio City Music Hall Rockettes.

"Time to see if Mr. McCluskey is out of his meeting," Pancake said.

He dialed the number, and in less than a minute, had station manager Richard McCluskey on the line. Pancake once again went through who we were, made the introductions, and laid out the purpose of our call. He concluded with, "As part of our research we came across your situation. I guess Tiffany Cole's predicament would be a better way to put it."

"You think it might be related to your case?" McCluskey asked.

"We do. As well as another one in Salt Lake City."

"That young lady that was murdered up there? What? A year ago?"

"That's the one," Pancake said. "She was also a TV reporter for a smaller station."

"That's what caught my eye when I read about it. But I never thought it might have anything to do with Tiffany."

"It might not," Ray said. "Tell us what happened there."

McCluskey ran through what was becoming a repetitive story. Started out as a fan with emails and texts and notes and benign gifts. Then after a couple of months escalated to more aggressive language. Beautiful roses became dead flowers. Other presents left at her door. Her home sprayed with foul graffiti. Car tires slashed.

I looked at Nicole. She was no doubt thinking what I was. This was looking more and more like a pattern. Like the same guy was roaming around and creating havoc along the way. Not to mention had tortured and murdered a young woman.

"Did she ever go to the police?" I asked.

"No. I tried to convince her to do that, but she'd have none of it."

"Why?"

"She told me that if she did, and if she angered him, he might do something."

She was right. Salt Lake City proved that. If this was the same guy.

McCluskey continued. "I told her that the police might have arrested him. Then she would be safe." He let out a long breath. "I remember even as I said that, that it sounded very naive. Tiffany told me so. She said they probably couldn't even find him, and that even if they did, they wouldn't do anything. Maybe a restraining order but her feeling was that those were worthless. Even if he was arrested, he'd get bond and she'd be out there on her own with him pissed off."

Hard to a argue with that. The guy hadn't physically assaulted her, and other than some texts and emails, a little spray paint, and a couple of car tires, he hadn't really done any damage. That's not how I saw it, but that's how the law would look at it. He did have rights, after all.

Pancake hunched his shoulders forward and clenched both fists. I knew what he was thinking, and what he wanted. To be put in a small room with this dude so he could read him his rights. Something along the lines of: You have the right to broken ribs, a fractured jaw, and half your teeth in your lungs. You have the right to an ICU bed, a ventilator, and peeing blood for a month. You have the right to blunt-force trauma to your entire person. Pancake had a way about him.

McCluskey went on. "So, instead, she left the area."

"What about a marriage proposal?" Nicole asked. "Did he send one of those?"

McCluskey's intake of breath was clearly audible. "Yes. It came with a dozen yellow roses. Don't tell me this also happened in Salt Lake City?"

"It did. Here too."

"What does that mean?" McCluskey asked.

"That we just might be dealing with the same guy in all three cases," Ray said. "Which means we need to find him."

"Of course. What can I do?"

"We need to talk with Tiffany. She might remember something that could help."

"I doubt she'll talk to you or anyone else. When she left she was terrified and wouldn't give us even the merest clue what her plans were."

"Do you have any idea, even a guess, where she might be?" Pancake asked.

A hesitation. "She wouldn't tell anyone." He sighed. "But she has a sister near here. Over in Summerlin. She might know."

"Do you have a number for her?"

Another hesitation. "I'm reluctant to give it out."

"It might help," Nicole said. "It might save my friend's life."

"Tell you what, let me call her and see what she says. I'll give her your number and she can call if she wishes."

"Okay," Ray said. "Please let her know we'll absolutely protect her sister's privacy. That her sister just might have the key to taking this guy out of society."

CHAPTER 37

THE MINUTES DRIPPED by. As my granddad used to say, "Like black-strap molasses in winter." Nicole sat at the kitchen table, flipping through pages on her iPad. Ray across from her, his laptop open, concentration on his face. Pancake rattled around the kitchen as if lost. Obviously trying to decide what to eat. He settled on the fridge, rummaged inside, and came away with a foil-covered plate of leftover ribs and hot links. I was surprised there were any given Pancake's scorched-earth approach to food. He gnawed on a rib while bending over the sink. Nicole offered to heat it in the microwave to which Pancake responded, "Why?"

"They taste better warm."

"Takes too long."

That was another thing about Pancake's relationship to food. It was more a sprint than a marathon. Actually, it was both.

I stepped out on the deck and used the railing to stretch out my back. Bending, twisting, none of it helped. I noticed Jimmy Fabrick's boat slip sat empty. He was probably out on the water given it was another day made for sailing. Were there ever any days in The OC that weren't? It seemed that every time Nicole and I were here the weather was perfect. I never saw a drop of rain. Sure, some early morning dampness and drizzle from the marine layer, but that rarely lasted past noon.

By the time I stepped back inside, Pancake had cleaned the plate, licked and washed the excess sauce from his fingers, and dried them with a paper towel. His phone buzzed from the tabletop. He answered. Tiffany Cole's sister.

Pancake introduced himself and told her that he represented Longly Investigations. She responded that she was Sharon Wynter and that, yes, Tiffany was her sister. Pancake told her she was on speaker and then introduced each of us.

"Thanks for calling," Ray said.

"I almost didn't. I'm still not sure this is a good idea."

Nicole jumped in. "I completely understand your hesitation. All we want to do is ask a few questions. I promise we will protect your sister."

Sharon said nothing for a beat, and then, "Mr. McCluskey was a little vague about all this. What's this about?"

"A friend of mine," Nicole said, "here in Orange County, California, is in the same boat your sister was."

"You mean the same guy is there? Doing all this again?"

"We don't know that for sure," Ray said. "But based on our investigation, we think that your sister's case, another one a year ago in Salt Lake City, and the situation we have here might all be related."

"What makes you think that?" Sharon asked.

Ray explained the other cases, running through the stalker's actions and how things escalated in a similar pattern in each. He ended with, "I assume your sister is now safe and moving on."

"I'm not sure how far she's moved on. I have my doubts that she'll ever get over it. Maybe someday, but right now it's still too fresh to her. And safe? I'm not sure she'll feel that way until the guy who harassed her is caught. Maybe not even then."

"Understandable," I said. "These things do leave scars."

I thought of the baggage Nicole still carried around from her various stalkers.

"Mr. McCluskey said you're trying to reach my sister," Sharon said. "I'm not sure I'm comfortable with that."

"Like Nicole said, we'll protect her privacy," Pancake said. "That's an ironclad promise."

"I see." She sighed. "I don't want Tiffany to have to relive all this again. She's still fragile. Probably more so than you could imagine."

"I'm sure that's true," Nicole said. "My friend, who like your sister is a local TV reporter, is in the middle of a similar situation right now. She's scared and needs some help." No response. "I have some personal experience with these guys so I know what she's going through."

"How so?"

"I grew up in the movie business. I was an actress for many years. I managed to attract several of these guys. A couple that were more than an annoyance."

"Any as bad as this?"

"Let's just say that I've had my space invaded. I've been threatened and scared shitless, so I know how this works. I know how terrifying it is to have someone following you, taking photos and videos, and threatening you."

"Would you want to relive all that? Have it all dragged to the surface again?"

"No, I wouldn't. Like your sister, I'd avoid doing it if I could. But the difference is that I knew who was stalking me. It helped the police make each of them evaporate. Mostly with restraining orders and the authorities offering the guys forceful explanations and making sure they understood the consequences of continuing along their chosen paths. I even got one of them considerable jail time."

"That's where I wish Tiffany's stalker was. I—her too for sure—would feel a lot better."

"That's the point," Nicole said. "She doesn't know who the guy was or where he is. Or if he might reappear without warning."

"I think that's her greatest fear. It's the fact that he could be anyone that's most stressful. She's literally afraid of everyone."

"If we are dealing with the same guy and we can find him, wouldn't that make her sleep better?"

"It would."

"That's why we want to talk to her. If she can offer us anything that leads us to him, we hopefully can make that happen."

"I don't see how."

"It's what we do," Ray said. "We're pretty good at it."

Sharon seemed to mull that for a good half a minute. I understood. She wanted to protect her sister but she also wanted the guy identified and arrested. It presented a dilemma for her. Keep her sister isolated and safe or take a chance on some strangers who said they might be able to end the nightmare. I suspected that what she most wanted was for her sister to find an end to the horrible game the stalker had played. Even though Tiffany was in hiding, this guy still hung over her. He was out there in the dark. He might find her again and the entire ordeal would resume.

"Tell you what," I said. "Just as Mr. McCluskey did with you, call your sister and talk with her. Give her our number and if she wants to talk have her call."

"I don't know."

"Trust us," Nicole said. "We will protect her. Just call her and give her the choice. She might have some little bit of information that could make or break all this. If so, and if we can find this guy, that weight will be taken off her shoulders."

"Okay. No promises. It'll totally be up to her."

CHAPTER 38

AGAIN, WE WAITED. For a call that might never come. I didn't know Tiffany Cole. Really, nothing about her other than she was a TV reporter who had to weather a stalking episode. A stalker that scared her enough for her to completely abandon her life in Henderson. Cut and run stuff. What does it take to drive someone to do that? To leave a job, family, friends, and hit the road? If she was that scared, why would she talk with us? Why stick her head out of her foxhole?

The answer just might be that she wanted to put this guy behind her once and for all. She might take a chance that we, or someone, could find this guy and get him off the streets. So she no longer had to look over her shoulder, enter unfamiliar areas cautiously, and stare at the ceiling in the dead of night wondering where he was, did he know where she was, and was he even now planning to tighten the noose around her yet again?

It was the unknown that always weighed most heavily. Basic human psychology that was ingrained since birth. Was there a predator outside the cave? Was there a monster under the bed? Was it better to huddle in the corner or ball up beneath the covers, or confront the monster head-on?

The question became, which of Tiffany Cole's fears would win out? The fear of exposing herself by grasping the helping hand extended to her or the fear that regardless of how well she hid he was closing the gap between them? Take a chance on strangers to hopefully end this or burrow more deeply into the dark hole she had dug? I didn't envy her that choice. Either could be the right one—or could be a total disaster.

After a half hour of waiting, my confidence and enthusiasm waned. Nicole was sitting on her deck so I joined her, leaving Pancake and Ray at the kitchen table, working on computer stuff. I sat in the chair next to her.

"What do you think?" she asked.

"I think Ms. Cole is scared. I think she's paralyzed with indecision. I think she's not sure which path to follow—stay low or take a chance to end it all."

"Hopefully, it's the latter."

It was. I heard Pancake's phone buzz and him answer, followed by, "Ms. Cole, thanks for calling back."

Nicole and I joined Ray and Pancake at the table.

"It wasn't an easy decision," she said.

That was evident in the tension I sensed in her voice. Like she still wasn't sure and just might hang up and end the discussion before it even started.

"You did the right thing," Pancake said.

"I hope so."

Pancake introduced each of us, letting her know we were all in the conversation.

"My sister said you think the guy who came after me might be out there in California."

The phrase "out there" struck me as telling. If she were still in the Vegas area she would have said "over there" since Nevada was right next door. "Out there" to me suggested she was farther east. But, I could be overreading it.

"We aren't sure but we've found many similarities," Ray said.

Pancake ran through the chronology of what had happened to Megan.

Tiffany didn't respond immediately. She seemed to be trying to absorb what had been said. "It sounds like him, that's for sure. As you were laying it out, it was as if you were telling my story, too."

"That's why we think this might be the same guy," I said. "We're hoping you can offer something that might help us find him."

"I don't see how."

"You just never know what might be important."

"I suppose. My sister said you guys were from Alabama. Gulf Shores. How did you get involved in this if it's in California?"

"Megan, the woman here, is a friend of mine," Nicole said. "I've known her for years. She's good people and definitely doesn't deserve what's happening."

"Does anyone?"

"No. But this isn't rare. I have personal experience so I know what you went through and are still going through."

"Someone stalked you?" Tiffany asked.

"Actually, several someones," Nicole said.

"Are you in TV also?"

"Movies. I was an actress for a while."

"Anything I might've seen?"

"Probably not. I've moved to the other side of the camera. I write screenplays now."

I liked this. Nicole was gaining her confidence, lowering her tension, and drawing Tiffany out.

"Did you leave acting because of the stalkers?" Tiffany asked.

"That was part of it for sure. But also there's a lot of BS in that celebrity world. Being a writer and not an actor keeps me out of it for the most part."

"Were any of yours as scary as this guy has been?"

"Yes, and no. A couple were very aggressive. One ended up in jail. But the advantage I had was that I knew who was stalking me. It wasn't some phantom in the dark."

"That's what it seemed like. He just wafted in, did his damage, and forced me to give up my career. Really, my life."

"It's what they do."

"Things haven't been the same since."

"That's why we want to find this guy," Nicole said. "So you, and my friend Megan, can get back to a normal life."

"Normal? That seems so elusive. I mean, I'm a TV reporter, yet I can't do that job. That's all I ever wanted to do, and now I'm afraid to have my face seen anywhere. Scarfs and sunglasses have become my major fashion accessories."

"I remember those days well," Nicole said.

Tiffany let out an audible breath. "Okay. What can I tell you?"

"Run us through it," I said. "Tell us what happened."

She did. It was more or less what we already knew and, as she had said earlier, a carbon copy of what Megan was dealing with. The texts and emails, the gifts, the evolution from what seemed an infatuated fan to an angry and threatening menace.

"The worst part was when he came to my home. He sprayed-painted messages on my front door, my windows, my garage door."

"You never saw him, right?" I asked.

"No. I woke up that morning, got ready for work, like a normal day. Until I went outside and there it was. Big ugly red words. I was freaked. My neighbors were freaked."

"That happened here," I said. "He broke into Megan's condo and spray-painted her walls."

"Inside her home?"

"Yes."

"I would've died. It was bad enough on the garage door and windows. I can't even imagine." She sighed. "Of course, he might have been headed that way. Actually invading my home. I didn't give him that chance. I split."

"Did he do anything else?" Ray asked. "At your home?"

"He slashed a couple of my car tires."

"Same here with Megan," Nicole said. "Not at her home but rather at the studio where she works."

"I can see why you think this might be the same guy."

"I know you got a marriage proposal. Megan did too. So did the reporter in Salt Lake City."

"Yeah, I know about her. It was when I found out what happened to her that I split and came here."

"Good thing you did," Pancake said. "It now seems he might have ventured farther west and landed here."

"Lord. This guy is like a rolling plague."

I liked that. It seemed to describe this guy perfectly.

"Is there anything else you can think of?" Pancake asked.

"I think we've covered it."

"I'm sorry all this happened to you," Nicole said.

"Thanks. Me, too. I lost my career, my wonderful friends in Henderson, basically everything. But the one I really feel sorry for is Beth."

"Who's that?"

"She was my intern. She had been with me for three months. All this freaked her out. She left the area too."

"Your intern?" I asked.

"Yeah. Very nice young lady. I guess you could consider her collateral damage to all of this."

"What was her name?" Ray asked.

"Beth Macomb."

"Do you know where she is?"

"No. She was as freaked out as I was. Really took it hard. But she was a trooper. Not sure I could've weathered all this without her support."

"She left the area also?" I asked.

"She did. I don't know where she went but I wish I did. I'd like to talk to her and thank her for all she did."

"What did she look like?" I asked.

"Attractive. Long hair. Great smile. Everyone at the station loved her."

"Can we send you a picture?" Pancake asked.

"Of what?"

"Megan also has an intern," Nicole said. "Similar to what you describe."

"Really? What does that mean?"

"I don't know," Nicole said. "I'll text a picture of her. Take a look and see if she looks familiar."

"Okay."

"It was taken at dinner so it's not a close-up. More a group picture. She's on the left."

Pancake showed Nicole Tiffany's phone number on his phone's display. Nicole typed it in, attached the photo taken at The Cannery the other night, and sent it.

Took a couple of minutes, then Tiffany said, "Got it." Silence as she studied the image. Finally, she said, "It could be her. Can't see her face all that well. But this girl's hair is short and looks to be dark, maybe black. Beth's was long and lighter brown."

"Do you have a picture of Beth?" I asked.

"Not that I know. I'll double-check and let you know."

"But right now, you can't say whether the photo I sent is Beth or not?" Nicole asked.

"Not for sure. I mean, it could be, but I can't really say."

CHAPTER 39

"THAT'S INTERESTING," I said.

"Very. But is it a game changer?" Nicole asked.

"Could be," Pancake said.

"I have to admit that when she said she had had an intern it got my attention," I said.

"Could be a coincidence," Ray said.

Pancake grunted. Meant he didn't think so. He snatched up his phone, dialed a number, activated the speaker function, and returned it to the tabletop. After going through the secretary, Scott Hartman came on the line.

"Something new?" Hartman asked.

"Maybe," Pancake said. "Got a question for you."

"Let's have it."

"Did Dana have an intern? Someone who worked with her or for her?"

"She did."

My heart did a hop, skip, and jump.

"Who was it?" Ray asked.

"Uh, what was her name? Very nice young lady. Bright and a hard worker." He snapped a finger. "Liz. Liz Ingram."

"Is she still with you?" I asked.

"No. She left right after Dana's murder. She was totally spooked."

"How did she and Dana get along?"

"What's this about?" Hartman asked.

"Before we get to that," Pancake said. "Can I send you a photo?"

"Of what?"

"A girl. I want to know if she could be this Liz girl."

Since Hartman was on a landline and not a cell, Pancake got Hartman's email address and sent the photo. "She's the one on the left in the photo."

"Let me open it," Hartman said. He fell silent for a minute, probably examining the image. "Could be. I mean she seems about the same age, size, and build. Can't see her face all that well. But the hair is all wrong for sure. Liz had bright red curly hair."

Both Hartman and Tiffany had mentioned that Abby's face wasn't very visible. I hadn't noticed the single time I had looked at the photo. The night it was taken. Now I examined it more closely. Interesting. Abby had averted her head slightly to her right and downward. On purpose? Did she not want her picture taken? Did that mean we were on the right track? Or merely paddling in coincidental circles? Or maybe, just maybe, Abby was a chameleon, and a dangerous predator.

That didn't make sense. She had been present during many of the episodes. The texts and emails often came in while she was sitting right next to Megan. She was actually in the photo the stalker had taken on the beach in Malibu. Also, since she was with us at the time, she couldn't have scrawled the graffiti on Megan's living room walls.

But then, the stalker had never called Megan. Actually spoken to her. Was that to avoid revealing that the perpetrator was a woman?

It seemed that for every arrow that pointed toward Abby another pointed away. Maddening and confusing. As Pancake often said, "Evidence don't mean nothing until it does." I suspected that's

where we were. Sitting on the fence, not sure what was important, what was simply noise, and which side of the fence we should
focus on.

Another thought crept in. What if Abby wasn't acting alone? What
if she had an accomplice? Did that even make sense? Did stalkers work
in teams? How could two people be focused on the same target? Share
the same obsession? Talk about cosmic coincidences.

"What's this about?" Hartman asked again.

"In a similar case we found in Nevada and the one we have here in
California, the target of the stalker had an intern. With the Nevada
case, she also disappeared around the time the reporter in question
split."

"I see."

"As the old adage goes," Ray said. "One is an event, two a coincidence, and three a conspiracy."

"Are you saying Liz is this person?"

"Maybe. Do you have a picture of Liz?"

"I don't think we do. I can check with the staff and see if any of
them took any but we don't have anything official."

"That would help," Ray said. "Tell us about Liz. What do you know
about her?"

"Let me grab her file."

I heard the phone clunk on his desk, then the sound of drawers
scraping open and closed. "Let's see. She was from Lakeland, Florida.
Went to school at UCF and got a degree in journalism. She had no
real work experience, which is why she wanted an intern position to
get that experience."

"Did you check her out? Before you hired her?"

He sighed. "I'm afraid not. We probably should have but as an
intern she had few real responsibilities. She mainly shadowed and
helped Dana. I took her at her word."

"I understand," Ray said. "I probably would've looked at it the same way."

No, he wouldn't have. Not Ray. He would've done a colonoscopy on any applicant. But then he had hired—sort of—Nicole while sitting in a bar. Which was an interesting point. It meant that he had more or less accepted my vetting of Nicole as a good and honest person. The irony of that was thick. All my life Ray had held out the women I had spent quality time with as symptoms of my lack of motivation and inability to be more responsible and more like him. Yet, with Nicole, he seemed to have bought in. Or did he sense all that in her? Probably. Ray possessed an uncanny knack for reading people.

Ray continued. "I take it you haven't heard from her or have any idea where she might have gone."

"Nothing. I figured she was too spooked by everything and wanted to sever all ties to this place." He exhaled heavily. "Can't say I blame her. If you find her, tell her we still owe her for her final week."

"She didn't get her paycheck?" I asked.

"No. She just evaporated."

Pancake thanked Hartman and disconnected the call. He then called Richard McCluskey back.

"What'd you forget to ask?" McCluskey said.

"Beth Macomb."

"What?"

"We talked to Tiffany Cole."

"So, her sister came through. How is Tiffany?"

"Doing okay under the circumstances. She told us she had an intern while she was there. Really liked her."

"Everyone liked Beth. She was very pleasant, smart, and a good worker."

"Do you have a picture of her?" I asked.

"What's this about?"

Pancake ran through it. In each of the three cases in question, the reporter had a young woman for an intern.

"I can't imagine Beth has anything to do with this."

Nicole went through the picture thing again, sending McCluskey a copy of the dinner pic. Like the others, he agreed it could be Beth but he wasn't sure because he couldn't really see her face and the hair was all wrong. This was becoming a broken record. He concluded with, "But I'll see if anyone around here has a picture of Beth, and if so, I'll send it to you."

"What do you know about her?" Ray asked. "Where she's from, what her background is? That sort of thing."

"I'm afraid all I know is what was on her application, which isn't much. I have it right here in my desk drawer. Just a sec." A scraping noise followed by the rustling of pages. "Okay, here it is. She's from Des Moines, Iowa. She went to Iowa State and finished a degree in journalism. She was looking for work experience so she applied for an internship and we hired her."

This was an echo of what we had heard from Hartman about the mysterious Liz. The hair on my arms rose and that tingly feeling erupted on my neck. Like when a cool breeze ripples over a sunburn.

"Have you heard from her since she left?" I asked.

"No. She didn't even pick up her final paycheck."

Well, well.

Pancake ended the call.

I wasn't sure exactly how to process all this new information. What did it mean? How did Abby fit into this? If she did at all. Still too many missing pieces to see the entire puzzle.

But one thing was for sure—the game had just changed.

CHAPTER 40

"WHAT DO YOU think?" I asked.

"Too much for a coincidence," Nicole said.

"Unless it is."

"True," Nicole said.

We were driving up Newport Boulevard toward the Channel 16 studios to catch Megan's broadcast and then follow her back to the condo.

"The problem I'm having," I said, "is that I still don't see the whole picture."

"No one does. You heard Ray and Pancake talking. Abby doesn't fit the profile. She couldn't have done all the things the stalker has done. Hell, she was present when a lot of them occurred. The emails, the texts. She was with Megan when many of them came in. She was in the photo he took of us walking on the beach in Malibu. She was sitting at the breakfast table when the dead flowers were delivered to Uncle Charles' home."

"That crossed my mind, too." I turned off 19th street and into the parking lot. "She can't be in two places at once."

"Unless she's two people."

I slid into an empty slot and parked, switching off the engine. "You're pretty smart," I said.

"I know." She smiled. "But what makes you say that now?"

"Because I came to the same conclusion."

"Which is?"

"Either this is one hell of a coincidence and the fact that the other two, Dana and Tiffany, and now Megan had, have, interns is merely a cosmic ripple."

"Or Abby is all three of these interns and she has a partner," Nicole said.

"Exactly."

"But why? What's the payoff?"

"That's the big question." I tapped a finger on the steering wheel. "It makes no sense."

"Not yet," she said.

"Did she ever say anything about a boyfriend or anything like that?"

Nicole considered that for a minute. "Not that I know. She never said so around me anyway."

Nicole grabbed her purse from the floorboard and pushed open her door. "Be cool around Abby. Don't act suspicious or get all freaky."

I stepped out and locked the car. We headed toward the entrance. "I thought you liked it when I was freaky."

She bumped her hip against mine. "That's an entirely different kind of freaky." She shifted her purse to the other shoulder, flipping her braided hair out of the way. "Just act normal."

Don't you hate that? When someone says act normal, or natural? How do you do that? Being normal comes easy, acting normal is impossible. Every time someone says that to me I never know what to do with my arms and hands, or face, or really anything. Be casual, but not too casual. Be friendly, but not overly so. Don't say anything stupid. That was the hardest part.

Okay, time to get my game-face on. And act normal, natural.

I shoved my hands in my pockets. Didn't feel right. I tried one, then none, letting my arms hang loosely at my sides. They felt foreign. I decided it was best to ignore them and work on my face. I smiled, but that felt off. Forced and frozen. I tried to set my jaw and look cool but that felt worse.

To make things even more uncomfortable, as soon as we quietly slipped into the rear of the main recording studio, where Megan's segment was just beginning, we ran head-on into Abby. She held a clipboard in her hand. She looked up and smiled. I shoved my hands in my pockets, pulled them out, relaxed my shoulders, pasted on a smile. I hoped I looked totally normal and relaxed. Didn't feel that way.

"You guys made it just in time," she whispered.

"Jake needed to primp," Nicole said.

I started to respond with something clever, but nothing came to mind so I simply shrugged.

We watched Megan do her thing. She looked tense and tired, definitely not her usual perky self. It was a four-minute piece on the upcoming shows at the Orange County Performing Arts Center. When the producer ended the segment and switched over to a pre-recorded package, Megan unclipped her mic and came our way. We walked down to the office.

"Good show," Nicole said.

"Didn't feel that way."

"You were great," Abby said. "As usual."

"You're just saying that to be nice."

"No, I'm not. You worked hard on that piece and it showed."

"You did most of the research," Megan said.

"That's my job." Abby smiled. "It's a team effort."

"We do make a good team."

Now Abby beamed. "We do."

"What's new?" Megan asked as she flopped in her chair.

"Nada," Nicole said.

"I got three more texts today," Megan said. "One all loving and flattering, the other two the usual snarky stuff." She picked up her phone from her desk, glanced at me. "I'll send them to you." Megan's phone whooshed the send sound. "Done."

"I'll pass them on to Pancake," I said. "See if he can find anything useful."

"He's pretty smart, isn't he?" Abby asked.

"Oh yeah," I said. "Much more so than he looks."

"He's cute," Abby said. "I love his hair."

"It's his trademark," Nicole said.

"I wish I had red hair. I always liked the ginger look."

The first thing that popped in my head was that she might have been a redhead once. A year ago when she played the role of Liz Ingram, Dana Roderick's intern in Salt Lake City. When she kidnapped, tortured, and murdered her. That thought bubble collapsed quickly. The young lady who stood before me could not possibly have done that. Could she? She seemed so normal and from what I'd seen possessed no hard edges, or the slightest hint of that kind of depravity. But then, hadn't Bundy fooled everyone? Was Abby on a par with such a psychopath? I kept all this to myself though and instead said, "You can change it. Purple, green, red, whatever you want."

"True. I wonder what color would look hottest on me?" She laughed. Easy and relaxed.

Speaking of easy and relaxed. Nicole twisted the conversation back to intel gathering. "Do you have a boyfriend or significant other? You could ask him."

"I wish. I haven't been here long enough to meet anyone cool." She looked at Megan. "What? Three months?"

"That's right."

"I've had a couple of dates, but they seemed a bit self-absorbed."

"Welcome to The OC," Megan said. "Why do you think I'm still single?"

"Because you work too much," Nicole said.

"Isn't that so." Megan stood. "Let me go scrub off the makeup and then we can get out of here." She headed toward the women's room.

"I'm surprised you don't have a boyfriend," I said to Abby. "Pretty young lady like you."

"I don't even have a cat or a dog," she said. "Much less a dude."

"A roommate?" Nicole asked. "One of those at least?"

"Nope. But actually, I like it that way."

"There's something to be said for that," I said. "Roommates and significant others can be annoying."

"Oh, really?" Nicole said. She punched my arm.

"Nicole snores," I said.

She punched me again. Harder. "That's you."

Abby laughed. "If I had a relationship like you two seem to have, maybe I'd feel differently." She sat in her chair, placing the clipboard on her desktop. "But most of the guys I've dated in the past turned out to be jerks. So, just being alone with myself works pretty well."

"Where'd you grow up?" I asked.

"Portland."

"Brothers or sisters?"

"No. I was an only child." She shrugged. "Maybe that's why I do better on my own."

"Did you go to college there?" Nicole asked.

"Oregon. Down in Eugene. Not far from Portland."

"Good school," I said.

"It was. They had an excellent journalism program so it was my first choice."

"Have you had other intern positions?" I asked. "Or is this your first?"

"This is it. There's a lot of competition for these gigs. More than I thought there would be. I looked at several others but liked this place best. The facilities, the manager, Megan. It all seemed to fit."

"What other places did you look at?" Nicole asked.

Did she take in a breath, hesitate, or was I overreading it?

"Let's see. Lincoln, Nebraska; Indianapolis; and St. Louis. Oh, and Billings, Montana."

"The weather's better here," Nicole said.

"I know," Abby said. "I've never lived in this area. I've visited Southern California a couple of times but only briefly. The weather sure makes you want to stay."

"What is it?" I said. "Forty million? The number of folks who agree with you?"

"That's the down side. Lots of people around."

"So, you always saw yourself doing TV work?" Nicole asked.

"Yeah. Or print work. I like the writing. Not sure I'd do so well in front of the camera."

"You'd do fine."

"Maybe but definitely not as good as Megan. She's the real deal. I admire her so much. I envy her comfort level, particularly when she does live shows. It takes a special talent to do that. You have to be fearless."

"She is that."

Abby nodded. "Yeah, onstage anyway. But this—" she waved a hand. "This stalker stuff's hitting her hard. I can feel the fear. It seems to surround her like a negative energy field or something."

"Understandable," I said.

"She's more afraid than she lets on." Abby said. "I can almost taste it. She'll sit at her desk and simply stare at the wall, or her computer screen. I can see the tension in her shoulders."

"She hasn't been sleeping well either," Nicole added.

"It shows. She looks tired and her brain gets fuzzy at times."

"Megan said that you've been a great help to her. A big support through all this."

"I've tried. It's scary though."

"I think at first she thought you were overreacting," I said. "Making more out of it than it was. But it seems you were right. Almost clairvoyant."

Abby smiled. "I wouldn't go that far. But, yes, I sensed this guy would get worse and more dangerous. I think Megan has finally come to that conclusion also."

"You're right," I said.

Again, I tried to picture Abby as a stone-cold killer. One who would stalk and kidnap and murder someone. I couldn't see it. She seemed so nice and sweet. Again, Bundy came to mind, as did Jeffrey Dahmer who had been downright shy.

"It's the unknown that makes this so hard," Abby said. "Not knowing who's doing this and why. It adds another layer of anxiety."

"Why do you think this guy hasn't showed his face?" I asked. "Approached her directly? From what I've read, most stalkers do that because they want to get close to their target. To win them over as much as anything else."

"I don't know," Abby said. "But I believe, and I've told Megan this more than a few times, that he will. That she needs to stay vigilant and on guard."

"Not much fun living that way," Nicole said.

"No, it's not. But does she really have a choice? Not knowing who it is means it could be anyone. That's where the real anxiety comes from."

CHAPTER 41

BEFORE WE MADE it out of the studio, Pancake called, saying we should pick up something for dinner. Not only was he hungry, not a headline news story, but also that he and Ray had a lot to go over with us.

"What?"

"Too much to get into right now. Let's just say the thread connecting these events has thickened."

"Okay. Pizza good with you?"

"That'll work. One more thing. Do you know where Abby is from? Where she went to school?"

"Interestingly, we were just talking about that. She's from Portland and went to the University of Oregon."

"Okay. Grab the grub and we'll see you here."

Nicole rode with Megan and they headed to the condo. I swung by a local pizza joint and grabbed four fourteen-inch pies. Two for Pancake, two for the rest of us.

When I arrived, Megan had just finished showering and had changed into gray sweatpants and a yellow tee shirt. Nicole had slipped into a similar ensemble, hers lime green over black. I felt overdressed in jeans and a golf shirt.

Ray and Pancake had obviously gone shopping. Two bottles of Merlot and a quart of Buffalo Trace bourbon sat in the middle of the dining table. I placed the pizza boxes on the counter. We each slid a couple of slices on our plates. Except Pancake. He simply sat one box in front of him. Let the games begin.

Since Pancake was too occupied with eating, Ray went over what they had uncovered.

"What we knew before was that we have three cases with several points of identity. Small-station, limited-market reporters, stalkers, and each with a new intern. One murder and a second situation that just might have been rolling in that direction."

I noticed Megan's back stiffen, her chewing slowed. It wasn't difficult to guess where her head was at. Was this situation spinning toward her murder? Was that the endgame here? I wanted to tell Ray to get on with it and spit it all out. But Ray was methodical if nothing else. He needed to lay out the full picture in a deliberate manner so that the context of each fact could be easily snuggled against the others and a clear picture would emerge. It was his way.

Ray continued. "Though no one involved in the other cases can say for sure, each at least said that the photo of Abby was similar. That defies the odds. I mean, what are the chances that the interns involved in these three would even look similar? You'd expect at least one of them to be an outlier. Totally differently in size, shape, age, something. So, the next step was to see if these other two interns were real or manufactured." He glanced at Pancake.

Pancake, who had already motored through half of the pizza before him, wiped his mouth with a napkin. "Liz Ingram in Salt Lake City. According to station manager Scott Hartman, she was from Lakeland Florida, and went to UCF. But the city of Lakeland, hell the state of Florida, has no record of her. She has no paper trail at all. She was never a student at UCF."

"She made up her resume," Nicole said, not a question.

"Looks that way."

"A lot of folks do that, don't they?"

Ray nodded. "They do."

"Then there's Beth Macomb," Pancake said. "I found no record of her in DesMoines. Like Liz Ingram, no tax info, no driver's license, no voting registration, no employment record, no social media presence. She also didn't go to the Iowa State like she told the folks at the station there."

"A pattern," I said. "I think I know the answer to this, but what about Abby?"

"She ain't from Portland. Again, no record of her existence there. She never attended the University of Oregon."

Megan appeared to deflate and sink into her chair. Her shoulders, her face, even her hair, seemed to fall limp.

I spoke up. "So, we have three fake interns in three different cities who look sort of alike and who work for a TV personality who is being stalked. Is that about it?"

"It is." Pancake shoved the remnant of a pizza slice into his mouth.

"If that's the case, she has an accomplice," I said.

"What?" Megan asked. Her shoulders rose, furrows creased her forehead.

"Nicole and I talked about this earlier. She couldn't have done this on her own. She was with you when many of the messages and gifts arrived. With you on the beach when the photo was taken and sitting next to you when the dead flowers were delivered up in Malibu."

"She was with all of us when your condo was broken into and spray-painted," Nicole added.

Stunned didn't cover the look on Megan's face. Sprinkled with a dose of confusion, and fear. No doubt, to her mind—mine too—this upped the ante.

"Who on earth could it be?" Megan asked.

"That's the question," Ray said.

"She said she didn't have a boyfriend or a roommate or any family here," I said.

Pancake grunted. "Doesn't mean she doesn't have a partner."

"But why?" Megan asked. "Why would she do that?"

"She's a terrorist," I said.

Megan gave me a quizzical look. "What does that mean?"

"I thought about this last night. After Nicole quit pestering me and I had time to think."

"Pestering? That's what you call it?"

"Monopolizing my attention, then."

"Not a difficult task."

I gave a headshake. "What I meant was that if Abby is the one, the same person in each of these, then she feeds off terror. She creates it, has a partner to keep the wheels turning, and she's present to see the result. Up close and personal."

"But she's been great to me," Megan said. "Always there and always calming me when I would get wound up. She's been a rock."

"Which gives her a chance to play the hero," Nicole said.

"Which makes her less of a suspect," Pancake said. "The supportive friend couldn't be the bad guy, or gal. A very good head fake."

"Also," I said, "wasn't she the one that sounded the alarm the earliest? Didn't she say that you should be worried about, even afraid of, this guy? Didn't she say it would get worse?"

Megan nodded.

"Nothing ramps up fear more quickly than those around you being afraid," I said. "That's why horror movies are scarier in the theater than they are at home on TV."

"Herd mentality," Ray said. "Even if the herd is only two."

Megan seemed to consider that before speaking. "I just find all this hard to believe. I mean, Abby seems so sweet. Not the kind of person who would even consider something like this."

"But she's not who she says she is," I said. "Who you think she is, is a creation."

Megan leaned her elbows on the table and buried her face in her hands. "I don't freaking believe this."

"I just had another thought," Nicole said. "What if the guy is actually stalking Abby? What if she has moved and changed her ID and background to hide from him, but he keeps finding her?"

Megan looked up.

"Go ahead," Ray said.

"He knew her from somewhere. Maybe he's an old boyfriend or maybe he's completely anonymous. Maybe he's simply trying to wreck her life by keeping her off balance and afraid. Not by going directly at her but by going after those close to her. In these cases, the person she's interning for."

I liked that. As crazy at it sounded, it wasn't any more off kilter than Abby and some unknown dude doing all this. Either scenario seemed improbably improbable but not impossible. I gave Nicole an atta-girl nod.

"I saw a few cases like that," Pancake said. "One was a high school kid who was dumped by his girlfriend so he set about stalking and harassing her mother. Made her life hell for nearly a year before he was caught."

Ray leaned back in his chair and folded his arms over his chest. "I don't buy it. If that were the case and if Abby were truly innocent, wouldn't she have told you about it?" He looked at Megan. "That she had some mysterious stalker and that this person was harassing you as a tact to make Abby uncomfortable?"

Megan nodded. "I believe she would have."

"I do too. She would be looking for the support from you that she's apparently been so generous giving to you."

Okay, I had to admit that that made more sense that Nicole's suggestion. If Abby was in hiding, she would need allies. She would need a support system. Megan would have been a prime candidate for that role.

"The big question is—do stalkers work as teams?" I asked.

"Don't know for sure," Pancake said. "But if you mean like the typical obsessive, infatuated stalker, I'd think probably not. Seems to me that it would be very unlikely that two people would share the same obsession for the same person."

"But if inflicting terror, and reveling in that, is the goal, then a team could make sense," I said.

"Good thinking," Ray said.

Ray actually said that? Had the world reversed its spin? I started to comment on that but quickly disconnected my brain from my mouth. See? I was getting better.

Ray continued. "That would also explain why the supposed stalker hasn't called or showed up. The Trojan horse, Abby, was always inside the castle walls."

"She has a front-row seat to the terror she and her partner have inflicted," Nicole said.

Megan took a deep breath and exhaled it slowly. "I find all this hard to believe."

"I know," Pancake said. "It's a lot to get your head around. But things are starting to look like that could be the deal." He opened his hands. "There's something rotten in the state of Denmark and it ain't the marriage of Claudius and Gertrude."

"What?" I asked.

"*Hamlet*. You need to read more."

Where does he store all this stuff? Pancake's big, very big, and even his head's big but still, it only has so much storage space. Yet, he comes up with crap like this all the time. Not that I knew what he was talking about. Hell, I didn't even know who Claudius and Gertrude were and barely knew much about *Hamlet*. I do remember a skull in there somewhere. I started to ask him to explain but wasn't sure I could listen to an English Lit lecture right now, so instead, I asked, "What's our next step?"

"Pancake and I have more research to do. Why don't you and Nicole do a drive-by of Abby's apartment? Get the lay of the land. Maybe take a few pictures."

"Why?" I asked.

"It's intel we might need down the road. Don't let her see you and don't go near her place. Just check out the area."

"We can do that," Nicole said.

Of course we can.

"I'll go with you," Megan said.

"Might be better if you stay here," Ray said.

"I need to do something. I'd be an extra set of eyes. Besides, I know where she lives."

"We do too," Pancake said.

"Yeah, but I live here. I know the area."

CHAPTER 42

SINCE ABBY HAD seen our Range Rover, even ridden to Malibu in it, Ray suggested we take his rental car. It was a gray Chrysler 300 so we wouldn't stand out. I drove, Nicole shotgun, Megan in the back.

"This is so insane," Megan said. "I still can't believe it's not just a series of coincidences."

"A lot of coincidences," I said.

"I just don't see Abby as capable of something like this and I'm not sure I buy her doing all this just for kicks. That seems too strange to be true."

Nicole twisted in her seat and looked at Megan over her shoulder. "You might be right. This might be a wild goose chase and Abby might be completely innocent."

"Except she faked her identity," I said.

"Maybe it's what Nicole said," Megan responded. "She's being stalked. She's trying to hide."

"I just threw that out," Nicole said. "I'm not sure I buy it, but it's at least possible. That said, I agree with Ray. I think that if that was the case, she would've told you what was happening."

Megan considered that. "Maybe she wasn't sure."

"She'd have to be. If she is all three of these fake people, she'd know exactly what was happening. She would've been through it before so would know this guy had found her again."

"I agree," I said. "She would've told you about it rather than continually feeding your fear and making it seem as if you're the target."

"I'm not sure she's doing that. You know, adding to my concern. She's just concerned herself."

"Did she ever say that things weren't so bad?" Nicole asked. "That you're right not to be overly worried?"

"Not that I remember."

"So she feeds your fears," I said.

Megan exhaled a deep breath. "I suppose."

"The question is, is she the cause of your fears?" Nicole said.

"Turn left up here," Megan said. "Two blocks to the four-way stop, then right. We're almost there."

It was nearing nine p.m. A couple of cars passed, headed the other way, but otherwise the streets were quiet and dark. Three minutes later, we rolled past the Creekside Apartments. Also quiet. Nicole lifted Ray's Nikon, leaned past me, and snapped a few pictures through the driver's window.

"I'll turn around and give you a better angle."

At the end of the block, I made a U-turn and slowly worked my way back down the street.

"That's Abby's place," Megan said. She pointed. "First floor. Next to the end."

Nicole adjusted the zoom. "Number 8?"

"Yes."

The apartment building paralleled the street and extended nearly the entire block. Two-story white stucco, stacked above a half-submerged parking area. Put the first-floor walkway about five feet above the ground, steps leading up at intervals along the row of apartments.

I found an empty space and pulled to the curb behind a pickup truck. Abby's apartment was now only forty feet away. Interior lights illuminated the closed curtains. A shadow moved by. Then another.

"There're two people inside," I said.

"Did Abby say anything about having company?" Nicole asked.

"No," Megan said. "But then I didn't ask."

I switched the engine off. "Let's hold here for a few minutes."

My cell buzzed. It sat on the console. I spotted the caller ID. It read "Tammy." Before I could grab it, Nicole did.

"Oh, good." She then said to Megan, "You're going to love this."

"Don't answer," I said.

"She'll just keep calling."

"Turn the phone off."

"Who is it?" Megan asked.

"Jake's ex." She rolled her window up so the sound wouldn't carry outside and punched the answer button, placing it on speaker.

"Jake, what's wrong with you?"

"Nothing. But I'm a bit busy right now."

"Yeah, right. Doing what?"

"Staking someone out."

"Hope it works out better than last time. Barbara Plummer didn't do so well under your watchful eye."

She was never going to let go of that one. Sure, I was charged with watching the Plummer residence, trying to catch Barbara cheating, and sure she did get murdered right under my nose, but those things happen, don't they?

Tammy wasn't finished. "So I guess you're too busy to talk to Walter?"

"About what?" I knew but I just couldn't help myself.

"Do you ever listen to me?"

Even I knew this was a trick question. There was no right answer. So why try? "Probably not. It's a self-preservation thing."

"Don't be an ass. I need for you to talk Walter out of retiring."

I was thinking maybe he should retire, change his name, get plastic surgery, and move as far away from Tammy as possible. I didn't say that but rather said, "Walter's an adult. He can make his own decisions."

"Not when it impacts my life."

Ah, the joys of modern marriage. Tammy-style.

"Maybe Walter wants to lower his stress level." Getting the surgery done and running away would be a good start.

"Walter loves his work. It's not a stress for him."

"Maybe he has enough money squirreled away and he no longer needs to work."

"Are you kidding? Enough for the next forty years?"

I flashed on a courtroom scene. Walter in handcuffs, facing the judge. Actually, I saw Judge Ruth Corvas. I had stood before her hawkish glare before. I pictured her dark eyes piercing Walter, her saying, "The jury has found you guilty of colossal stupidity and I sentence you to forty years of solitary confinement in your home with your insane wife." Maybe I should write a screenplay. I wondered if Uncle Charles would be interested in a domestic thriller. Maybe tag Kirk Ford to play Walter. Casting Tammy would be more difficult. Maybe Grendel's mother was available.

"Maybe a budget could help," I said.

"You're an ass." She hung up.

"Wow," Megan said. "She's a trip."

"A trip to the psychiatrist," I said.

"I love it when she calls," Nicole said.

"Look." Megan pointed toward the building.

The curtain to Abby's apartment slid open a couple of feet, followed by the glass slider. A man stepped out, phone to his ear, a cigarette dangling from his mouth. He wore cargo shorts and a tee shirt. His hair looked fairly long and unkempt. While he spoke, he scanned the street but apparently didn't focus on us. Just three folks sitting in a car, talking. He turned profile, flicked an ash from his cigarette over the railing, and continued his conversation.

Nicole lowered her window, raised the camera, and snapped several pictures. She worked the zoom and took more.

"Who is it?" Megan asked.

"Don't know," Nicole said. "Looks to be around thirtyish."

Based on the slider behind him, I guessed he was just over six feet, fit, maybe around 170. "Looks like Abby has a man in her life."

"Is that him?" Megan asked. "The guy?"

"Could be," I said. "No way to know."

"Maybe he's a neighbor or something."

"Yeah. Just dropped by for a cup of sugar and a smoke."

"If he lives there," Nicole said, "it sort of blows her having an anonymous stalker out of the water and puts an accomplice in play."

"Spoken like a true screenwriter," Megan said.

Nicole smiled. "Thriller of the week."

"Thrilled isn't exactly what I'm feeling."

"Are you sure she never mentioned that she was seeing someone?" I asked.

"No. Never. You heard her earlier today, talking about how few guys she had even dated."

"I get the feeling this guy isn't just a visitor or a neighbor. He looks comfortable, like he belongs."

The guy ended his call, tossed his cig over the railing, and stepped back inside, pulling the slider closed. Shadows moved behind the curtain, then the front door opened and the guy stepped out. I could see Abby just inside before the door swung shut. The man bounced down the nearby stairs, turned into the entrance of the underground parking, and descended down its ramp. He walked along the row of cars. From our vantage point we could only see the roofs. He appeared to stop behind the fourth one in. A silver something, but from this angle and distance, I couldn't determine the make. He popped the trunk, rummaged around, lifted a backpack, slung it over one shoulder, closed the trunk, climbed the ramp, the stairs, and went back inside.

Nicole snapped a couple of dozen pictures of him. It was dark so I wasn't optimistic any would be very detailed, but it's the best we could do.

"Do you recognize him?" I asked Megan.

"Never seen him before."

Nicole pushed open her door and stepped out.

"What're you doing?" I asked.

"Wait here."

She walked maybe a hundred feet up the sidewalk, crossed the street, veered toward the building, and backtracked to the garage entrance. She descended the ramp. I saw her approach the car and snap a few pictures.

Two minutes tops and she was back in the car.

"Got something for Pancake to use," she said. "Toyota Celica. Colorado plates."

CHAPTER 43

"WHAT DID PANCAKE say?" Nicole asked.

"Nothing."

"He was up late last night and then again this morning working on tracking that car and you're telling me he's found nothing?"

We were headed up Newport Boulevard, following Megan to the studio.

"He didn't say that. But he wouldn't tell me anything. He did say he was close but didn't want to talk about it until he had it all tied up."

"He'll find out who the dude is. Or at least who owns the car."

"He will."

"Those donuts smell good," she said.

This morning, Megan had been nervous about going in and having to face Abby. Now that she knew things just might not be as they had seemed only a few days ago. What if she slipped up and said something that created tension, or worse, made Abby wary? Nicole and I tried to assure her that all would be okay.

"But what if she senses I'm suspicious of her?" Megan had asked.

"She won't," I said.

"Just be yourself," Nicole said. "Focus on work and don't force anything. Act as if everything is normal. Just another day."

See? There it was again. Act natural, normal. Impossible to do.

So, we devised a plan. Nicole and I would go in with her to be a buffer while Megan settled in. On the surface, it seemed strange that she needed to get comfortable at her own job, in her own office, but I understood. It's hard to unring the bell of knowledge. With everything that Pancake had unearthed, Megan now knew that Abby was not who she said she was. Abby Watson didn't exist but rather was a manufactured person. Which, of course, changed everything. What we didn't know was whether she was also the other two interns, Liz Ingram and Beth Macomb, or whether she was a serial stalker, or worse, truly dangerous.

Rather than simply barging in with Megan, we decided to grab a box of donuts for the staff. Always a distraction, a great icebreaker, so to speak, and the last thing we wanted here was for any frost to appear in Megan's relationship with Abby. As Ray would say, we needed to be cool. Ray-speak for not showing your hand, gathering intel and not delivering it, and in the end acting naturally.

See, it cannot be escaped.

I lifted one of the two boxes of donuts from the Range Rover's rear seat. Yes, we were smart enough to double up so we could take one box to Pancake. If we hadn't, he would have smelled it on us—yes, he can do that—and then we'd have to put up with his complaints and ultimately have to head back out to get another dozen. Better to be preemptive.

Inside, Phyllis P oohed and aahed over the donuts, before selecting one with multicolored sprinkles. The others we ferried to the office where Abby and Darren Slater did their own oohing and aahing.

"You guys are the best," Abby said. "I was starving. I didn't have time for breakfast this morning." She pulled a chocolate-covered cake donut from the box and took a bite. "Hmmm. Wonderful."

"Late night?" I asked.

"Stayed up too late reading," Abby said.

"Anything I might like?"

"Uh, no. A trashy romance." She smiled. "You don't impress me as the romance book type."

"I'm romantic. Tell her, Nicole."

"He is. In a rude, crude, guy sort of way."

"Yet you never complain," I said.

Nicole laughed. "That's because I don't require romance. My needs are more basic."

Now, Abby laughed. "Oh, I want to hear more."

"When you're older," I said.

"Yeah, right."

"Here I was hoping you stayed up late because you had a hot date," Nicole said.

Abby wiped chocolate from one corner of her mouth. "If you know of anyone, my schedule is open." She raised an eyebrow. "Maybe Kirk Ford?"

"Afraid you'd have to stand in line," Nicole said. "Kirk is—how to put this—in high demand."

"I'd be surprised if he wasn't. He's hot and then some. But, then again, right now I'm not that choosey. Anyone will do." She smiled. "Well, almost anyone."

"Still hard for me to see why you don't have a boyfriend," I said. "Smart, pretty young lady like you."

"Flattery works," she said. "Almost as well as donuts."

Everyone laughed.

Mission accomplished. Ice broken, relaxed atmosphere in place. We left them to their work.

Back at the condo, Pancake pounded down four donuts and was licking his fingers before I could get a word in.

"What did you find out about the car?" I asked.

"A lot."

"Is it a secret or are you going to tell us?" Nicole asked.

"First," Ray said, "how're things at the station? More to the point, how's Megan? Any awkwardness?"

"She was nervous but she did great," I said. "We took donuts and that seemed to get things settled somewhat."

"Good idea. Good distraction."

"Great distraction," Pancake said, as he took a bite from a butter-milk bar. In less than half a minute, it too disappeared. He washed his hands at the sink and dried them on a paper towel. He sat at the dining table and flipped open his laptop. "Okay, here's what I have."

Nicole and I sat and listened. Ray took a few notes. The more Pancake rolled out, the more impressed I was. Not surprised though. Pancake had a way of sniffing out things that were dead and buried and way off the radar.

The car was registered to a Greg Morgan. It was purchased used on the fringes of Denver in Aurora, Colorado, just over a year ago. For cash. Registered with Morgan's Colorado driver's license. The address listed was an apartment, also in Aurora. Morgan had rented it for a year as was required according to the manager. He paid his rent in catlike clockwork. Never late. But after four months, he forked over the remainder of the year's rent, and disappeared.

"That would've been around the time the burner phones were purchased, wasn't it?" I asked.

"Correct."

"Which would make it around the time things ramped up in Salt Lake City. Right?"

Pancake nodded. "Sort of a timeline, it seems."

"Any evidence of him in Salt Lake?" Ray asked.

"None that I've found so far."

"Who is Greg Morgan?" I asked.

"Don't have much yet but he's twenty-seven and was born in Springfield, Illinois. Apparently, after he finished high school, he worked around the area for a few years. At a bank, then a savings and loan, and finally an insurance company. Must be a pretty smart kid to get those jobs with no college degree. Then, his tracks became scarce. No jobs or taxes paid. No voter registrations. No criminal record. No credit cards. No bank accounts. No home purchases. Rental data will be harder to come by, but I'm still looking into that. Other than this driver's license from Colorado, it's been a pretty quiet three years."

"If he doesn't have a job or a bank account and no credit cards, how does he live?" I asked. "You know, pay for stuff?"

"Don't know, but I'm not through looking."

"I don't like the feel of this," Nicole said.

"Me, either," I said. "Any connection between this guy and Abby?"

"You mean other than the fact that he's apparently hanging out at her apartment?" Pancake said. "Haven't found anything from before last night."

"Is that him?" Nicole asked. "The guy we saw? Could it be someone else who's using this Greg Morgan's car?"

"It could be," Pancake said with a shrug. "But it ain't."

He tapped a few keys, then spun his laptop toward us. Greg Morgan's Colorado driver's license stared back.

"Sure looks like him," Nicole said. "This is all strange and more than a little scary. For Megan."

"Okay," I said. "Here's what I think." Everyone looked at me. "We're assuming, or at least entertaining the possibility, that Abby is each of the other interns. Means she's lived under several false identities for the past year, maybe longer. Now there's this dude, who she obviously knows on some level, who has left few footprints for the past year or so. To me, that means he could also be living under false identities."

"Except for the Colorado licenses and the Denver-area apartment," Ray said.

I thought about that. "True. But to operate the vehicle, maybe even to buy it, he'd need a driver's license. To get that, he'd probably need an address. Since he has a clean record, according to Pancake, getting a license was easy."

Ray nodded. "After four months, he dumped the apartment and moved on."

"To Salt Lake City?" I asked.

"Possible. In fact, I'm getting the feeling that that's exactly what happened. Now, he might be living in the shadows. Like Abby."

"You're thinking they've been traveling together?" Nicole asked. "As made-up people?"

Ray shrugged. "Could be. The problem we have with proving that is that we have Greg Morgan's real name but not his aliases, if he has any, and we have Abby's aliases but not her real name. Makes marrying them to each other over the long haul difficult."

"But they must be," I said. "It's too much of a coincidence for him to be here with her right now. I mean, we have two people who're apparently very secretive. Abby using aliases and this guy keeping his head down for whatever reason. Now they end up here, hanging in the same apartment. All that seems too coincidental for them to not be connected."

"You found nothing to put him in Salt Lake City or Henderson, Nevada?" Nicole asked Pancake.

"Not yet."

"I can't shake the feeling that these two are connected and have been for a while," I said.

"I agree." Ray nodded. "But to make a case, we need more."

Everyone fell silent for a minute.

"Should we bring this to Detective Mills?" Nicole asked.

"And tell her what?" Ray asked. "That we believe Abby isn't who she says she is? That she knows some dude who seems sketchy? Not exactly major crimes there."

"But if they're stalking Megan and they've done it before, even killing one of the women involved, wouldn't that be something she needs to know?"

"We're assuming, actually guessing, that they're connected," Ray said. "We're also assuming that Abby is indeed these other two interns. Lastly, and most importantly, we're assuming that these two have been roaming around doing very bad things to very good people. That's a lot of assumptions and we have nothing that makes them true."

"But you agree," I said, "that this is starting to look like they might be a team?"

"I do," Ray said. "But like I said, we have to prove it."

"How?" Nicole asked.

"I have a couple of ideas."

CHAPTER 44

MEGAN SAT AT her desk, touching up the script for a show set to shoot next week. Her concentration wavered and her mind kept wandering, what if?, what if?, what if? fragmenting every thought. Even the words on the screen before her made no sense. She read and reread each line, but it all seemed nonsensical.

She felt flushed, her heart thumping overtime, pulsing against the back of her eyes. Had Abby picked up on her anxiety? Had she sensed that things had changed? Relax, she told herself. Don't panic. Everything had been more or less normal all morning. Except for the war going on inside her head. Had she betrayed that in any way?

On the positive side, at least she hadn't melted down or said anything stupid. Jake and Nicole bringing in donuts had helped. They lightened the beginning of the day and gave her time to lower her heart rate enough so that she could breathe. All night, after she had learned about the other cases, Megan had dreaded facing Abby. Dreaded even more the need to act normally. As if nothing had changed. The truth? Everything had changed. Or had it? Part of her couldn't grasp the idea that Abby was a serial stalker. Maybe even a killer. Why would she? What the hell was the thrill? The payoff?

It made no sense.

But facts were facts. Abby wasn't Abby. At least not Abby Watson from Portland who went to the University of Oregon. No such person existed.

Who was she? Why did she need to create a fake persona? Surely there was some rational explanation and not the one that stared her in the face. Surely she was hiding from someone and wasn't some stalker herself.

Then there was the guy at her apartment. Who was he? He certainly didn't seem like a one-night deal. She flashed on him coming out on the walkway, casually smoking a cigarette, and making a phone call. He acted as if he lived there, belonged there.

The truth that stared her in the face was that if Abby was her stalker, then he must be her accomplice.

How could she unravel this without exposing her suspicions? Pancake had warned her not to dig or even ask questions, but rather to simply act as if it were a normal day and leave the digging to him and Ray.

She found that easier said than done.

Her brain sparked and sputtered. She couldn't concentrate or think straight. It was as if a flock of birds, fluttering and swirling in no discernable pattern, had invaded her mind.

She felt the need to do something, to ask something, to say something, and not simply sit by passively and let her life dissolve into a jumble of frayed nerves and fear. She searched for a way to find the truth. To get Abby to talk and come clean.

Her chest felt heavy, the air she breathed thick and harsh. She sensed a scream building inside. Yet somehow she managed to hold it together and not do or say anything stupid. So far anyway. It helped that Abby had spent much of the last two hours in one of the studios, helping with a public service piece and then serving as the de facto script girl for two other packages.

But now she was back and ensconced at her desk only ten feet from Megan. It didn't help that the sugar rush from the donuts had waned, making her feel weak and fuzzy. Megan stared at her computer screen, trying to remember what she had been working on. She had three docs open but the words on each seemed to be mostly nonsense.

Get a grip, Megan.

Abby spun her chair toward her. Megan jumped, recoiled, her breath caught.

"What is it?" Abby asked.

Megan took a deep breath. "Nothing."

"I'm sorry. I startled you."

"No, it's me. I'm just all wound up."

Abby rolled her chair toward her, laid a hand on her arm. "I'm so sorry. This guy's really getting to you, isn't he?"

Megan nodded. Moisture blurred her vision. She felt light-headed.

"Are you okay? You look pale."

"I'm fine. I shouldn't have eaten that donut. Sugar always makes me goofy."

Abby squeezed her arm. "Did something change? About any of this?"

Megan froze. Her throat tightened.

"Did your friends uncover something new?"

Megan was afraid to open her mouth. Afraid if she tried to say anything it would come out wrong. Was Abby's question mere curiosity or had she become suspicious? That's the last thing she wanted to happen. The one thing Pancake and Ray had warned her not to allow. They had told her to be calm and casual. As if that were so easy to do. Had she now blown that completely out of the water? She fought the panic that rose inside her.

She had to say something. She couldn't simply sit here, fingers trembling, cold sweat building along her back, tears pushing against her eyes.

"Tell me," Abby said. "What is it?"

Say something, Megan.

"It's nothing. I think this has simply worn me down."

Abby rolled her chair closer. Hugged her. "I'm sorry."

"I'm just being a ninny and acting like a child."

"No, you're not," Abby said. She squeezed her tighter. "These things take a toll. What can I do to help?"

There it was. An opening. One that might diffuse her suspicions.

Megan pulled away. She grabbed Abby by her shoulders. "You've been amazing. My rock, really. You've been here for me every step of the way."

Abby brushed a strand of Megan's hair off her forehead. She smiled. "You'd do the same for me."

Megan broke down. She began to sob. Abby hugged her again and let her get it out. Finally, Megan broke the embrace, swiped tears from her eye, and sat up straight. She sniffed.

"Look at me," Megan said. "Acting like this. It's just not me."

"These are stressful times. I'm amazed you've held it together so well."

"Did you feel this way? When that guy was stalking you?"

Abby rolled her chair back. She gave a weak laugh. "Oh yeah. I was a lot worse than this. I spent a lot of time in my apartment, peeking through the curtains and wondering where he was."

"You knew who he was. Right?"

"Yes. That made it easier. A little anyway. I can't imagine what you're going through. Not knowing. To me, that's the terrifying part."

It is, Megan thought. She tried to read Abby's face. Was she enjoying this? Was her concern real or was she that good an actress? Was she the source of Megan's terror?

"Did you ever consider running away?" Megan asked. "Changing identity and disappearing?"

She immediately regretted the questions. In her head they seemed innocent but when said out loud, they felt more intrusive, even accusatory.

Abby didn't react as if she felt that though. "I did. Move away, that is. I hoped that would end it, but when he continued sending me messages, I did look into changing my name."

"But you didn't?"

"In the end, I decided I liked being me." She smiled. "I wasn't going to let some deranged fool take that away from me."

"He eventually gave up?"

She nodded. "He did. At least I haven't heard from him for years."

"Do you ever worry he might reappear?"

"I do. I did anyway. It's been so long I doubt I'm of interest to him anymore."

"Maybe he found someone else?" Megan said.

"Maybe."

Megan's cell buzzed. She answered. It was Nicole.

"Hi," Megan said. "What's up?"

"Can you talk?"

"Sure."

"Part of Ray's new plan," Nicole said. "Invite Abby to dinner with us tonight."

"Okay."

"I'll explain the details later."

"Okay."

"Six thirty. The Cannery."

"Sounds like fun," Megan said. "I'll let her know." She ended the call.

"That was Nicole," Megan said. "Group dinner tonight if you're free."

"Free? Me? I'll have to check my busy schedule."

Megan smiled. "I take it that's a yes."

"It is." She raised an eyebrow. "I assume Pancake—I still can't get over that name—will be there?"

"Yes."

"Good. He's cute."

CHAPTER 45

"THIS LOOKS GOOD," Ray said.

"Of course it does," Pancake said. "It wasn't too hard to rig."

It wasn't. It had taken Pancake all of thirty minutes to cobble it together. The petition was to block the destruction of two apartment complexes, including the one where Abby and perhaps Greg Morgan lived. It was totally bogus. Pancake hatched the idea as a way for Ray to see the dude face-to-face and to make sure he was indeed Greg Morgan. In reality, they knew it was, but verification never hurt. Besides, Ray wanted to get up close and personal and get a better handle on this guy. Threat assessment was Ray's take.

Since Ray was new on the scene, there was less chance that Morgan had seen him before. The risk wasn't zero since they had no idea what kind of intel and surveillance Morgan had been doing while they had no idea he existed. But it was lower than Pancake or Jake doing the door knocking.

An added benefit of his plan was that with Ray looking Morgan in the eye, Morgan couldn't surprise Pancake while he did his thing. His thing being placing a GPS tracker on Morgan's car.

The problem was that they had done a couple of drive-bys and the Toyota wasn't there. They parked in a convenience store lot a block from Abby's place, a location that gave them a direct view up the street to the complex, including the parking area entrance. They settled in to wait. Pancake worked on a bag of Cheetos—the large family size—and a massive cup of Coke. Ray worked on a can of Mountain Dew.

"What if he's gone?" Pancake asked.

"Then we're wasting our time."

"Not like we ain't done it before." Pancake slurped his Coke. "We've been involved in some crazy shit before, but this is right up near the top."

"It is," Ray said. "Maybe not Billy Wayne Baker crazy, but this's an odd deal."

Dear old Billy Wayne. A serial killer now biding his time in Union Correctional in Raiford, Florida. He had hired them to prove he had only killed five of the seven women he confessed to killing. That was still number one on the hit parade, but this had the potential to slide into second place in Longly Investigation's long list of weird cases.

"I hope to hell he's not gone." He crunched some Cheetos. "I'd love to wring his neck and watch him flop around."

"Very visual."

"I'm a freaking poet."

"A regular Walt Whitman."

"I always liked Coleridge."

"I don't think he's gone," Ray said.

"Sure he is. He died a couple of hundred years ago."

Ray laughed. "I mean Morgan. If they're a team, which might or might not be true, they haven't reached the endgame."

Pancake grunted.

"I know. I don't like to dwell on that either. But maybe tracking him will give us what we need to drop some charges on them before they do something stupid."

"Hopefully when we finally run him to ground, he'll have that phone in his pocket," Pancake said. "Sort of put a bow on this whole deal."

"Odds are it's gone and he's moved on to another one."

Which is what the stalker had done. In each of the three cases. Smart enough to use one phone a dozen times or so and then dump it. Never to be heard from again. Actually, pretty clever and made getting any kind of fix on him almost impossible.

"It'd still be fun to pick him up and shake his pockets clean," Pancake said.

"It would."

"Probably not the smartest move."

"No," Ray said.

"But it would be a hoot."

"At least that." Ray finished his Dew and crushed the can in his fist. "I meant to ask earlier after you spoke with Graham Gordy. Anything useful come up?"

Pancake shook his head. "Of course, he couldn't use the NSA computers and had to do it all from home on his own time, but he managed to determine that the guy wasn't plugged into a VPN or anything like that." He grunted. "I didn't think he was. He also said he'd done a pretty deep dive into the dark web but didn't find any evidence of this guy tickling those wires."

"Makes sense," Ray said. "For this, all he needed was a basketful of burner phones and he could remain more or less invisible as long as needed."

"Low tech," Pancake said. "But highly effective."

Pancake gripped the steering wheel. He hated waiting. Stakeouts were part of the job and he had done it way too many times, but he still didn't like it. Felt like it was unproductive time.

The minutes crept by.

"What do you think their play will be?" Pancake asked.

Ray shrugged. "Based on previous adventures, they'll try to nab Megan and take her off somewhere. If Dana Roderick is any yardstick, it won't be pretty."

"Maybe we should just shoot this guy in the head and be done with it."

"I thought you wanted to wring his neck?"

"Either way's fine with me. So, when and where? Best guess?"

"Soon and I don't know. With Megan either at work or with us, they don't have many opportunities. Making the transit from point A to point B would be her most vulnerable time."

"Lots of traffic out there," Pancake said. "Pretty much all the time. At least from what I've seen."

"Makes it risky. A citizen in the right place at the right time could mess it all up," Ray said. "Or get killed themselves."

"Which means they'd be in the wrong place at the wrong time."

"It's all perspective."

"True that."

Pancake completed his demolition of the defenseless Cheetos and wadded the bag.

"Feel better?"

"I do." Pancake pointed up the street. "Showtime."

The silver Toyota rolled up the street in their direction. It turned and disappeared down the parking ramp. A couple of minutes later Greg Morgan came out, climbed the few steps to the first floor, and entered the apartment.

As planned, Pancake did a drive-by, made a U-turn, and when he again reached the complex, he descended into the parking area. It was mostly empty, everybody at work or off doing errands or whatever. Pancake slid into the empty slot next to the Toyota.

Pancake slipped his Bluetooth earpiece in one ear. Ray called him. He answered.

"All good," Pancake said.

Ray slipped his phone into his shirt pocket, where it would pick up his conversation with Morgan, or whoever this was. He walked up the ramp and out of sight. Pancake reached into the back seat and grabbed a black canvas bag. Inside he found the device and set about prepping it.

He heard Ray's knock and then Greg Morgan's voice.

> MORGAN: "What do you want?"
>
> RAY: "I have a petition I hope you'll sign."
>
> MORGAN: "Not interested."
>
> RAY: "It would greatly help if you would."

Pancake stepped out of the car and inspected the area. All clear. He knelt next to the front wheel well of the Toyota.

> MORGAN: "Help who?"
>
> RAY: "You and the other tenants. You see, they want to tear down this complex and another one just up the street. To put in another shopping center. What we need is more housing, not more concrete and coffee shops."

With a rag, Pancake wiped the dust and grime off a portion of the frame.

> MORGAN: "I don't live here. I'm just visiting. So I don't really give a shit."
>
> RAY: "Maybe the renter is here?"

MORGAN: "She's not. Have a nice day."

Pancake heard the door slam just as the magnetic GPS snapped against the metal frame. He checked his iPhone app. A blinking red dot stared back at him.

Ray came down the ramp. "All good?"

Pancake nodded and climbed in the car. "Let's roll."

"It's him," Ray said. "No doubt now."

CHAPTER 46

NICOLE LIKED RAY'S plan. It seemed simple and straightforward, and just might work. If she didn't screw it up, that is. She would head over to the The Cannery and hook up with Abby while everyone else laid back and waited at her condo. So she could have some girl-girl time and see what she could pry out of Abby about her life. Hopefully, she'd say something useful or slip up on some fact or maybe even drop clues about her newly minted "roommate," or whoever the dude was. Worth a try anyway. Phase two of the plan would await Pancake's arrival.

As Nicole walked almost literally across the street to the restaurant, she felt tension gather in her back. Not that she was afraid of Abby or anything like that. After all, she had a bunch of Krav Maga classes under her belt. Her goal was to trick Abby into revealing something she wanted to keep hidden. Something that would create a connection to Salt Lake City and Henderson, Nevada. Nicole simply had to do so without revealing the suspicion that now surrounded Abby. No pressure there.

Megan had done her part today. She had played it cool and casual and had gotten Abby to join them for dinner. According to Megan, Abby hadn't hesitated to accept the invitation and hadn't conveyed an ounce of suspicion. Now it was up to Nicole. She slapped her game face on and called on all her acting classes to play the role of clueless friend. She climbed the stairs to the entrance door.

When she entered the bar, she saw Abby. She sat on a barstool, looking at her phone, her purse on the bar top.

"Hey there," Nicole said.

Abby twisted toward her. "Hey." She looked beyond Nicole. "Where is everyone?"

"They're coming. Ray and Pancake are doing some last-minute stuff on some case they have back in Gulf Shores. Jake and Megan are primping. I decided to come on over so you wouldn't think we had bailed."

"I just got here myself."

Nicole climbed up on the adjacent stool. "I'm buying. What are you drinking?"

"I haven't decided."

"I'm thinking maybe a margarita."

"Hmmm. That does sound good."

Nicole waved to the bartender. He came their way and Nicole ordered a pair of Cadillac margaritas.

"So, Jake's primping?" Abby smiled.

"Yeah. He takes twice as long as me."

"He doesn't need it."

"He is pretty, isn't he?"

Abby laughed. "He is."

Nicole shifted her braided hair so that it hung over her other shoulder, the one away from Abby. "Megan's moving slow. This's all wearing her out."

"I know. I've seen it progress day by day. Particularly since we got back from Malibu."

"Yeah. That was creepy. Guy taking pictures and delivering those dead flowers. Way up there. Then coming back to find her condo had been broken into."

"It's more than creepy," Abby said. "It's scary and makes her feel vulnerable for sure."

The margaritas arrived. They toasted and took sips.

"Your guy?" Nicole asked. "The dude that harassed you? How long did that go on?"

"Several months. Around seven or eight."

"Did you ever consider pulling up stakes and running away?"

Abby eyed her. "Megan asked me the same thing this morning."

Uh-oh. Had Megan slipped up? Dug where Ray had asked her not to? Was that suspicion she saw behind Abby's eyes? She scrambled for something to say, finally landing on, "She did? You don't think she's thinking that way, do you?"

"Do you?"

"She's never said anything like that to me," Nicole said. "I think if she was leaning that way, she'd have talked to me about it."

"I agree," Abby said. "She really admires you."

"As I do her." Nicole took a sip. "So, did you? Ever consider running?"

"Sure did. I couldn't sleep. I looked over my shoulder all the time. Everywhere I went I felt like I was being watched."

"You called in the cops, right?"

"For what it was worth. They couldn't do much. Sort of like now with Megan. In my situation, they couldn't, or wouldn't, do anything until the end when he became truly threatening."

"What exactly did he do that was so threatening?"

"His texts became more personal, and crude. Telling me all the things he was going to do to me." She shrugged. "Sexual things. But the final straw was when he confronted me in a mall parking lot. He grabbed my arm and tried to drag me into his car."

"My God," Nicole said. "What did you do?"

"I screamed and hit him with my purse. The police showed up in a couple of minutes and took him away. After that, they took my complaints seriously. But for the first six months, I was on my own."

"Stalkers have rights, I guess."

"It felt like he had more than I did." She stirred her margarita with a finger and then licked it. "What about you? You had more than one episode. Were the cops very helpful?"

"Actually, they were. But the Beverly Hills Police take that sort of thing seriously. It helped that my parents and Uncle Charles, of course, carry a bit of weight in that town."

"You lived in Beverly Hills?"

Nicole shrugged. "That's where I grew up. 90210 all the way."

"Sounds idyllic. Well, except for the stalkers."

"It was. I was lucky. I chose my parents well."

Abby laughed. Easy and relaxed. If she was acting, she had some chops. Nicole saw no hint of stress or concern or, more importantly, suspicion.

"It sounds more glamorous than it was," Nicole continued. "Sure, the neighborhood was cool. Lots of actors, producers, and other Hollywood folks were in and out of the house all the time. But I still had school and boyfriend issues like every girl. They just dressed better and drove better cars."

"Why did you move down to Alabama? Did the stalkers have anything to do with that?"

"They did."

That was a lie, but Nicole sensed it's what Abby wanted to hear. If she was involved in this, and had a partner who fired the salvos while Abby was near Megan and could feed off the terror that followed, she would probably get a similar thrill from hearing the fear and terror someone else had faced. Maybe the game was to drive Megan to give up her job and her life as Tiffany Cole had done. Or was her plan to kill her like Dana Roderick? Be cool, Nicole told herself.

"Bet that was tough," Abby said.

"It was. But at least I got to live in Uncle Charles' place back there. It's impressive."

"Based on his Malibu home, I imagine it is."

"Also, I got this screenplay finished. So, all was not lost."

"To your movie's success," Abby said.

They clinked glasses again.

"What about you?" Nicole asked. "You grew up in Portland, right?"

"I did."

"I've been there a couple times. Nice city. I really loved that area where all the cool restaurants and bars are." Nicole snapped her fingers. "What's that called?"

"The Pearl District."

"That's it. Fun area."

"I got into my share of trouble," Abby said with a laugh.

"What about your family? Any brothers or sisters?"

A slight hesitation. "No. I'm an only child."

"Me too." A sip of margarita. "Were you in Portland when you came here for this job?"

"No." A headshake. "I left there right after school and moved in with a distant cousin in Chicago. I stayed for nearly six months, but I couldn't find a job there. Well, except for waiting tables or serving coffee, neither of which is my thing. Then I met a guy and moved with him to Tampa. That didn't work. He was a dick."

"As guys are wont to be," Nicole said.

"True. That's when I decided to actually use my journalism degree and maybe get into broadcast news. I did some research, found this gig, and moved."

"By yourself?"

Another hesitation. "Yeah. It was scary as hell. All the way across the country to a place where I didn't know anyone. I wasn't sure I'd like the job or the people. There were lots of unknowns."

"Ballsy move."

Abby shrugged. "It was but I'm proud of myself for doing it. Then meeting Megan? That was the icing. She's great and has really been a good friend and mentor."

"She's good people."

"You've known her a while?"

"Years."

"How'd you get in this P.I. business?" Abby asked.

"Only peripherally. It's really Ray and Pancake. But Jake and I hang around with them a lot."

"Have they come up with anything new? Or anything at all?"

"Not really. This guy's pretty clever. He doesn't leave many footprints."

"Sure seems so."

"There's two pretty ladies."

It was Pancake. As planned.

"Either of you looking for a tall, handsome, witty, redhead?"

Nicole and Abby laughed.

"I just might be," Abby said.

"Well, you found him."

The bartender appeared and took Pancake's drink order. Took only a minute to pour a dose of bourbon over ice. Pancake lifted his glass. "To friends."

Nicole and Abby returned the toast.

Pancake slipped his phone from his pocket and passed it to the bartender. "Take a picture of us. I can't have too many pictures with hot chicks on my Facebook page."

Abby's back stiffened slightly. She glanced around. She looked like she might flee. But Pancake laid one hand on Nicole's shoulder, the other on Abby's. He leaned forward so his head was between theirs, and the bartender snapped a couple of photos.

Phase two complete.

Jake, Ray, and Megan showed up.

CHAPTER 47

"How'd it go?"

"Not well." She placed her purse on the coffee table and flopped on the other end of the sofa. "They're suspicious."

"How?"

That was the question she'd asked herself as she drove from the restaurant to the apartment. Where had the mistake been made? Or was she overreading everything? She had run back through all the bar conversations, and those over the dinner table. No, she had read it correctly. She had good instincts. She always had and she knew to listen to her gut. Right now it said it was time to shut this down and move on. Too bad since they were just getting to the fun part. She had plans to amp things up, create even more fear, make it thick enough to taste. Her favorite part. Well, except for the end. When the pain and terror was right in front of her and she had total control over every ounce of it. That was definitely worth the price of admission. The months of planning, the months of worming into Megan's life, and now that the payoff neared, they might have to cut and run. Not before the finale but before she had rendered all she could from this project.

Project. She liked that word. It seemed to fit.

"Did we do something wrong?"

"No. I think it's those friends of hers."

Greg Morgan sighed. He eyed his sister, Stacy. "I looked into them. Longly Investigations out of Gulf Shores, Alabama."

"Yeah. Things changed, at least to me, when Ray Longly showed up. His son Jake and his big redheaded friend seemed okay. Not a real threat as far as I could tell. But the dad? He's no fool. You can see it, sense it, in his mannerisms, body language, face, the whole thing. It was like he was always absorbing information. Even when he was making small talk. I don't think much gets by him."

"They have a good reputation as far as I could tell. What did they ask you?"

"It was mostly Nicole. She came early. Actually, on time I guess, but she said the others were delayed and would be along soon. Looking back, I think that was the plan. For her to be all friendly and see what she could get out of me."

"Okay, again, what did she ask?"

"Where I was from. Where I went to school and where I worked and lived. Did I have any siblings? That sort of stuff." She stood and walked to the kitchen. "Want a beer?"

"Sure."

She grabbed a pair of Bud Lights, returned to the sofa, handing one to her brother. She twisted off the cap and chugged nearly half of it.

"What'd you tell her?"

"The usual bullshit. I kept everything vague and gave her nothing that was real or would lead back our way."

"What's the plan?"

She sighed. "As much as I hate to, I think we'll have to end this."

Greg nodded. "Tomorrow?"

"Yeah."

"Here's the million-dollar question. Do you think they know anything about me?"

Abby/Stacy considered that. "I don't see how. We've followed our blueprint perfectly. You've never showed your face. We've never been in public together."

"True."

She took another slug of beer. "I hate to have to do this. We were just getting to the fun part."

"Oh, we have a few fun parts left."

She gave a half nod. "Yes we do. Is everything set?"

"Sure is. I have the house all set. It's isolated and abandoned. Out the Ortega Highway a ways. It's dusty and ratty but it has some furniture. A bed, sofa, a few other things. The water and electricity are on and working. Everything we'll need."

"Sounds lovely."

"We've stayed in worse places."

"I have the plan to grab her all ready to do. Send her a couple of texts in the morning. Maybe make them all lovey dovey. Keep her calm right now."

"Will do."

"What do you want to do with my car?"

"The usual. Since we bought it for cash and never changed the registration, we can dump it."

"Not here."

"No, not here. We'll wipe it down and drop it on a street or in a parking lot. Leave the keys so it'll be stolen and probably chopped."

"When?"

He glanced at his watch. "It's ten now. After midnight or so, we'll head out and leave it where it'll be stolen again. Done deal."

She finished her beer. "Okay. Tomorrow morning you can drop me a couple of blocks from the station. I'll text you when I get things set up with Megan. Say around eleven."

"Sounds good. I'll load up the ice chests and grab some supplies. Then I'll hang in the area from ten thirty on. I'll only be a minute away."

She stood. "Guess we better get packed up and then get to wiping down the car." She waved a hand. "And this place."

CHAPTER 48

THE NEXT MORNING, Nicole and I followed Megan to the studio, then down the ramp into the parking area. When she pulled into a slot, I slid up behind her and lowered my window.

"Get your game face on," Nicole said.

"Will this ever end?" Megan asked.

"Just be cool," I said. "Pancake said he had something and was digging a little deeper. Hopefully it'll be something we can use."

"When is your filming?" Nicole asked.

"Eleven thirty, noon, something like that."

"We'll be back for that," I said.

"That's really all I have today so I'll be ready to go after that."

"Just relax," Nicole said. "Be yourself."

There it was again. Act normal.

Megan shifted her oversized purse to her other shoulder. "That's what you said yesterday, and I spent all morning wound into a knot."

"But you managed," Nicole said. "In fact, you did great. Today is simply more of the same."

"I guess I don't really have a choice, do I?"

"Unless you skip school," I said. "Pancake can create a doctor's note for you. He has experience along those lines."

Megan laughed. "I'll see you guys later."

"We'll call if and when we have anything new," I said.

We watched her climb the stairs toward the studio and then headed toward the condo.

"I hope Pancake has worked some of his magic," Nicole said.

Boy, had he ever.

When we walked in, Pancake and Ray were at the dining room table, laptops open.

"What's new?" I asked.

"Lots," Pancake said. "Give me a minute."

A minute turned into an hour. Nicole and I retreated to her deck since we had nothing else to do. Jimmy Fabrick was backing his boat out of the slip. He had a young lady on board. A different one than the one we had seen before. Boy did get around. He waved and then motored up the channel toward the open water.

"Did Megan seem more distracted to you?" Nicole asked.

"She's been like that for several days," I said.

"It seems worse."

"Can't say I blame her. I think the pressure and the unknown is weighing pretty heavy right now. I just hope she doesn't panic and say anything stupid."

"She's tough," Nicole said, "She'll be okay." She clasped my hand. "I hope I didn't screw up last night."

"What do you mean?"

She let out a breath. "I don't know. While I was asking Abby questions, about her background, that sort of thing, I felt that she was becoming more wary. Like she knew what I was doing."

"She seemed fine at dinner. Like her usual self."

"You're probably right."

Pancake appeared at the open slider. "Let's talk."

Once we were seated at the table he began and unfolded a story and then some.

"You already know that Greg Morgan was from Springfield, Illinois, and after high school worked various financial jobs. He rented an apartment there until three years ago. Then we lose track of him until just over a year ago when he rented an apartment briefly and snagged a Colorado driver's license in Aurora. Then he again dropped off the radar."

"How long was that before Dana Roderick was murdered in Salt Lake City?" I asked.

"Three or four months."

"Which is about how long her intern Liz Ingram worked with her. Right?"

"Exactly," Pancake said. "Now to the good stuff."

I had seen the look Pancake now gave us on his face before. It meant he had found something we might not like, or maybe we would. Either way, it would be unexpected. He always had a flair for the dramatic. Anticipation elevated the hair on my arms and scalp.

"Seems his parents died in a house explosion," Pancake said. "Gas deal."

"Really?" Nicole asked.

"Looks like someone left a stove burner on and, well, things went kablooey."

"Morgan wasn't hurt?" I asked.

"He was already out of the house, working, living on his own in an apartment." Pancake caught my gaze. "With his sister."

"Sister?"

"Named Stacy Morgan."

"Okay."

"So I dug into their high school yearbooks. They were posted online. Lucky us." He spun his computer toward us. "Here's his picture."

The page held a dozen faces. One was Greg Morgan.

"This was his senior year." Pancake flipped to another screen. "Now three year later, here's Stacy's senior picture." He scrolled through several pages, stopping on one.

More faces and right smack in the middle was Stacy Morgan.

The person we knew as Abby Watson.

She was obviously younger then and her hair was longer but the eyes, the mouth, the contour of her chin left no doubt.

Nicole took in a breath. "Oh no."

"There's more," Pancake said. "Just to be sure, I sent the photo the barkeep took of us last night to Scott Hartman in Salt Lake and Richard McCluskey in Nevada. Both were ninety percent sure that Abby was the same person as the interns they'd hired. I also sent it to Tiffany Cole. She said that even though the hair was different, she was virtually one hundred percent sure that Abby was her intern Beth Macomb."

"Looks like our little Abby's been a busy girl," Ray said.

"A bad girl, too, it seems," Pancake continued. "Shortly after their parents' death, that would be just over three years ago, they dropped out of sight. You know about Greg, but Abby—or Stacy—went even deeper underground. No footprints. No tax or voting records. No jobs I could find. No residences. No driver's license. No accounts. No credit cards and phones. No social media presence. No nothing."

"Are you thinking they killed their parents?" I asked. "By exploding the family home?"

"They inherited a pile of cash," Ray said. "Nearly two million."

I whistled. "Adult money."

"Money that also disappeared," Pancake said.

"What do you mean *disappeared*?" I asked.

"Once the insurance paid out. Life, home, even the two cars in the garage, the cash went into one account. At a bank where Greg had previously worked." He shrugged. "Then poof. It went away."

"He cashed out?" Nicole said.

"How do you cash out millions?" I asked. "Where do you put it?"

"Not easy on either count," Pancake said. "But possible. I haven't gotten that worked out yet but the cash means they have the where-withal to disappear."

"Or go on a killing spree," Ray said. He stood, walked to the sink. He turned, leaning against the counter, arms folded over his chest. "It's actually brilliant. Stacy, or whoever her persona of the month is—here being Abby—is the face of the operation. She's on the inside, up close and personal, where she can revel in the fear and anxiety the duo creates. Greg is completely off the radar doing all the mischief. That gives her a solid alibi."

"Like being in pictures made in Malibu?" Nicole said.

"Exactly. The perfect alibi. Plus being present when flowers were delivered the next morning and being with all of us when Megan's condo was invaded. Not to mention that she was right by Megan's side when most of the texts and emails came in."

"Amazing," Nicole said. "And diabolical."

"I like diabolical," Pancake said. "I've been asking myself for days that if Abby—Stacy—was involved, what was the payoff? Now I think we know. She wanted to be near the damage to see and feel the panic she and her brother created. Acting like the supportive friend while relishing every moment."

"Which would place them in the thrill killer category," Ray said. "What they did to Dana Roderick was psychopathic and very personal. Something only someone who enjoyed it would do."

"Do thrill killers work as teams?" I asked.

"Sure do," Pancake said. "In fact, the case that more or less defined this was a team effort. Back in the 1920s, Nathan Leopold and Richard Loeb killed Bobby Franks just to see what it was like. I think that's when this type of killing was first labeled as such."

He shrugged. "There have been others. Even husband and wife teams."

"Sort of redefines diabolical," I said.

"This is amazing," Nicole said. "You simply can't make this up."

Pancake smiled. "Somehow I think you could." He raised an eyebrow. "Maybe your next screenplay."

"Bottom line is that it looks like they're a team," Ray said.

Now things made more sense. We had been thinking there must be more than Abby involved in this. Nothing else fit. But this? These stalkings, now in three different states, weren't obsessions. Not someone falling in love with a TV image. Not some feverish infatuation but rather they were the work of a pair of miscreants seeking pleasure.

"What now?" I asked.

"A visit to Detective Mills," Ray said. "If we show her everything we have, I think she'll see how all these are connected. Salt Lake City, Henderson, the situation here with Megan. Maybe it'll be enough for her to secure an arrest warrant. Or at least get her team more deeply involved."

"If she can't?" Nicole asked.

"Then we fix it," Pancake said.

"How?"

"Personally, I'd start with a hard interrogation of old Greg." He smiled.

Ray raised an eyebrow. "He never did sign the petition. We could always give him another chance."

"Yeah, that was rude of him," Pancake said. "Boy needs some manners."

CHAPTER 49

NICOLE AND I followed Ray and Pancake to the Newport Police Department. On the way, Nicole called Megan. She put it on speaker.

When Megan answered, Nicole said, "Can you talk?"

A brief hesitation. "Yeah."

"Don't react. Pancake uncovered some very interesting facts."

"What?"

"Don't want to go into it right now," Nicole said. "Laugh like I just told you something funny."

Megan did, following it up with, "That's wild."

"What's wild?" It was Abby's voice in the background.

"Oh, just Pancake doing some silly stuff," Megan said. Then back to us, "So, what are you guys up to?"

"Heading over to see Detective Mills."

"Sounds good."

"Then hopefully she'll be with us when we head your way. Maybe dragging a pair of handcuffs with her."

"Really?"

"We wanted you to know that another hour or so and maybe this'll be over with," I said. "All you have to do is hang in until then."

"Got it covered."

"Laugh again," Nicole said. "Then say you'll see us before noon."

Megan did. She then added, "I got two more texts from Mr. Wonderful this morning."

"And?"

"He was all upbeat and said he loved me madly. Seems he still wants to get married."

"No threats then?" I asked.

"Sounds like he's in a good mood today," Megan said. "Maybe he's mellowing."

"We'll see you soon," Nicole said. "Be cool until then."

"Will do."

Nicole disconnected.

"She's good," I said.

"She is. But she's scared. I could hear it in her voice."

I had felt it too. "Hopefully Abby, or Stacy, or whoever the hell she is, didn't pick up on it."

"Hopefully."

We parked a block away and walked back to the PD. I had an uncomfortable feeling but I wasn't sure why. To me, everything Pancake had uncovered screamed that Abby and her brother—boy, did that come out of nowhere—were dangerous stalkers and murderers and should be locked away for a long time, if not forever. That seemed obvious. But I also knew that cops and district attorneys and judges saw the world differently than I did. Would Mills think we had enough to slap the cuffs on? Would a DA sign off on it? Would a judge issue a warrant? If so, great. If not, where were we?

I knew how Pancake would answer these questions. He'd say it was time to kick the door down and have a heart-to-heart with Greg and Stacy. A heart-to-heart with Pancake usually involved pain. That would actually be fun to watch.

We found Detective Claire Mills in her office.

Pancake and Ray went through everything. Pancake used his iPad to show her the pics and news reports and other scraps of information he had collected. While they unpacked it all, I saw the creases in Mills' forehead progressively deepen.

"How'd you uncover all this?" Mills asked.

"That's sort of what we do," Pancake said.

"Want a job? We could use this kind of thing around here."

"We're set up a couple of thousand miles away," Ray said. "Tough commute."

"You could move."

"Can't," Pancake said. "We'd be too far from Captain Rocky's"

Mills gave a quizzical look.

"My place," I said. "In Gulf Shores."

"Jake lets me eat and drink for free."

"Can you say bankruptcy?" I said.

Mills laughed.

"What do you think of all this?" Ray asked, getting back to business.

"It's a hot mess," she said.

"Enough for a warrant?" I asked.

"If it were me, I'd go over there and smack them around. Convince them that confessing was less painful." She smiled. "But rules are rules. Even if they're maddening at times. To answer your question, I think this will work. I know a couple of friendly judges, and prosecutors. Let me get on it."

"Time might be critical here," Pancake said.

"Give me an hour and I'll know by then."

"Sounds good."

"What are you going to do in the meantime?" Mills asked.

"Keep an eye on Megan," I said. "We're headed over to the studio now."

Mills looked at Pancake. "Don't hurt anybody."

"You're no fun."

CHAPTER 50

CURIOSITY, PLUS A healthy measure of anxiety, gnawed at Megan to the point that her temples throbbed and her stomach felt queasy. More than once she feared she'd have to rush to the restroom and empty her stomach of the coffee she had consumed. Too much coffee, in fact.

Nicole had said she had news and from her tone it sounded big. What had they found? Was it truly the game changer they needed? Would Detective Mills actually show up with handcuffs? Would this finally be over?

Megan tried to stay busy, or at least appear that she was. She couldn't concentrate so she mostly pecked away at her computer and tried to avoid as much interaction with Abby as possible. No small task since Abby sat a mere five feet away, tapping away at her own computer.

Darren came in. "I have some images for you." He spread them on his desktop.

Megan rolled her chair that way. Abby walked over and stood behind her, peering over her shoulder. The images were for a piece they were creating on Roger's Garden, a local, very high-end, nursery in Newport Beach. More than that, it also housed one of those farm-to-market restaurants called Farmhouse. Popular and also high-end.

"I like this one and that one," Abby said, pointing.

To Megan, the images were mostly a blur. Her eyes and her brain refused to focus. She took the easy out. "I agree."

As she rolled back to her desk, Abby asked, "What time are we shooting today?"

"The crew said they'd be set up around eleven thirty," Megan said.

"What do you have after that?"

"Nothing. Short day."

"Okay," Abby said. "After we wrap, I'm going over to the Roger's Garden to meet with the head chef. I told him I'd let him know what time."

Abby sat at her desk, scooped up her phone, and began thumbing a text. "Okay. All done." She spun her chair toward Megan. "Oh, I almost forgot. I have your coffee maker down in my trunk."

"Coffee maker?"

"You know. I told you I'd look into Keurigs for us. I found a good price so I bought us each one."

"You didn't have to do that."

"I wanted to." She stood. "Come on. Let's run down and we can put it in your car."

Megan hesitated. Glanced at her computer.

"Might get busy later," Abby said. "Or I might forget again."

"Okay." Megan glanced at Darren. "Back in a sec."

"Need any help?" he asked.

"I think we can handle a coffee maker," Abby said. "You have enough to do."

Megan followed Abby down the stairs and into the parking deck.

"I'll get it," Abby said. "Pop your trunk open."

Megan punched the button on her key fob. As the lid rose, a jolt pierced her neck and took her off her feet. The world spun, faded, not completely to black, but rather to a murky gray. She was vaguely aware of car tires squealing and someone moving around her. She felt her ankles and wrists being bound. Duct tape? That's what it felt like. Then someone pressed a broad strip across her mouth. As the world began to sort itself out, she felt herself lifted and placed on the back seat. A blanket dropped over her. Thick, heavy, and coarse, it seemed smothering.

The car engine churned as the vehicle rose from beneath ground and humped over the speed bump at the top. A couple of turns, accelerating, decelerating, a few more bumps, traffic noise, a car horn. Then the whine of the tires as the car reached what she assumed was freeway speed.

The fog began to clear and everything returned to a sharper focus. The thick blanket allowed no light to filter through. The car continued at high speed, the ride now smoother.

Megan had no illusions about what was unfolding. Wasn't this what happened up in Salt Lake City to that girl that was killed? She was also a TV reporter. What was her name? She knew. Pancake had told her, but she couldn't retrieve it. Is that what would happen to her? Would people forget her name?

She tested her bindings, tugged and twisted, but found no play whatsoever. Tears pressed against her eyes accompanied by a wave of nausea, followed by a new fear. What if she got sick? She'd drown in her own vomit.

Relax, she told herself. Think.

They were definitely on a freeway. For fifteen minutes, maybe more, they had moved at a steady clip. Where were they taking her? Up the 55? North or south on the 405?

"There's a cop up ahead." It was Abby talking. "Slow down."

Megan felt the car slow slightly. Did the cops know she was here in this car? Were they pulling them over? She heard no siren, only the hum of tires on concrete.

"He's giving a ticket." A male voice. "He isn't even looking at us."

"Still, best to stay well below the speed limit. Getting pulled over now would be a problem, don't you think?"

"I know. I'm just anxious to get there."

"Me, too," Abby said. "But we got away clean. Let's not press our luck."

Anxious to get there? The man's words echoed in her head. Get where? For what purpose? A sob lurched against her chest and she let out a low moan. She tried to sit up, but a hand pushed her back down. The blanket slipped down a few inches, and she found herself looking Abby in the face. She had leaned into the gap between the two front seats and now stared at Megan.

"Don't fucking move," Abby said. "I'll taze you again if you try anything stupid."

The blanket again fell over Megan's face. She couldn't see, or breathe. She felt as if she'd been buried alive.

CHAPTER 51

AFTER LEAVING THE Newport PD, Nicole and I headed toward Channel 16 to see what was going on and to prop up Megan. Our feeling was she was getting shaky and could do with friendly faces and moral support while we waited for Detective Mills to call. If she called. If she could secure a warrant. Seemed a no-brainer to me. With all that Pancake had cobbled together, Abby/Stacy and her brother, Greg, looked as guilty as homemade sin.

But what did I know?

After Ray admonished us to "be cool," of course, he and Pancake opted to drop by the condo so Pancake could look into a couple of things while we waited on news from Detective Mills.

Nicole and I pulled into the parking lot out front of Channel 16. Everything appeared normal. Not sure why I expected it wouldn't be, but on the way over I felt tension in my neck. As if some disaster loomed beyond the windshield and that we just might roll into chaos. I hate that feeling.

Inside, Phyllis P greeted us with her usual smile. A good sign that all was well in Channel-16-land. Now, I felt stupid for getting all wound up in my what-if thoughts.

"I think everyone's back in their offices," she said. She glanced at her watch. "They have another half an hour before the studio will be ready for them."

We walked down to the office. No Megan. No Abby. Darren Slater was hunched over his desk, nose buried in an array of photos.

"Hey," I said.

He jumped.

"Sorry."

"No problem. I was lost in all this stuff." He waved one hand over his desk and then leaned back and massaged his neck with the other.

"Where's Megan?" Nicole asked.

He spun his chair. He seemed to be surprised she wasn't at her desk. "Oh, she and Abby went down to get a coffee maker."

That made no sense. "What coffee maker?"

"Apparently they both wanted one of those Keurig things." He pointed toward the machine in the corner. "Abby picked up a couple and they went down to transfer Megan's to her car."

An electric prickle crept up my back. I glanced at Nicole. Her face betrayed that she felt the same thing. Okay, take a breath. This is nothing big. Merely a friend doing a favor for another. Except that Abby wasn't Megan's friend. I was sure of that now.

"When will they get back?" Nicole asked.

"I thought they were." He looked at his computer screen. "Oh, they've been gone over half an hour."

We were out the door, down the stairs, and into the underground parking in what seemed less than a second. Megan's car sat in its usual slot. The trunk lid stood open. No Megan. No Abby.

That prickly feeling spiked, rose into my neck, over my scalp, and flashed down both arms.

"Look," Nicole said. She pointed.

Megan's keys and fob lay near the rear tire. Nicole picked them up. I called Ray.

CHAPTER 52

MEGAN HAD LOST track of time and determining where she was became virtually impossible. The thick, heavy blanket blocked all vision, even light. Maybe a faint glow but that might be her imagination. It smelled like wool and its abrasiveness underlined that belief. Hearing and feeling, the only senses available to her, weren't helpful.

She had tried to follow their travels as best she could. They had been on a freeway for maybe twenty or thirty minutes, but she had no idea of how far they had gone, or in which direction. Then they slowed and took an off-ramp. No doubt about that as the car rose up an incline before coming to a stop. She could feel as much as hear the engine's idle. They moved forward and swung left onto a more uneven road. She felt what seemed to be several lane changes and could easily hear the engines of other cars.

It was at that point that she concluded that she had to do something and that this just might be her last chance to do so. Not that she had many options, but maybe if she sat up, kicked at a window, and made some kind of fuss, someone alongside would see her, all wrapped up in a blanket and struggling, tape across her mouth. If so, they might alert the police.

She struggled to rise but didn't get very far. A hand against her chest pushed her back against the rear seat.

"I told you to stay down," Abby said. "Or do you want some more of this?"

She heard the sizzle of the taser.

She tried to say something, but it came out as muffled grunts and squeaks.

"What's the matter? Cat got your tongue?" Abby laughed. Then she said, "Relax. We're almost there."

Relax? Was she freaking serious? Abby and whoever was with her and snatched her from the parking area, had bound her like a carpet roll, and covered her with a blanket that blocked all light and seemed to suck the oxygen from the air. Relaxing wasn't an option.

Abby had also said that they were almost there. Where was there? More importantly, what would happen then?

Soon the sounds of traffic and civilization fell away. The road began to wind. Right, left, up, down, bouncing her against the seat. Her head banged against the door panel.

Could she open that door? How? And then what? Slither out? To where? The road, a ditch, under the moving car. Even if by some miracle she survived that, she wouldn't be able to run or fight or scream or anything. She felt tears gather in her eyes.

Think, Megan. There must be some way out of this.

Did Nicole and Jake know she had been taken? Did they call the police? Even if they did, how would they ever find her?

The car slowed and turned uphill onto a rough and serpentine road, bumping and gyrating over ruts, gravel pinging the undercarriage.

"This is in the middle of no-fucking-where," Abby said.

"Told you. No one ever comes up here it seems. I've been here four times now. Never seen anyone."

"Rugged for sure."

"Oh yeah. Nothing but hills and scrub brush."

Where could they be? What part of Orange County would have that kind of terrain? Most of it was houses, and parks, and golf courses, and shopping malls. And Disneyland.

The car took a left and a hard bounce, then accelerated up a steeper hill.

"There it is," the man said.

"Not as bad as I envisioned," Abby replied. "Pull around back."

"Why? Nobody's going to come up this way."

"You never know. Better if the car's hidden from the road."

"If you say so."

"I say so. We got this far and got away with all our other adventures because we've been overly cautious, overly prepared, and left nothing to chance."

A minute later the car jerked to a stop and the rear door opened. The blanket slid away and Megan looked into the man's face. He smiled.

Abby appeared at his side. "Let's get her inside."

The man grabbed her beneath her arms, tugged her from the car, and stood her up. Hard to balance with her ankles taped together. She wobbled but he held her up.

She looked around. She was indeed in the middle of nowhere. Rolling sandy hills and scrub brush in every direction. No houses or any signs of civilization in sight. The house was dirty, dingy stucco that had once been tan. The roof was flat and made of corrugated metal that was rusted and bent along the edges.

Her stomach knotted. No one would ever find her here.

The man lifted her over his shoulder, told Abby to grab the ropes, and then carried her inside. She swiveled her head, taking in everything she could see. They moved through a kitchen, an empty dining room, and down a short hallway to a bedroom. He dropped her on the bed. The mattress was flimsy, lumpy, and sagged under her weight. It had no sheets or other coverings. The frame was sturdy and seemed to be composed of rusty metal.

"Let's get her settled and then we can bring in the supplies," the man said.

They unwound the tape from her ankles and wrists and then used the ropes to bind her spread-eagle to the bed frame. Her heart leapt against her chest as if trying to escape. She suddenly felt as if she couldn't breathe. Air whistled in and out through her nose.

Abby smiled down at her. "It's showtime."

CHAPTER 53

NICOLE COULDN'T STAND still. She shifted her weight from foot to foot, her head constantly on a swivel. "Where the hell are they?"

"They'll be here in a minute," I said.

She let out a breath. "I can't stand this."

We had pulled the Range Rover down into the underground area and parked next to Megan's car, where we stood, waiting for Ray and Pancake to arrive. I hugged her. Her chin rested on my shoulder.

"Relax. The calvary's on the way."

"But then what? She's gone."

"Remember? Pancake put a tracker on the car."

Nicole broke my embrace and stepped back. "That's right. I forgot." "We'll find her."

Unless the tracker fails, or falls off, or was discovered and discarded, or they were in a different car. In which case we are screwed. I thought that but said nothing.

"There they are," Nicole said.

Pancake's car raced down the ramp and jerked into an empty space next to us. He and Ray hopped out. Ray retrieved a canvas bag from the back seat.

"Let's go," Ray said. "We'll take the Range Rover." He yanked open the rear door.

"Up the 55, south on the 405," Pancake said.

We piled in, Ray and Pancake in back, both working their phones. I zigged over to Newport Boulevard and then on to the 55 freeway. Fortunately, the sparse traffic allowed me to bump the speed to seventy-five.

"Where are they?" Nicole asked.

"Maybe thirty miles from here," Pancake said. "Off the 74. Looks to be a rural and unpopulated area."

"Moving or stopped?" I asked.

"They've been stationary for the past fifteen minutes." Pancake looked out the window. "Can you go a little faster? Or maybe Nicole should drive."

"I like that idea," Nicole said.

Of course she did.

I top-gunned it through the broad sweep of the connecting ramp and onto I-5. Once I merged, I accelerated to eight-five. Which basically matched the rest of the traffic. Speed limits on California freeways were similar to stop signs in Italy—merely suggestions.

Fifteen minutes later—seemed much longer—I could sense Nicole willing the Rover to go faster—we reached the exit to Highway 74, the Ortega Highway. To the right was downtown San Juan Capistrano and the famous San Juan Mission, where the swallows returned every year. Sort of. They had been a bit sparse in recent years from what I had read. I turned left. Two miles later the traffic and signs of civilization faded and the road became narrow and serpentine.

The Ortega Highway was one of the most dangerous roads in California, actually the nation. Once you left the residents of San Juan Capistrano behind, the highway—that was being generous— narrowed to a two-lane blacktop. It rose, fell, twisted, and tilted through scrub brush–covered hills with rocky hillocks and often deep ravines on either side. Fatal accidents, head-ons, and tumbles down hillsides weren't rare. Add the fact that people liked to test their driving skills as if it were Le Mans, and dudes hurled rocket bikes along the road like it was a video game, often reaching triple-digit speeds.

To me, it also looked like a good area to dump a body.

"Take the next right," Pancake said.

The road, also a generous description, was called Tenaja Truck Trail. An apt name as it looked more like a trail than a road, and a truck was definitely the vehicle of choice. Ratty, rutted, and poorly maintained, it wound up hill, then down, then back up, and so on.

I was getting motion sickness.

"We're close," Pancake said. "Slow down."

I eased my foot off the accelerator, reducing the Range Rover's speed to a crawl. A paved driveway veered off to the left and I could see a house maybe a hundred feet away. It looked to be well kept, the drive flanked by shrubs and bougainvillea. A white sedan sat in front of the house.

"Here?" I asked.

"No. Keep going."

Another two hundred yards and a dirt track spurred to the left.

"That's it," Pancake said.

I stopped.

"They're maybe two hundred yards up that way." He pointed up the incline.

The dirt drive rose up a hill and disappeared from sight beyond its crest. Off to the left sat an old and very rusty metal shed. At least what was left of one.

"Pull over there by that shed," Pancake said.

I did. We climbed out.

My cell buzzed. I answered. Detective Mills.

"Jake?"

"Yes."

"What the hell is going on? I'm at the studio. They said something about Megan being missing."

"She was kidnapped from the parking deck."

"When?"

"Less than an hour ago," I said.

"Why didn't you call?"

"We've been busy. But I think we've found them. I'm going to put you on speaker. We're all here."

"Where is here?"

"Off the Ortega on a side road called Tenaja Truck Trail."

"How did you find them?" Mills asked.

"Pancake put a tracker on Greg Morgan's car. We followed it here."

"So what's going on?"

"This is Ray," Ray said. "We just rolled up. Can't see the car yet but it's nearby. There's an abandoned shed here where we are and I suspect we'll find some kind of structure once we move in."

"You're a little out of my domain but tell me where and I'll get the OC Sheriff's Department rolling your way."

Ray hesitated, then said, "Okay. But tell them to come in quietly. No lights or sirens and for sure no helicopter. I don't want them to know they've been found. It might not go well for Megan if they feel cornered."

"Got it."

Ray told her exactly where we were, then said, "We're going to move closer, see what we're dealing with."

"Might be better to wait on the sheriff."

"Might be," Ray said. "But we aren't."

"Somehow I figured you wouldn't. Shouldn't take them more than fifteen, twenty minutes."

"We'll have it scoped out by then. Tell them to look for a green Range Rover on a dirt track off the left side of the road. The house is just over the hill from there."

"Got it."

"I'm curious," I asked. "Did the warrant go through?"

"No, the judge said we didn't have enough probable cause."

"We got all the probable cause we need now," Pancake said.

"You did before," Mills said. "I suspect the judge will agree now that we're dealing with an abduction. I'll get things rolling on this end."

Ray ended the call and handed me my phone. He lifted the canvas bag from the rear seat and zipped it open. He tugged out a pair of Glocks, handing one to Pancake.

It still seemed odd to me that Ray could fly with handguns. He did it all the time. So did Pancake. They, of course, possessed all the proper credentials, and licenses, and whatever was required. I guessed US Marshals and FBI agents and others of their ilk did so also, but it still seemed strange for Ray and Pancake to do so. I didn't have such problems. I only traveled with baseballs.

Ray then tugged out a small zipper bag that held half a dozen communication mic/earpiece combos. He fitted each of us with one and we tested them. All good.

Ray led us up the hill to the crest. The trail then gently descended to a stucco house. Dingy and dirty, the sun reflected off its metal roof. No car was visible.

"It's there," Pancake said. "Signal is five by five. Must be hidden behind the structure."

Ray scanned the area, his gaze finally settling on the hill that rose twenty feet above us to the left.

"Wait here," Ray said.

He climbed the hill, weaving through the brush and around a few boulder-sized rocks. We lost sight of him for a few minutes, then he reappeared.

"It's there."

"Okay," I said. "So Megan's in the house. What's the plan?"

CHAPTER 54

MEGAN FOUND HERSELF alone and securely attached to the bed by coarse, abrasive ropes that bound each ankle and wrist to the metal frame. She tested them but found no play. Helpless didn't quite cover what she felt.

Abby and the man came into the room, Abby walking to the bedside, the man leaning against the doorjamb, a beer in one hand. Each appeared relaxed and casual as if this were a daily occurrence. Or at least not a new experience. She guessed Salt Lake City and Henderson, Nevada proved that.

Abby reached for her. She recoiled as best she could.

"Relax," Abby said. She then ripped the tape from her mouth. "Better?" She waded the tape into a ball and tossed it toward the corner of the room. "Don't even think about screaming. No one will hear you out here anyway, but Greg finds it annoying." She smiled. "You don't want him annoyed."

Megan glanced at the man. He tipped his beer bottle toward her as if to say, that's a fact. She returned her gaze to Abby.

"Why are you doing this?" Megan asked.

"I think you know."

"No. I don't." Even to Megan, her voice sounded foreign. It came out pitched too high and stretched too tight, betraying the fact that she was on the cusp of full panic.

"Because it's fun." Abby laughed. She glanced toward the man. "Isn't it, bro?"

He again tilted his beer.

"Meet my brother, Greg. He thinks this's fun, too." She laughed. "Almost as much as me."

"Are you insane?" Megan said. "Look, Abby, you don't have to do this. Let me go. I won't say a word."

Abby sat on the edge of the bed. "Oh, trust me, I know you won't say a word." She smiled. "Oh, and my name isn't Abby. It's Stacy."

"What?"

"You're so freaking gullible. By far the easiest person to fool we've run across." She rubbed Megan's arm. "So nice, so trusting. Sure as hell made all this easier."

"Though shorter than we had hoped," the Greg dude said.

"Yeah. Your friends fucked it all up. We had a another couple of weeks of fun planned before we got to this point." She shrugged. "But, then again, here we are."

"You won't get away with this."

Greg dragged a chair over and sat near the opposite side of the bed from his sister. "Looks like we already did."

"Not yet." Megan glared at him.

"I love this part," he said. "When all the threatening and blustering goes on."

"Followed by the whining and begging and pleading and bargaining," Stacy said.

"Just so you know," Greg said. "This isn't our first rodeo."

Stacy laughed. "Not even close."

Megan felt a chill ripple through her. "What does that mean?"

"This is my favorite part," Stacy said. "Story time."

Megan looked at her, glanced at Greg, then back to Stacy. "What the hell are you talking about?"

"The part where we enlighten you as to who we really are. What we need. What we've done." She grabbed Megan's hand and squeezed. Hard. "The fun part is that we get to watch the fear eat you up." She laughed. "For me, that's really the payoff."

Greg took a gulp of beer. "I like the hammer better."

"You would."

"What are you talking about?" Megan asked. Tears now gathered in her eyes.

"Let's not get the cart before the horse," Stacy said. She looked at her brother. "You want to start off story time?"

"Sure." He pulled a pack of cigarettes from his pocket, shook one up, and lit it with a cheap red service station lighter. "Let's go back to the beginning. I was a junior in high school, Stacy in the eighth grade. There was this girl."

"Sally Whitmire."

"Yeah, dear old Sally. I didn't really know her. Well, until the end anyway. But she was a real bitch."

Stacy/Abby nodded. "Rich, haughty, and the prettiest girl in the school. She knew it and acted like it. Like she was so much better than everyone else."

"She had her little clique, which didn't include Stacy."

"Didn't include anyone that wasn't in her little self-admiration club," Stacy said. "They thought they were so fucking special."

Greg took a drag and let the smoke tumble from his mouth and nose as he spoke. "Sally, the ringleader, needed a lesson in manners." He shrugged. "We gave her one."

"Did we ever," Stacy said. "I can still see her. Crying, begging, even apologizing for being such a bitch. Can you imagine that? How wonderful it felt to see her that way?"

"What did you do to her?" Megan asked.

"Let's see," Greg said. "We tied her to a tree and stoned her to death."

Megan gasped. Stoned to death? He said it so flat and unemotional as if that were normal behavior.

Stacy smiled. "Yeah. Big old rocks. Took a half an hour for that bitch to die."

"We took our time," Greg said.

"She was a whore," Stacy said. "So we treated her like a medieval whore. Isn't that what they did to whores and witches back then?"

"We dumped her body in an isolated cave," Greg said. "Way in the woods. They never found her. So you might say we were good at this from the beginning."

Megan began to whimper.

Stacy squeezed her hand. "That's my girl. Let it out."

"You're a monster," Megan said. "How could you?"

"Very easily. The bonus was that we discovered something about ourselves." She smiled, raised an eyebrow. "We liked it. Really, really liked it."

"Next up were our parents," Greg said. "They weren't all that good at the parenting thing anyway, so it was no great loss."

"Not to mention the money," Stacy said. "Lots of money."

"We don't really count those though," Greg said. "Sally and our parents. Sally was pure revenge and our parents we did for the money."

"Maybe partly for revenge," Stacy said. "For being such douches. They were too stupid to live."

"Hard to argue with that," Greg said. "Still, not like the other seven and a half. Those were for fun."

Stacy must have sensed the question behind Megan's eyes. "The half was for the one that got away. That bitch in Nevada. We only got to have half the fun with her."

"You've killed that many people?" Megan asked.

Stacy patted her hand. "So far."

Greg took a final puff from his cigarette. "I feel like breaking something. Where're my hammers."

He leaned over and stubbed out his cigarette on Megan's foot.

She wailed, tried to twist from her restraints.

Stacy laughed. "Now we're talking."

CHAPTER 55

RAY'S PLAN WAS simple and, as he always said, fluid. It could change on the fly.

The house sat at the end of the trail, surrounded by a circle that had been cleared of brush. Maybe a hundred feet in diameter. Nicole and I would veer off the dirt drive to the right and wind our way through the brush and rocks, staying out of sight, and approach the front of the house. The plan was to get within a hundred or so feet and then hunker down and wait for Ray's commands. Ray and Pancake would go left, circle to the back, and hopefully get close enough to see what the interior layout was and where all the players were. The hope was to isolate Greg and neutralize—Ray's word—him first, and then deal with Stacy.

Seemed vague to me, but I didn't have anything clever to offer so off Nicole and I went. We worked our way into the scruffy vegetation. It grabbed at our clothes and scratched our arms. By the time we got into a position where we could see the front of the house, I looked like I'd been in a fight with a bobcat. Nicole on the other hand was pristine. Like she'd been walking through a park. How did she manage that?

We squatted behind a bolder that had a pathetic bit of shrub glommed to its side. I lifted the binoculars Ray had given me and scanned the two windows that faced us. One with closed curtains, while the other looked into what seemed to be an empty living room. I zoomed in and now saw a chair and the very top of what appeared to be a sofa. Beyond, I saw light coming through a windowed door. To its right sat a refrigerator. Obviously the kitchen.

"In position?" It was Ray's voice in my left ear.

"All set," I said.

"Got anything?"

"Looks quiet from here. Two windows. One has closed curtains. The other seems to look into the living room."

"Same here," Ray said. "A window to the kitchen area. Another window with curtains. I suspect that's a bedroom. Maybe where Megan is being held. Hold your position and keep your eyes open. We're going to work a little closer."

I kept scanning the windows. No movement that I could see.

Nicole was getting antsy. She wanted to do something. I'd seen this before. Once she even tackled a guy who had a gun. Another time she Krav Maga-ed an armed guy in the throat. She had that coiled posture right now.

"Relax," I said.

"I am."

"No, you're not."

"We should do something."

"You should stay where you are," Ray said. "We've made it to the car. Still don't see anyone."

"Us either."

"Pancake flattened two tires just in case they get a chance to run for it."

"What if they had another car?" Nicole said. "Dumped this one and took off."

I hadn't thought of that. Probably should have but I hadn't.

"Could be," Pancake said. "But I don't think so."

"Based on?" Nicole asked.

"Gut feeling."

That was good enough for me.

Apparently not for Nicole. "What if your gut's wrong?"

"It ain't."

Then I saw something. Movement through the living room window. "Got something," I said.

"I see it," Ray said.

A man came into view, bent over the sofa, and seemed to be messing with something. When he stood and turned, he had an object in his hand. Took me a microsecond to recognize it. A hammer.

"He's got a hammer," I said.

"Okay," Ray said. "Phase two in motion."

Phase two of Ray's plan was to take place once we were in position and knew where the players were. We weren't completely there, but the hammer changed things. I flashed on what had happened to Dana Roderick in Salt Lake.

"All set," I said.

"Do what you do best."

Ray designed phase two as a distraction and an assault.

The first part was to hopefully bring Greg out front and separate him from Megan and give Ray and Pancake a chance to take him down. I had collected several fist-sized, more or less round rocks as we pushed through the brush.

I stood, made a best guess as to the distance and trajectory, and hurled one high in the air toward the house. It seemed to hang against the clear blue sky as if defying gravity and then plummeted. It struck the corrugated metal roof with an explosive bang. I released a second one. Same result.

Greg appeared again. This time he stood near the window, half hidden, peering around the molding. I watched him, concealed by the scrap of brush that sprouted from our rocky hiding place. He eased out of sight. Then I saw him move toward the back, into the kitchen area.

"Coming your way," I said.

"Got him," Ray said.

"Lock, load, and fire," Pancake said. "Something a little more dramatic. Draw him to the front again. I'm coming in the back. Time to put this boy down."

"You sure?"

"Do it."

I stood. I could see the shadow of Greg Morgan. Still in the kitchen, still gazing out the back. I gripped the next rock, automatically looking for a seam, finding a slight ridge. I then hurled an excellent fastball. Definitely a strikeout pitch. This time, directly through the front window. It shattered.

Greg spun, ducked, scurried toward the front again. Low, peaking over the windowsill.

Damn, this was fun. Or could be if Megan wasn't in danger.

Things happened quickly then.

The kitchen door exploded. Greg stood, rotating that way. Nicole took off on a dead run toward the house. What the hell? I followed.

Two shots exploded inside the house. I caught Nicole, dragged her down. She kicked me. In the shin. It hurt. She was back up and running toward the front door. I caught her just as she swung it open.

Pancake stood in the middle of the room, his Glock to his side. Greg Morgan lay on his back, a red splotch dead center of his shirt, an amazingly clean round hole in his forehead. His lifeless eyes seemed to stare at the ceiling.

"Greg." Abby's voice came from through the door near the corner of the living room. "What the hell's going on?"

Pancake moved that way. We followed. Ray appeared behind us.

In the room, Megan was in four-point restraints on the bed. Abby/ Stacy sat near her head, a large butcher knife at her throat.

"Stay where you are," she said. "I swear to God I'll cut her fucking throat."

"I'll shoot you in the head," Pancake said.

"Where's my brother?"

"Sorry," Pancake said. "I did shoot him in the head."

"Put the knife down," I said. "Let's talk about this."

"Don't see we have much to talk about."

"You haven't harmed Megan yet. But if you do, things won't go well for you."

"Right. Like you don't know about the others."

Well, there was that.

Nicole stepped toward her. "Abby, you don't want to do this."

"Actually, I do. And I will."

Another step forward brought Nicole to the foot of the bed. "Give me the knife and let's stop all this before it gets any worse."

"Ha." It seemed to explode from her lungs. "Gets any worse? Are you an idiot? A fucking bubble-headed blond? Dumb as dirt like Megan here? How could it get any worse?"

Another step forward. "Things can always get worse."

"Don't take another step or Megan is done for."

"I don't think so," Nicole said. She took another step. This to her right, clearing the bed frame. She had a free run at Abby now. "I think you want to end all this."

"You don't know shit. Now back the fuck up."

Stacy fisted the knife, raised it high, and set her shoulders to plunge it into Megan's chest.

Nicole moved, a single long stride. Stacy recoiled; her attention now diverted as Nicole closed on her.

The explosion from Ray's gun was deafening. Abby's head jerked, and a black hole appeared just above her right eye. She shivered slightly, and then slumped forward.

"Let me see your hands."

Two deputies stood in the doorway; weapons leveled at us.

CHAPTER 56

"LET ME GET this straight," Detective Claire Mills said. "This duo killed a classmate, their parents, seven TV reporters, and failed at two others? Including Megan Weatherly?"

"That's right," I said. "At least it looks that way."

Nicole and I were in Mills' office. It was the morning after the fiasco out off the Ortega Highway. No, we didn't get shot by the OC Sheriff's deputies who burst in on us, but that surely looked like a possibility at the time. I mean, they had been dispatched to the location and were probably told something bad was going down. Even that small arms fire was possible. What did the two amped-up deputies find? Us. In an abandoned house with two corpses, Pancake and Ray with guns, Nicole with the knife she had snatched from Abby/Stacy's dead hand and was using to cut Megan loose, and me with a rock. Okay, so I was severely underarmed. All that meant was that I would likely be the last one they'd shoot.

"I've seen some crazy shit in my career but this is high on the list," Mills said.

"We wanted to drop by and thank you for your help," Nicole said.

"I'm afraid I didn't do all that much."

"You sent the Sheriff's department out."

And almost got us shot, I thought.

"Ray said he'd let you know what else we uncovered," I said.

"Which is what so far?"

"Pancake looked into the murder of Sally Whitmire, Stacy Morgan's classmate. He talked to the detectives back there and brought them up to speed. They were shocked, but grateful. They'll go see the girl's parents."

"Maybe that'll give them some closure," Mills said. "If there's such a thing."

"We called all the interested parties in the Salt Lake City and Henderson, Nevada, cases," Nicole said. "Including Tiffany Cole. Maybe now she can reclaim her life and sleep a little better."

"Pancake also found three other cases that fit the pattern," I said. "All back East. Hopefully, they'll pan out and he can find the other three and wrap this up."

"How's Megan doing?"

"She's okay," Nicole said. "She's a tough lady."

"Seems so."

"I might have something that'll put a little sunshine in her life."

"What?"

Nicole smiled. "Can't say. It has to do with my movie though."

"Now I am intrigued." Mills raised an eyebrow. "You mentioned you were doing a movie. What's that about?"

Nicole explained that she had written the screenplay and a little about the story behind *Murderwood* and who all the players were.

"Kirk Ford? Charles Balfour? I'd say you have a built-in blockbuster."

"You never know. Remember Dustin Hoffman and Warren Beatty made *Ishtar*."

Mills laughed. "I forgot about that."

"Most other people did, too."

"When do you start shooting?"

Nicole thought for a second. "Wow. Only ten days." She looked at me. "We've been so tied up with this that I forgot to get nervous about it."

"There's still time," I said.

She slugged my arm.

CHAPTER 57

NICOLE AND I sat in a pair of those tall director's chairs, just to the left and behind Lee Goldberg, the real director. We didn't get our names on ours like he did.

Uncle Charles and Nicole's parents, Bob and Connie, had been in and out of the sound stage all morning. They were excited about the happenings but had other irons in the fire so had to step out to make calls and whatever else they did.

Nicole did get some good news. Uncle Charles had made her an executive producer on the project. Apparently, he had done so since its inception but held it back as a surprise. What it meant was prestige and money. Lots of money. Want to know why movies cost so much? Watch the credits. Each of those executive producers that seem to roll on forever get well paid. Now Nicole would, too. Deservedly so.

I leaned over toward her. "How does it feel to be an executive producer?"

"Great actually. Unexpected for sure."

"Now you can buy me a Lamborghini."

"I could."

"But, you're not."

"No. It's not your style."

"I could change."

"Too late for that."

The excitement on the set began to ramp up. We had already been there for three, mostly boring hours, while the tech types fiddled with the lights and cameras and sound equipment and set decorations. Making movies can be tedious. But now, Goldberg had finished herding all the cats and everything was set. The scene was labeled number eight and wouldn't come until eighteen minutes into the movie, yet it would be the first scene filmed. I never understood why scenes weren't done in sequence, but then again what did I know? I figured Uncle Charles and Director Goldberg knew what they were doing.

Nicole was now visibly nervous. I reached over and grabbed her hand. The actors were in place. The star detective, Kirk Ford, was interviewing a witness, played by Megan Weatherly. A bit part for her, but it was her debut. She didn't look nervous at all. With what she had survived, this was a walk in the park.

"And action," Lee Goldberg said.

Murderwood was off and running.

PUBLISHER'S NOTE

We hope that you enjoyed *The OC*, which is the fifth in D. P. Lyle's Jake Longly Thriller Series. If you haven't read the first four in the series, here's a recap that we hope will pull you in.

Jake Longly and Nicole Jamison first appear in *Deep Six*. Jake has owned a restaurant on the Gulf shore of Alabama ever since an injury sidelined his career as a major league pitcher. But when his P.I. father cajoles him to help out, he reluctantly agrees only to have his surveillance target murdered right under Jake's nose. That's about when he meets Nicole and the fireworks start.

A-List takes Jake and Nicole to New Orleans, where a young girl is found murdered in the bed of a movie star. DNA plays a tricky role in this one and Jake and Nicole are at the top of their game. Nothing is easy in the Big Easy.

Sunshine State throws Jake and Nicole into the bizarre case of a convicted serial killer who now claims he only murdered five of the seven victims he'd originally claimed. They are in Florida now, trying to figure out whether this convict is lying for attention or if there is still a killer out there. Dark clouds loom in the Sunshine State.

Rigged finds Jake and Nicole trying to sort out the murder of Jake's best friend Tommy "Pancake" Jeffers' first love from back in the sixth grade. There's a soon-to-be-ex-husband involved and two guys she's been dating. Complex relationships, a plethora of motives, a huge modicum of danger—and with all that, the easygoing humor that infuses all Jake Longly thrillers.

We hope you will dive into this series, get to know Jake and Nicole and Jake's dad, Ray, and iconic friend, Pancake.

D. P. Lyle is a humorist, yes; but he is also an expert in forensics and never fails to generously sprinkle both in his novels. We hope that you will read the entire Jake Longly Thriller Series and will look forward to more to come.

For more information, please visit the author's website: http://www.dplylemd.com.

Happy Reading.
Oceanview Publishing